GIANT SLAYERS

JEFF ALTABEF & KEN ALTABEF

GIANT SLAYERS
Copyright © 2016 by Jeff Altabef & Ken Altabef
Cover Art Copyright © 2016 by Sarima
Contact Sarima at **http://envuelorsante.com**
Edited by Stevie Mikyane

All rights reserved. No part of this book may be used or reproduced in any manner whatsoever, without written permission, except in the case of brief quotations embedded in articles or reviews. Contact the author for more information.

ISBN: 1535509252
ISBN-13: 978-1535509251

Cat's Cradle
Press

New York

This is a work of fiction. Except in the case of historical figures, all names, characters, places, and incidents are the product of the author's imagination or are used fictitiously, and any resemblance to actual persons, living or dead, business establishments, events or locales is entirely coincidental.

ALSO BY JEFF ALTABEF

CHOSEN
Book 1: Wind Catcher
Book 2: Brink of Dawn
Book 3: Scorched Souls

SHATTER POINT

www.JeffAltabef.com

ALSO BY KEN ALTABEF

ALAANA'S WAY
Book 1: The Calling
Book 2: Secrets
Book 3: Shadows
Book 4: The Tundra Shall Burn!
Book 5: The Shadow of Everything Existing

FORTUNE'S FANTASY:
13 excursions into the unknown

www.KenAltabef.com

ONE

David frowned. Storm clouds had rolled across the sky, sudden as death, as if a dark smoky hand had smothered the sun. *Creepy.*

"It's going to rain again," said Abby.

David's little sister looked miserable as she peered at him from beneath a soggy linen shawl draped loosely over her head. Long black hair, tangled and wet, trailed down from the edges. Not that she ever combed her hair neatly — she was too much of a tomboy for that — but now it looked like a soggy bird's nest. At eleven years old, she barely came up to the middle of his chest.

She kicked him in the shin.

"Owww!" he said, playfully. "What's that for?"

She shook her head at the boggy pass. "That stream's going to be flooded for a week. We'll never get the flock back through the valley tonight."

"We'll go around, then. Just look at it as an adventure." He smiled at her, but she scowled back at him.

"Relax," he said. "I know a shortcut through the hills."

"You're the only person I know whose shortcuts are longer than the usual way."

He shrugged. "The usual way is boring."

"I don't see what's so exciting about this."

Tall rocky cliffs with jagged points like bony fingers held sway on either side of the valley. The startling colors of the rocks, varying from deep crimson to golden-brown, cut across each finger as if they wore giant rings of glittering gemstone. No two were the same—each unique in shape and color.

"When I first saw this place I knew I had to show it to you, Abby. Don't you see? Look at the way the cliffs curve up toward the sky as if they were the first things carved into the face of the world. They're... magical."

Abby puffed out her lower lip in a defiant pout. "It won't feel so magical tonight, sleeping in that cave with a rock for a pillow and a wet cloak for a blanket."

"We'll be all right." David smoothed a few soggy locks of auburn hair from his face. "You didn't have to tag along, you know."

"Yes I did. If I'd stayed home, Mom would've had me weaving baskets and listening to old women talk all day. They just repeat the same tired old stories. If I hear one more time about having babies, I'm going to scream."

Their flock of twenty sheep and a handful of goats mulled along beside them, taking water from the stream.

David shook the rest of the water from his shoulder-length hair and whistled a shrill herder's call. "All right, that's enough! Especially you, Eli." He whacked Eli on the rump. He'd named the largest goat after his eldest brother Eliab. The goat was just as lazy but only half as stubborn. "You've drunk enough. Let's go. I want to get home before supper."

"Think Dad will be angry we won't make it home tonight?" Abby asked.

"As long as I bring back all the sheep in the morning he won't care. They're all much too busy harvesting the wheat to worry about little David."

"And Abigail," she added.

"Abigail? Who's that?" He swung his head back and forth, searching the air above her as if she were invisible.

"Stop that. You're glad I came with you, and you know it."

He smiled at her. "Oh there you are. I thought I heard a bird squawking." He *was* happy to have her with him.

"If you got to choose, what would you rather do?" she asked. "Swing a hoe in the field or watch after the flock?"

"Neither. I'd be a soldier like Eliab, and Abinadab, and Shimeae. Defending the kingdom. That's what I want to do. Not spend all my time with twenty stinky sheep, four goats, and one little sister who asks questions all day."

"Well, I'm sure I'm more fun than a bunch of sweaty soldiers," she chuckled. "You're too young to fight anyway."

David kicked a stone down the trail. "I'm sixteen. That's old enough. Dad just won't allow it."

"He can't let all his sons go off to war. Someone has to look after the flock."

That's the story of my life, he thought. *Our family has eight sons – three soldiers, four farmers and me. I always get the worst jobs, but it won't stay that way. Not forever.*

"And besides," she added, "you don't even know how to use a sword."

"How hard can it be?" He swung his staff in a wide arc, enjoying the whooshing sound it made as it cut the air. "That seems about right."

"Watch out before you smack one of the sheep."

"Shhh!" David heard a rumble in the distance, a low growling sound that meant trouble.

Abby's face turned white. 'What's that?"

"Mountain lions sometimes creep down from the rocky hillside. I've avoided them in the past, but this one sounds close. Don't wander off."

He herded the few last reluctant goats in a line down through the pass but kept his eyes on the ridge, looking for trouble.

He couldn't spot the mountain lion, but he heard another growl, and his flock certainly knew trouble had found them. The sheep began bleating wildly and scattered down the pass, splashing red mud behind them.

David raced after his charges, counting them as he went. Only nineteen sheep in the pass. One of the lambs was missing. He sprinted forward, his sandals slipping on the wet stone as he urged the sheep along the trail.

The narrow pass widened as it flowed down toward the valley. The flock had followed it downhill, but one lamb was still missing. David spotted a small break in the trail to his right where the missing lamb had wandered toward the cliff face.

A snarling mountain lion had cornered it against the rocks. The lamb tried to climb the rocky shelf, but its hooves scraped hopelessly off the smooth stone.

David waved at Abby. "You stay back!"

"David! Leave it alone. It's dangerous.

"Go after the other sheep! You'll be safe there."

The lion tensed for a leap. Its mouth opened wide, flashing long, pointed fangs. The lamb wouldn't stand much of a chance against those teeth.

David darted between them. "No! Get lost you mangy cat! You're not eating anything here!" He swung his staff at the mountain lion and struck it in the jaw.

Enraged, it spun around and growled at him. The lion's snarl was the scariest thing David had ever seen. Its fangs looked as long as daggers and just as sharp.

He stepped between the lion and the sheep, but the big cat still eyed its prey. Hissing and snarling, it swung its head back and forth between David and the lamb. Before David could swing again, the mountain lion jumped up the rock face and leapt past him to reach the lamb.

David whirled and cut it off just in time. He chopped down with the staff, which struck the ground in front of the mountain lion's nose with a thud. The beast skidded to a stop, growled and bared its fangs. Its legs tensed for another leap, but the lamb had a clear path down the pass toward the flock and scampered away.

The wild cat growled, its tongue lolling and saliva spilling from its mouth.

"Get! I'm warning you!" shouted David.

Now that the sheep had escaped, David got the uneasy feeling he was the next item on the animal's menu. His heart raced. He swung the staff in front of him, slicing it through the air. The cat lunged, ducking under the staff, fangs ready to rip into his flesh.

David sidestepped the charge and bashed the cat on the head. The blow sent it rolling away on its side.

"Warned you."

The mountain lion growled one last time, turned and disappeared up the slope.

"Ha! David! David's my name. Remember me. Next time we meet, I won't be so easy on you!"

David grinned. His record would stay intact. He had never lost a sheep and today would be no different. He headed toward the wider pass to find his sister and collect his flock when he heard Abby scream.

He spun. Her shout came from the ravine below the trail. He jumped over the edge and slid halfway down the slope, scraping the back of his legs on the rocks.

Abby stood frozen, her eyes locked on the mouth of a small cave carved into the cliff wall.

David smelled trouble. *Big trouble.* A dusky shadow crossed the mouth of the small cave, and his hair stood on end as an enormous black bear lumbered toward Abby.

David's blood froze. He grabbed his sister and shoved her behind him. "Run!"

He could run for it, but that would only put Abby in danger. She wasn't as quick as him. The bear would follow them and overtake her.

He had no choice but to tough it out. He puffed out his chest, lifted himself on his toes, and whipped his staff in the air. "Come on big fella! Are you scared yet?"

The bear caught the pole in its teeth, bit down, and snapped the rod in half. It spit out the shattered wood.

"I guess not," muttered David. His entire body trembled. The creature was a full head taller than him and could snap him in two in its powerful jaw.

The beast swung a massive paw that grazed his shoulder, carving a nasty gash in his skin.

David fell backward, sprawled on the ground, helpless.

The animal rose on its hind legs and stood over him.

I'm going to die, he thought. I'm going to die.

A violent buzzing sound filled his ears as if the world had suddenly become a gigantic hornet's nest with him trapped at its heart. He clapped his hands over his ears to shut out the noise.

Time seemed to have stopped. The bear stood frozen on its two hind legs, ready to throw itself at him in a deadly lunge, its blackened lips curled back from sharp yellow teeth. Its eyes beamed down a pointed snout. But it didn't move. It couldn't.

David tried but he couldn't move either.

The bear's fur began to ripple and blur. Each hair glowed red, every bit of flesh flared into a separate point of light like countless burning embers in a vast hearth.

The bear screamed, a high-pitched tortured wail.

Its face glowed orange, then red. The light flared hotter and brighter as the face dissolved away, from skin to meat to bone in an instant.

The bear vanished, leaving nothing behind but a few drifting embers and the stink of scorched meat.

A deathly silence replaced the buzzing sound.

David scrambled to his feet and sucked air in short violent gasps, his heart still pounding.

A driving rain began to fall.

"What happened to it?" Abby looked bewildered, her eyes wide and her mouth agape.

"I don't know."

TWO

Look closely at a woman's face and you can read her entire life story. It's all there in the crevices and contours, the tiny expressions and doubts. Such little things, but they combine to give away her secrets. Men's faces, however, were still mysteries to Michal. She'd spent so little time with men that their lines seemed written in a foreign language, unique and indecipherable.

In Hadi's face, Michal saw rivers flowing down cheeks rich with experience. The canyons carved into her forehead spoke of a tough life, one without the blessing of children, where she had served as a house servant for as long as anyone could remember. The old woman's walnut eyes sparkled with a hint of summer wheat, still sharp and bright and full of mischief, and the wrinkles creeping from the corners of those eyes had been etched by laughter.

Michal frowned at the way Hadi's tunic drooped over her shoulders and hung low on her thin frame. She had lost weight in the past month, and her back seemed more sharply stooped than it had been only a few weeks ago. She must be ill, thought Michal. But whenever I try to summon a priest for help, she shrugs me off.

Hadi slid close to Michal. Her whisper sounded coarse, as if age had stolen its smoothness. "This is too dangerous. I should never have told you about the staircase."

"It's too late for that. You know I've been waiting my whole life to see the Ark."

"Your whole life," Hadi chuckled. "You're just fifteen. Barely a babe. Only yesterday, you were toddling around learning your first prayers."

"That was a long time ago. Tonight's my only chance to see the Ark before everything gets turned upside down for the festival. Who knows how long I'll have to wait if I don't go tonight?"

Hadi sighed and shuffled farther into the cellar. Her small lamp cast just enough light for them to make their way, brightening small swirls of dust ahead. The cool air smelled both sweet from raisins and acidic from the large oak casks of wine. It created an odd mix and Michal wondered if it meant a good omen or a bad one.

She followed close behind Hadi, her footsteps tentative in the unfamiliar cellar. As they traveled deeper into the storage area, her heart quickened and her imagination started to race. Witches formed in the shadows and wolves lurked behind every storage bin—dark images she chased away only with great effort.

Hadi led her to the farthest corner of the cellar, around two crates of melons, three baskets of figs, and a few bushels of recently harvested wheat. The cellar was filling with food for the upcoming feast.

"It's a high crime for a woman to look upon the Ark," warned Hadi as she paused next to an enormous cask of wine. "If you get caught, you could be stoned or exiled—princess or not. I may not worship your God, but I've learned your ways while I've worked in your father's house, child. He *will* punish you."

"The Ark belongs to all of us." Michal folded her arms across her chest. "It's not just for men." She saw doubt waver in Hadi's eyes and added hastily, "No one's around at this time of night anyway. Only my father can unlock the room, and he's fast asleep by now. No one will know. Besides, what about all those stories you've told me about women doing the unexpected, protecting the honor of their houses? I'm not going to shrink away now just because I might be punished. I have to do this."

A twinkle of mischief chased the doubt from the old woman's eyes. Those stories could not be untold now. Hadi pointed behind the tall cask of wine next to Michal and sighed. "There's a rectangle cut into the clay in the corner, close to the floor. You'll find two gouges in the clay you can use as finger holds to pull it from the wall. Once you crawl through the opening, you'll find a narrow staircase that will take you upstairs to the room where your father has the Ark. At the top of the stairs you'll find another piece of clay cut into the wall you can push through."

"Thanks, Hadi." Michal kissed her lightly on her cheek.

"And don't forget to put the clay panel back in place, child. No one else knows about this tunnel but my dead brother who built it, and I'm pretty sure he won't be telling anyone else about it."

"Why did he build the secret passage, anyway?"

Hadi's lips frowned, but her eyes smiled. "He died before he could use it, so that's none of your concern." She handed Michal the small oil lamp. "Take this with you. I've spent enough time in the cellars that I can get out on my own, even in the dark. Be careful."

Michal took the lamp. "Make sure you leave right away," she said, wagging her finger in her best imitation of the old woman. "You could get in trouble for wandering around the palace at this time of night, you know."

"Fah! No one pays much attention to me anymore. I'll be fine."

Hadi would wait for her. It would take an earthquake to move her, so Michal thanked her one last time and snuck behind the cask of wine, her arm scraping against the clay wall as she squeezed through. When she squatted low, she couldn't find the rectangle cut in the clay, but her eyes lit upon two gouges high in the wall that could be used for handholds. With a deep breath she grabbed them and pulled. The stubborn clay held in place. Determined, she braced her feet against the bottom of the wall and strained until she yanked the panel free.

Stale air gushed toward her. She wrinkled her nose at the foul smell, and for the first time wondered whether she should continue. No woman had ever set foot in the chamber where her father kept the Ark.

The remains of the original stone tablets inscribed with the Ten Commandments rested inside the Ark, given from the hand of God to Moses himself. Her father told stories of how he'd heard God's voice when in its presence, how he knew God's strength just by standing beside it. If it was fair for men to feel that strength, then it must be right for women also. After all, God had created men and women.

I will see the Ark and feel God's power for myself, she thought. *Why not?*

The staircase was steep and narrow, just barely wide enough for her thin frame. Once she reached the top, she found two handles in the clay wall, grabbed them and pushed. This time, the small section of wall slid out easily.

Pushing aside a tapestry that draped over the secret entrance, she crept into the small room, and suddenly remembered to inhale. She'd been holding her breath without realizing it. This was the holy chamber that housed the Ark! No other woman had ever been this close to it.

A draft of fresh air gusted through a pair of slits cut high into the wall, blowing out her little lamp. Only the slightest hint of moonlight trickled through the slits, leaving the room mostly dark.

The Ark stood in the center of the room only a few feet away. If she hadn't been frozen in place, she could take three steps and touch it. But she *was* frozen. The air in the room shimmered against the darkness. A tingling sensation rippled across her skin like a million tiny needles pricking her all at the same time. It didn't hurt, but she felt the presence of something so great, so holy it sent a shiver down her spine.

From where she stood, she could only glimpse the pair of

winged sphinxes that adorned the top of the Ark. The sacred relic was housed within a chest of orange-colored acacia wood with four golden legs. The box wasn't as large as she expected, but it looked strong and solid.

Michal moved toward the Ark, but stopped mid-step when she heard the lock to the door twist with a metallic click.

Her heart stopped.

Her legs went weak as the door swung open.

Her father, King Saul, and her brother, Jonathan, stepped into the doorway. Jonathan lit their way with a lamp twice the size of the small one Michal had brought. He was tall for a Benjaminite, with broad shoulders and an athletic build. Long, light brown hair flowed down his neck and onto his shoulders.

As tall as Jonathan was, her father still towered over him, nearly a full head taller. They shared the same wide, almond-colored eyes, strong chin, and hawkish nose. Unlike Jonathan, her father's hair was dark brown and cut short in a ring around his otherwise bald head. Both men had tight beards, but her father's was darker and peppered with gray. He was the tallest man she had ever seen. Some even whispered that a little giant's blood flowed in his veins.

The door closed behind them with a thud.

Fear rippled through her like wind through a field of long grass. If she got caught now, her father would punish her severely. She backed up to the wall, sank down to the floor, and tried to make herself small, to become nothing more than a shadow.

"Every time I see the Ark, I get the same chills I had the first time," said Jonathan. "I've never looked upon anything as beautiful."

Michal thought the same thing as she saw the Ark, now emblazoned in the full light of the lamp. The golden sphinxes glowed a warm orange as if they'd been set on fire. The granite body of the Ark, where it peeked up out of its case, glittered in the light like gemstone.

Saul touched his son on the shoulder. "And you never will. This was given to us by God to do his will."

The two men stared at the Ark in silence for a long moment.

Saul broke the silence, his voice uncertain, hesitant. "I've brought you here for a reason. I used to hear God speaking to me when I gazed upon the Ark. Often, He gave me advice on how to fight the war against the Amalekites, but now...ever since Samuel's betrayal, His voice has gone silent."

The breath froze in Michal's throat. She had never heard doubt in her father's voice before. He always spoke with a King's voice, full of certainty and authority. He never wavered, but now in the presence of the Ark, he shared doubts with his oldest and favorite son.

"We've won the war, and Samuel is an old fool," said Jonathan. "He's lost his senses. I hear he's spreading treasonous rubbish in the mountains, looking for a new king among the peasants. Few can even recognize him at this point. He looks like a crazed demon with a long unkempt beard and a wild fire in his eyes. No one believes the nonsense he spews."

"I've placed a bounty on his head. I can't have him sowing seeds of doubt against my authority. But still, God hasn't spoken to me since I banished him." He hesitated, his eyes flickering between the Ark and Jonathan. "What do you hear, son? Do you hear His word?"

Jonathan stepped toward the Ark, still holding the oil lamp.

Michal knew she had to leave, and right away. If her brother took another step, the light from the lamp would find her. She kept her eyes locked on the lamp while searching desperately for the opening in the wall behind her with her hands.

The light snaked toward her.

A few more heartbeats, and she would be caught. She had nowhere to hide. Just as the light swung into her path, she found the edge of the panel and crept back into the passage.

"What do you hear, son?" asked the King again. "Tell me."

"I feel an energy in the air." Jonathan dropped to his knees. "It's as if I feel His presence, Father, but I hear no voice."

Saul rubbed his beard. "One day you will be king. And then God will speak to you through the Ark. I am sure of it."

From the safety of the tunnel, Michal slid the clay cutout carefully back over the opening in the wall, but it brushed against the tapestry. The hanging squeaked as it swayed. Her heart leapt.

"I heard something," said Jonathan. His boots scraped against the floor as he advanced.

She tried to force the clay into place in front of her, but the angle was off and it wouldn't close.

"The door was locked when we came in. No one else could be here," said Saul.

Michal heard Jonathan step around the Ark. He swung his light toward the tapestry. Sweat stung her eyes as she twisted the clay panel, struggling to find the right fit.

"Perhaps demons or ghosts," suggested Jonathan as his footsteps came closer.

She finally fitted the clay in place and pulled it tight. Her brother swept aside the tapestry on the other side of the wall and she held her breath. Would he notice the cracks that marked the hidden door, or hear her breathing?

Her father laughed. "Look at us, making mice into devils. Come, let's go. It's late."

"Do you smell that?" asked Jonathan.

"Smell what?"

"It smells like perfume. It's faint but I could swear I've smelled that fragrance before."

"I bet you have, son." Saul chuckled. "Come let's take leave of the Ark."

The door clicked shut, leaving Michal alone in the dark passage. She had finally glimpsed the Ark, but she was still quite uncertain whether she'd found what she was looking for.

Had God really turned His back on her father? And if so, who did He favor now?

THREE

Revenge.

Alzsheba, the Witch of Endor, knew quite a lot about revenge. The need for revenge was an itch she suffered most keenly, a burr beneath her skin that did nothing but burn and prod. A need unfulfilled. But that would change, starting today.

The Philistine camp buzzed with activity: weapons clattered, mules brayed, men shouted, boasted, argued. Little men who thought raised voices and bluster made them less pathetic and small. *Blind, stupid, stinking sheep. The entire lot of them. They fight and die for a king who cares nothing about them. King Farrah sits on a thrown far away and doesn't even know their names. Mindless sheep! Are they stupid enough to believe General Bulgossa, the bloated idiot the King has put in charge, is their shepherd? Do they think it is Goliath, who leads them in battle, towering above them like some bronzed god? Do they even suspect another unseen shepherd, one who guides them quietly, carefully, from the shadows?*

Her mind spun in tight angry circles. Enough! She had work to do. Twilight had come, and twilight was the only time for the things she must do. When day met night, when light succumbed to darkness, when the mists settled on the fields and the walls between the worlds were at their thinnest.

Alzsheba strode away from the camp—a tall beauty with high cheekbones, arched eyebrows, and dark stain on her lips. Her sheep were well served for the night. Let them drink, and gamble, and bicker and boast. None saw the lone figure of a woman, young and athletic, dressed in skin-tight leather breaches and bodice, heading toward the cliffs of chiseled basalt. They wanted only to feed their bellies and drink their fill and tell tall tales. Then they would sleep. But sleep would not find her, not while the need for revenge consumed her, that maddening itch still unfulfilled.

She squeezed into a narrow cleft in the rocky cliff face. Inside, she had dug out a tiny chamber, an earthy crypt where, even kneeling, the top of her head scraped the dirt above. She struck flint, lighting a pair of incense stands, and the pungent aromas of burning opium, poison hemlock and spice inflamed her senses.

A small wooden stand filled the center of the narrow chamber in the rocks. On top sat a small stone altar that had been captured from one of the Hebrew towns. The horns at the four corners had been broken off, the winged disc symbol on the front defaced. Dried blood crusted the burnished copper plate on the corrupted altar.

The witch emptied a small pouch of human ashes onto the plate, arranging the burnt offering in a circle. She felt power flow from the ashes, the murders still fresh.

She caressed the lines of the carving, tracing a bull's head with a man's chest and arms, then knelt before the altar, bare feet tucked beneath her thighs. Long black hair fell like dark fire across her shoulders. She drank the incense deep into her lungs, surrendering herself to the soothing influences of the tears of the poppy. The room blurred and faded away.

Alzsheba felt dizzy and weightless as all her cares melted away—all except the most pressing need, the prickling, aching, burning need for revenge.

Floating on a tide of colored mists, Alzsheba relaxed into the dream-like trance state that gave access to the Third Eye.

The Eye opened. And she saw. Her enemy—Saul, anointed King of the Israelites. Through the hazy mist and the swirling colors of the Third Eye, she saw his bedroom. He lay on his bed, but rest did not come easy for him. The crown sat upon a troubled brow. She hovered above the royal sleeping chamber, unknown, unseen, probing deeper. The Third Eye turned its bitter gaze upon the King's inner being. Stirring among the muck and mud of the King's soul, she would find what she needed.

The King could not conceal his doubts and fears from her now. They had ruled him ever since he was a child. The young Saul, though tall among his people, was small in his father's eyes. His father never believed he would amount to anything at all. How could such a boy, a sad and confused little boy, ever take up the solemn responsibility to rule the nation of Israel?

Doubts, doubts. How they fester over the years.

The prophet Samuel had anointed him in secret, on the outskirts of town. The first King of Israel had been chosen by a game of lots. A game of chance, which happened to fall upon the weak Benjamite farm boy, who knew nothing about politics or kingdoms. When Samuel called his name, Saul tried to hide himself among the baggage! Alzsheba cackled dryly. They dragged him from his hiding place, insecure, unsure, and thrust him unwillingly into the high seat. Unworthy.

Yes, she thought, that's the one. Let me pull that strand and see what dark spider tumbles out.

Saul had been caught in the divine lottery, like a rabbit in a snare. Doubts, doubts, the King of Israel had nothing but doubts.

Alzsheba intoned the words that called forth Molech, begging the dark lord for his aid and poisoned favor. She reached a long, clawed hand into the fiery depths of the pit. And, reaching into that seething nest of vipers, she pulled the first demon out: a slender snake, midnight blue with small black wings.

The demon, doubt incarnate, hissed and twisted in her grasp. The vile thing turned to sink its fangs into her wrist but stopped short of her flesh.

Alzsheba had no doubts. Not today. She cast it forth, and it disappeared into the night.

Alone in his bedchamber, Saul groaned.

But it wasn't enough. The witch turned the Third Eye upon the king once again. What else lurked hidden in his soul? Yes, there it was. Indecision. Overcome by power he didn't know how to wield. Overshadowed by his own son, Jonathan, a natural-born warrior, who strikes down their foes while Saul broods, unsure, beneath a pomegranate tree. His general, Abner, whispers the plans of battle in his ear, and Saul wonders if they are good ones, for he knows little of these things himself and cannot decide. Indecision. Oh yes, that was a good one. A puppet king of the prophet Samuel, uncertain, unsure, always relying on divinations and oracles. Always on the point of giving up or turning away. The witch cackled. The Israelites were nearly defeated already.

She reached again into the darkness and the fire. This one burned, scorching her very soul, but she did not flinch from it. Indecision. A fiery red cobra, fanged and furious, with silver wings. A second demon sent forth.

Saul gagged in his sleep.

Still, it wasn't enough. She sought out another weakness, the greatest of all. Fear. The King's hand shakes and his mind freezes. He tries to conceal it, but he can't hide his fears from the witch. Not from her! Her Third Eye sees all. The King's puppet master, the prophet Samuel, has abandoned him and turned away. Cast aside, cast aside. With nothing left but fear.

Fear. This was the freshest one, the biggest viper, so round and ripe and bursting with venom. Oh yes, she must send that one to the king's bedchamber, but it wanted a piece of her first. She struggled and strained to control it, but it sank its fangs inside her, for she was no stranger to fear. Its bite stung and she screamed.

"Fear me!" Molech's gravelly voice threatened from inside her head, and she felt his hideous touch. The viper stung her again and again, but she refused to succumb. This demon was meant for Saul, the one she hated above all others.

Hate, that hideous dark power, rules over fear. And so she restrained the demon and sent it to Saul. A black viper with yellow wings. It's eager to go to him, to tighten its coils around his throat and squeeze until he feels like he can't even breathe. Oh yes, go forth.

Saul screamed.

Still not satisfied, Alzsheba flew into a rage.

Where was the guilt?

The blood of her sisters was on his hands. The Third Eye could see. See all the crimson stains. But he felt no guilt for them. Not for Razana, not for Szandara.

The Witch of Endor and her sisters had been born Israelites, in the town of Tekoa. Alzsheba was the youngest of three girls. Her mother died giving birth to her and her greedy uncle murdered her father for their land when she was thirteen.

Alzsheba and her sisters found themselves tossed onto the streets. The older girls had to sell themselves to filthy men for food, until they finally decided they'd had enough and gave themselves over to dark forces. The devil and his demons gave them the things they needed. The sisters set up a shop selling medicines and other potions. For a little extra money they spun curses on people's heads, withering their crops or sapping their strength and good health.

Then King Saul decided to purge the Israelite cities of all the cultists, root peddlers, and conjurers. An angry mob dragged Alzsheba and her sisters from their home in the middle of the night. They killed Razana and Szandara, stoned them to death in the street. Only Alzsheba escaped, abused and humiliated by the mob, scrambling through the mud and rain—a despised outcast at the age of fifteen. She fled at last to Endor, a Canaanite city much more tolerant of outsiders.

Saul felt no guilt, but his hands were dirty. *Filthy with the blood of Razana and Szandara!*

The Third Eye grew tired, its festering lid heavy. Alzsheba took one last look before the eye closed. Saul roiled in torment on his bed as the demon snakes took their toll. Still it was not enough. She wanted more.

The blood of her sisters stained his hands. And she would make him pay.

FOUR

By the time David corralled the last of his sheep into their low-walled pen, it was well past noon. He broke into a run. *I hope I'm not too late.*

The spicy fragrances of the mid-day meal caught his nose, and his stomach growled. Abinadab's wife knelt before a cooking fire in the open courtyard midway between two small brick houses. As the youngest of his brothers' wives, she was usually the last to join them to eat.

"You're late," she said, stirring the pot. "Your father said if you didn't get them all in before noon, no supper for you. You'd better hurry."

The sun rode high over the rooftops of Bethlehem. Maybe his father wouldn't notice he was late. With some luck, he might still have a little time left.

"Great," he muttered as he bolted inside the main house and kicked off his sandals among the others at the doorway.

The rich smells of black cumin and coriander brought a smile to his face. He crossed the long central room, sidestepping his mother's loom, and hustled past the mules and donkeys. They were already settled in their stalls on both sides of the room, chewing hay between mud-brick pillars.

He raced up a rung ladder to the second floor. With all three of his soldier brothers visiting, the upper room was crowded. His family sat on the floor around platters of couscous and biscuits laid out on a mat in the center.

David's father, Jesse, was flanked by Eliab, David's eldest brother, on one side and his mother, Nitzevet, on the other.

While his brothers were busy laughing, he scooted beside his mother and next to Abby. Jesse, sharp-eyed as ever, shot him a look but thankfully said nothing about his late arrival.

Abby handed him a piece of fresh-baked pita from a wicker basket. He eagerly tore off a corner and scooped up a gob of couscous from the pottery tray. The spicy black cumin warmed his stomach and he smiled.

He loved his mother's cooking, especially when the entire family gathered together. He closed his eyes for a moment and just listened. Eliab teased Abinadab about his sword play, Mom fussed over Abby's untamed hair, and Dad lectured Shimeae about the proper way to chaff wheat. He breathed easy, finally able to relax after the long day. He was home.

Abinadab's wife joined them, carrying the pot of stew.

"That stew certainly took a long time to finish," said Jesse.

"You can't rush a good stew." She winked at David as she placed the pot next to the couscous.

His dad took a sip of wine and waved the others to silence.

David recognized that look in his eyes. Whenever the entire family gathered, his dad liked to make grand proclamations.

"The Festival of Weeks begins tomorrow," Jesse announced as if everyone didn't already know. "Now that the wheat crop is in, we'll head for Gibeah right away. I want to get started first thing in the morning. That way we'll be one of the first families to arrive. The Bedouins will already have made the crossing from Jordan and they'll be waiting for grain to load on their camels. We should be able to sell our entire harvest right away." Jesse leaned back and smiled.

Most of his front teeth were already missing, but David loved his father's smile. He had never seen a man who could display such joy in his face with so few teeth. At sixty-three, Jesse was an old man with a stooped back that constantly pained him. His hair fell straight to his shoulders in thin, gray strands.

"I've never seen a camel," said Abby.

"Filthy creatures," said Abinadab. He wore the gray tunic and white loincloth of a man of Saul's army. "One bit me on the arm at last year's feast."

"You mean a camel or a Bedouin?" smirked Eliab. He wore the same gray tunic but also a loose vest of dark leather with blue shoulder straps to denote his higher rank.

"That's not the point," said Jesse. "They'll need grain and we'll have it. We'll sell two lots of parched wheat for the price of three." He grinned. "And a few days later, we'll use the same silver to buy back twice as much at the usual price from the other families who arrive late. Just you wait and see, Nitzevet, if our wagon isn't twice as heavy when we come back as when we set out."

Nitzevet rolled her eyes. His father was always coming up with schemes that rarely went the way he hoped. He constantly talked about planting a vineyard but never had time to build the retaining wall or money enough for the vine cuttings. At last year's festival he'd bought three fancy new plough heads, certain he could resell them for twice the price. They still sat gathering rust in the barn.

"Just make sure you don't come back with less," she said warily. "And we need oil for the lamps."

"And we'll bring Abigail," Jesse added.

Abby broke out in a smile as bright as the sunrise.

"What for?" asked Eliab. "To feed to the camels?"

David nearly choked on a mouthful of goat milk.

Abby elbowed him in the ribs, her face turning red, transforming from sunrise to sunset in an instant.

"What for?" A sly grin snuck across Jesse's face. "She'll be eleven this season."

"I am eleven!" said Abby.

Jesse's grin morphed into a full-faced smile. "Of course. She'll be twelve this season. Twelve!" He glanced around at the faces of his many sons and their wives, but they all stared back at him with blank faces. "Well, sometime soon we'll have to think about marrying her off. And it wouldn't hurt if some wealthy land-owner at the festival took a liking. Now would it?"

David glanced at Abby. He doubted anyone else noticed, but he saw the way her lower lip trembled.

"Dad has high hopes for you," said Eliab. "He's not going to make the same mistake he did with Zeruiah. Her bride price included a promise of two men at harvest time, but they never bother to show up."

"And I'm keeping track of it, you should know," said Jesse. "They're going to pay me back for all that missed work, every bit of it."

"Dad won't be happy until he marries you off to a prince," added David in a reassuring voice.

"Well I guess that wouldn't be so bad." She pushed an unruly curl of hair from her eyes. "I'd make a good princess, so long as the prince was young and handsome and kind."

Jesse talked around a bite of pita bread. "Kings and princes only marry for alliances. You know that, Abby. We'd do well if he owns land."

Eliab scoffed. "You'll probably have to make do with the old man who runs the mill. He's sort of young-looking for seventy if you squint your eyes and don't look straight at him."

Abby's face twisted sourly. "Very funny."

"We've time yet," said Nitzevet, her voice low and sad, a frown darkening her face.

She's already lost one daughter to a bad marriage, David thought. She doesn't want to lose another. And he didn't want to lose his sister either. Not yet anyway. Sure she could be annoying, but she made him smile, and she was the only one who bothered to really listen to him.

"Sure, sure," said Jesse. "But these things take time. And the festival is only once a year. Everyone's in a good mood, having a good time. It wouldn't hurt for our Abigail to be seen, that's all." He nodded at his wife and grinned confidently.

"Don't expect you'll get near the house of Saul," said Eliab. "I know some of the men stationed there. Now that's a sweet assignment I'd give my right arm for. A lot less blood and a lot more wine than patrolling the straits, as I hear it. Not that I mind marching up and down the straits of Aijalon like a pack animal, swallowing dirt all day. It's just a man's got to think of comfort sometime."

David smirked. He knew how much his brother hated marching on patrol. Eliab constantly talked about a promotion to the house guard, which never came.

"You won't get inside the palace, Father," Eliab added. "Saul has two unmarried daughters, remember? He even has guards watching the guards."

"It's not the daughters I'm concerned with." Jesse took another scoop of couscous. "And we don't need to actually enter the palace. Everyone visits the festival grounds at some point. There must be a cousin, an uncle—someone—hanging about." He paused to stare down another scolding look from his wife.

"Anyway, that's not the main thing," he added. "It will be good for her to celebrate at the festival. We'll bring David with us, too. He can play his lyre for bits of silver in the square."

David grinned. For a second he'd been worried he would be left out.

"How much did he bring in last year?" joked Abinadab. "What was it—all of half a shekel?"

His brothers laughed, but Jesse cut them off. "Half a shekel," he said, "is half a shekel." He favored David with a little nod, for the first time really noticing him. "What happened to your shoulder?"

"I'm all right. It's just a scratch."

Eliab jumped in. "Did you take a beating from one of the bigger boys down at the mill again?"

"I usually give as good as I get!" answered David sharply. "But this was different.. A mountain lion came down as I was bringing the sheep through the mountain pass."

"What?" asked Jesse. "How many did it get?"

"None. I chased it away with my staff."

"Serves you right, for going through the mountain pass," said Abinadab. "That's completely the wrong direction. Can't you tell east from west? You were lucky."

"I know." He couldn't explain why he'd wanted to show Abby the beautiful rock formations in the mountains. If he tried, it would only serve as fodder for more of his brothers' snide remarks. They'd never understand.

"Stay on the flats, little brother." Eliab spoke slowly as if he were talking to the stupidest person in the world. "If you go down the valley, you have to climb up the other side." He illustrated his point with an exaggerated tilting motion of his hand while walking two fingers across it. Eliab and the others broke out laughing.

"Thanks, I think I've got the idea." David took another sip of goat's milk so they wouldn't see his face reddening.

Jesse pointed to the cut on his shoulder. "A mountain lion did that?"

"There was a bear too."

His mother leaned forward. "What? You were attacked by a bear?"

"Must have been a really small bear," joked Eliab.

"And you fought it off with your little staff?" asked Abinadab as he cracked an almond shell between his teeth.

"No," admitted David. "Something strange happened. The bear…" He couldn't quite think what to say.

"Kissed your feet and slunk away?" suggested Eliab with a smirk. "Or maybe you started to sing and he fell into a swoon?"

"No. The bear… caught fire all of a sudden. One moment it was there and the next it was gone."

"This is the most ridiculous excuse for coming home late I've ever heard," said Eliab. "A bear that disappears. Do you expect us to believe that?"

"I saw it too," said Abby. "And it did happen, just like he said."

Eliab sneered. "What a pair you two make. What will it be tomorrow? A dragon or a sphinx?"

"We did have that sudden storm," said Jesse. "It could have been a flash of lightning."

David's stomach tightened. He'd had an unsettling feeling all the way home that something else was happening, something bigger than a storm, something more powerful. Weirder still, he felt like he'd been chosen for an important role in what lay ahead.

"Maybe God intervened?" said David's mom.

Eliab laughed. "What would God want with our little David?"

Abinadab waved his hand at Eliab. "I met a traveler once who swore that God had saved him from a poisonous snake bite. He said..."

David shook his head, feeling foolish.

What would God want with me? I'm just the boy who looks after the sheep.

FIVE

Michal's life was filled with ordinary days. Days spent baking flat bread, spinning fabrics, or weaving baskets. As boring as those days often were, she never complained about them. Her ordinary days were far better than those of other girls in Gibeah. Before her father had become King, her life had been considerably harder and the days longer. She didn't miss those times. Anyway, she often found little ways to cheat ordinary days of their boredom: an unexpected conversation with someone new, playing games meant only for men to play, or even an improvised visit into town with Jonathan to barter with the potion peddlers.

One week had passed since her adventure with the Ark. She hadn't told anyone, not even Hadi, about what she'd seen and overheard. She'd never imagined her father had such doubts about himself and his relationship with God. It worried her. His confidence had been shaken by Samuel's betrayal and the endless battles with the Amalekites. The war had taken its toll on him. Now that the fighting was over, she hoped her father would find his faith again. She wanted to help, but he would never talk about something so important with her.

Perhaps this festival is what he needs. Maybe it will bring a smile to his face again.

She chased thoughts of the Ark and her father from her mind as she peered at the horizon from her favorite spot in the palace. Well, maybe not in the palace. She stood on the rooftop garden beneath a pair of small, potted palm trees that provided shade against the midday sun. A thin bed of wildflowers lined the waist-high wall that edged the roof, adding flashes of color and fun.

The rooftop garden marked the highest point of the entire kingdom, as the palace had been built on top of a hill that towered above the sprawling municipality of Gibeah. The buildings in the town were clustered so close together on narrow lanes, their brown clay walls looked like facets of a beehive carved into the hillside. She loved wandering through the streets with her brother, dragging Jonathan into the shops and market stalls, especially the stores that sold fine pottery. At the bakery she always forced him to buy her a sweet fig pastry.

Her gaze shifted to the dirt road leading to the palace. There it was! Finally a sign that the ordinary days would soon end.

"Look Merab," she said, pointing to a short caravan traveling along the long road up the hill toward the palace. "The first revelers are coming!"

Her sister Merab squinted against the harsh sun. She was beautiful in almost every way. Her dark brown hair fell lush and wavy down her back while Michal's was curly and unruly. Merab's almond-colored eyes were two shades lighter than her own, and Merab's lips were as attractive and full as the rest of her body.

Hadi had promised Michal that one day she would become even more beautiful than her sister, but she didn't believe it. It was impossible.

"They're just common traders," said Merab. "Look at those shabby carts and half-starved donkeys. They can't be anyone important."

"Maybe they have fine Persian rugs or silks or pottery in that cart. Maybe they're musicians or dancers or jugglers." Michal's heart quickened. She felt lighter than usual, the upcoming feast having already swept away some of the heaviness of the ordinary days.

"I doubt it," said Merab.

"Anything is possible, and it doesn't matter what they're bringing. They're only the first. Just think, in a few days the festival grounds will be full of interesting people with interesting stories they'll want to share with us."

Merab didn't look happy. Instead, she clenched her jaw tight and kept her gaze distant as she rubbed her hands together, twisting and turning them.

"What's wrong, sister? Aren't you looking forward to the feast this year?"

Merab leaned against the ledge. "No, it's not that. You know I love the feasts. It's just that everything feels different this year."

"Different how? The wheat harvest is in, and the grapes too. The same old decorations hang on the walls. Mother is fussing over every little detail as always. It all looks the same to me."

Merab glanced back at the travelers, her face suddenly grim. "Do you think they could be Amalekites?"

"I don't know. Why worry about them, anyway? That war is finally over. We won."

"That's precisely why I'm worried."

Michal instantly realized what was bothering her sister. Royal weddings usually followed after a war. Lands had to be consolidated, treaties forged. A few months shy of her seventeenth birthday, Merab would be matched soon.

"Father wouldn't," said Michal. "Not to an Amalekite. You don't have to—"

"Of course I do," snapped Merab. "I have to uphold the honor of our house. A King's household! We aren't just peasant farmers any more. I won't dishonor this house. I won't. If arrangements have been made…" She took a deep breath, then added, "Anyway, the Amalekites are probably no different from us. We're only taught to hate them because they raid our villages. We do the same to them."

Michal looked back at the small caravan, her chest growing tight. *What if they are Amalekites, and what if Father has already betrothed Merab to one of them? How far would she have to move away?*

"Has Hadi said anything?" asked Merab. "She has ears all over the palace."

Hadi did have a way of knowing things. She was always the first to learn when guests were coming, or which servants were pregnant, or when trouble loomed. But an engagement for Merab meant a new political alliance and was not something one of the servants was likely to overhear. Her father would keep something that important a strict secret. He wouldn't tell anyone until after the arrangements were already made.

Michal squeezed Merab's hand. "Hadi hasn't said anything. Have you asked Mother?"

"Mother will be the last to know." Merab frowned. "She'll probably find out after me. You know how she doesn't like to intrude on *men's* business."

"I don't understand how marriage is men's business." Michal felt heat flush her cheeks. "I mean, without women there would be no marriages. I think we're rather important in the process."

"Now don't start all that again."

"Why not?"

"Please."

"Fine. But we have to find out what's going on. There's only one person Father would confide in."

Both sisters turned to face each other and said the same name at the same time, "Jonathan."

"Can't you ask him?" Merab pleaded. "You've always been closer to him than me."

It was true. Merab and Jonathan rubbed against each other like two rough stones. Both of them could be so stubborn. Michal had a different relationship with him. She could talk to him and even change his mind sometimes.

"I know I'm stuck with whoever Father decides." Merab's voice cracked. "I'll do my part, but I hate not knowing."

"Don't worry. I'll figure out something. If Jonathan knows anything, I'll get it out of him."

"I just feel so helpless."

Michal flung her arms around her sister in a tight hug. As tears trickled down Merab's face, she hugged even tighter. She wanted to chase away her sister's worries by squeezing them out of her.

When they separated, Michal spotted another group of travelers quickly overtaking the merchants along the dirt track toward the palace. Dust swirled behind their horses in a long trail. Jonathan led the group. Three other members of the house guard rode with him. They surrounded a fifth man who rode a donkey.

"There's Jonathan," said Michal. "He looks tense, and who's that with them on the donkey?"

Merab leaned over the ledge. "I don't know, but look, his hands are tied."

The prisoner's head hung low, obscuring his face. "He's not an Israelite."

"How can you tell?" asked Merab.

"You see that symbol sewn in red on his robe? It looks like a bull's head with a man's chest and arms. That's a pagan symbol."

"How do you know that?"

Michal didn't answer. Hadi had warned her about that symbol once.

She felt the hair on her neck stand on end. Something was wrong, something important.

SIX

Michal's chest felt tight, her pulse quick. She needed to talk to Hadi right away.

She told Merab she suddenly felt ill and climbed down the wooden ladder into the courtyard. She began searching the palace. The house of Saul had become increasingly crowded. Servants crammed the hallways, cleaning the walls, bringing in provisions, or otherwise making sure that all foreseeable problems were, well, foreseen.

She wanted to race down the corridors, but running was unseemly for women and the last thing she wanted was for anyone to notice her distress. Where to look? She dodged a pair of maidservants carrying a tapestry out to the courtyard and narrowly avoided a farmer carrying a sack of wheat to the cellar. She didn't ask them about Hadi. Drawing attention to her housemaid was a bad idea. She wasn't quite certain why, but her instinct told her to find Hadi on her own.

She checked the courtyard, the cellar, the kitchens, and the arched entrance to the palace where servants waited to anoint guests' feet. Huge clay basins had been rolled into place on both sides of the archway in the grand foyer for the steady stream of visitors, but Hadi was nowhere to be seen. With her frustration rising, Michal paused in the courtyard with her hands on her hips. Where could Hadi be? Of course, she thought, I've searched everywhere but the most obvious place.

She climbed to the second floor, entered the royal residence wing, and opened the door to her small bedroom. Hadi sat on a corner of the bed, polishing a simple gold chain Michal would wear later that evening. She had laid out a formal shawl and a pale yellow dress with a red silk sash beside her. The dress wasn't her most elaborate; it was rather simple. She had many fancier ones, but this one was her favorite.

Hadi knew she would be nervous during the procession and knew exactly which dress would make her most comfortable. She always knew these things.

Hadi glanced up from polishing the gold chain. "What's happened, child? You look so worried."

Michal shut the door behind her. "I just saw that symbol you warned me about. The one that looks like a bull."

"A bull's head with a man's chest and arms?" Hadi's lips tightened into a thin line.

"That's the one. It was sewn onto the robe of a prisoner Jonathan captured. You told me to find you right away if I ever saw that symbol. What does it mean?"

Hadi turned from Michal and faced the narrow window that looked out the front of the palace. She placed her thin, careworn fingers on top of the windowsill.

Michal stepped toward her. "Hadi?"

"It could mean nothing, or it could mean everything," said Hadi, still gazing out the window. "But I suppose you need to know, so I'll tell you."

She turned, and Michal saw grief and sorrow had run down the long lines that dripped from the corners of her lips.

"I wasn't born in Gibeah. I was born in Tekoa. It's a small town three days' ride from here. When I was young, just a little older than your sister, I married. It was a good match."

Michal realized for the first time how little she knew about Hadi.

Why haven't I ever asked her if she'd been married? What else don't I know?

"He was older than me, but he was kind and strong and handsome. He had rust-colored hair. We were married so long ago that I can't even recall his face. I wish I could, but all I can remember is that beautiful hair and his strong arms and his smell. He smelled like the outdoors, like sand and wind and the sun. One day, he fell ill. It came upon him as sudden as a sandstorm. No matter what I gave him, he couldn't keep it down. Everything drained out of him. Nothing stuck."

She paused, her eyes roving the room as if searching back through time.

"What happened?"

"I was so desperate, I sought out the witches... A coven lived just outside the village. They worshipped this god, the one you've described."

"Witches?"

"Yes, witches." Hadi's voice hardened. "They could raise demons and curse enemies, but they could also heal. They had the power to save my husband, but I could not pay the price they wanted, so I let him die... I let him die."

Michal glanced at the gold necklace Hadi held in her hand, and Hadi laughed, but there was no joy in it. She lifted the thin golden links. "No, sweet child, gold was not the problem. My family had enough gold, more than enough, but they wanted something I could never give. Even now, if I had to do it again, I would still not pay their price. If those witches have business here, then we all need to be fearful."

"But... what did they want? What couldn't you give them?"

Two sharp knocks thudded against the door.

Jonathan sounded angry. "Michal, open up!"

Michal opened the door and Jonathan stomped into the room, his eyes hard, his hand gripping a torn piece of robe. He lifted the fabric so Hadi could see the bull's head symbol.

"Hadi, do you know anything about this figure?"

Michal recognized the deadly seriousness in Jonathan's clenched jaw and furrowed brow, and slid between her brother and her handmaid. "Why ask her? Just because she's not a Jew?"

"Not just that, sister. Besides, she knows exactly what this means." He waved the swath of ripped cloth like it was a flag. "It's obvious from her expression."

Michal glanced at Hadi, and the truth was written on her face. Her skin had drained of color; her eyes widened, and her lips pursed together. Even though they'd just been talking about it, the sight of the symbol frightened her.

She looks like she's going to fall down.

"Hadi's not saying anything until you promise me you'll keep her out of it." Michal's voice simmered. "She's loyal and always has been, but you know how Father's been lately. He's suspicious of everyone working in the palace these days. If he finds out that Hadi knows anything about this... symbol... he could turn her out, and I won't have that!"

"You don't understand. The stranger I found wearing this symbol murdered a whole family on a farm not far from here. They had two small children. He burned them. He won't tell me anything about this symbol or why he's here in Gibeah. He says he'd rather die. I'll gladly grant him that wish. But there could be others like him that mean us harm. This is serious. I don't need my little sister meddling in such matters."

"Hadi is part of my family." Michal crossed her arms over her chest and stared defiantly at her brother. "If Father turns her out, I'm going with her."

"I could lock you in the cellar until you come to your senses," said Jonathan, but conviction had begun to wane from his voice.

Michal knew she was getting to him. "I'll escape the first

chance I get, and you know I'll do it."

Jonathan groaned and his shoulders drooped slightly. "Sometimes I'd rather face a dozen Philistines with drawn swords than *you*. What do you propose? How do I keep this secret?"

Michal nodded toward the window at the newly formed line of travelers arriving at the palace grounds. "You can tell Father you got the information from someone at the festival."

"I don't like deceiving Father."

"Come on, Jonathan! You know we've nothing to fear from Hadi."

Jonathan sighed. "I must be crazy, but you win, sister. Okay? You win. I won't mention anything about Hadi."

Michal shot a reassuring glance at her housemaid and Hadi nodded back at her.

Jonathan's voice regained its sharp edge. "So Hadi, what does this symbol mean? And why would someone rather die than tell me?"

"It's the emblem of Molech. He's a very powerful god. If his followers have an interest here, no one can be trusted."

"There is only one God," said Jonathan.

"Others believe differently. There are witches that can summon Molech's power. They use it to control the innocent and make them do their bidding."

Jonathan smirked.

"You shouldn't take them lightly. That would be a mistake."

"Where do these witches come from?"

Hadi hesitated for a beat, but continued. "There used to be a coven in Tekoa."

Jonathan paced anxiously across the bedroom. "Tekoa. My father drove all the witches, magicians, and necromancers out of Tekoa ten years ago. They're all gone."

"Maybe," said Hadi, "but who can be certain?"

"Who would these witches ally themselves with? The Philistines? The Amalekites?"

"They have no sworn allegiances. They trust no one, but they would use anyone if it furthered their interests."

Jonathan looked hard at Hadi. "Surely you don't actually believe in this nonsense?"

"Gods are mysterious." Hadi shrugged. "They operate in ways we don't always understand. Even your own God suffers dark spirits who attempt to foil him."

"I believe in the power of our one God." Jonathan tucked the torn swath of robe into the folds of his tunic. "He will protect us from all other spirits."

"Without winter we would never appreciate summer," said Hadi. "Don't take Molech lightly. I've seen these witches use his power before. They're dangerous."

Jonathan smiled. "Yes, but the sun always drives away winter and brings spring back. Always. Is there anything else I need to know?"

Hadi shook her head, but Michal saw fear in her eyes. Even if Jonathan wasn't worried, she knew Hadi was, and that was enough to make her uneasy.

After Jonathan left, she whispered to Hadi, "All those years ago—when your husband fell ill—what did the witches want from you that you couldn't give them?"

A look of utter hatred swept across Hadi's face, so pure and fierce that Michal took a step backward.

"They wanted an innocent child. They get their power from burning children."

SEVEN

David couldn't shake the salty taste of dirt from his mouth. He tried to spit it out, but a fine grit coated his tongue. They'd been traveling since first light, and it was now well past midday.

He rode on a high seat at the front of the ox cart, sandwiched between his father and Eliab. His brother drove the oxen with a pointed rod, jabbing the animals viciously whenever they slowed. The old cattle barely paid attention to him as they plodded slowly along the dusty road, kicking up small swirls of red dirt with each step. The heavy cart had a tall sheepskin cover draped over a thin wooden frame. Its wheels creaked from the strain. Not only was the wagon packed with grain, but Abinadab, Shimea, and Abby rode inside.

The cart followed a trail that wove between sprawling household farms and long stretches of untended land. As he was only vaguely familiar with the area, the gentle slopes of the rugged hills all looked the same to David. His father, wanting to get to Gibeah early, had chosen a little-used shortcut. Eliab had cautioned against it, but Jesse wouldn't listen. He never did.

David's eyelids grew heavy. He'd started out wide-eyed and excited, but the long hours and the summer heat made him sleepy.

His eyes closed, and he dreamt of Gibeah, its mouth-watering smells, exotic foods, and all the interesting people from foreign lands he was sure to meet.

A sharp elbow from Jesse woke him. Three rough-looking men blocked their path. Eliab pulled on the yoke and stopped the cart well short of them.

"What goes on here?" Eliab shouted.

The men spread out. One stepped directly in front of them while the other two moved slowly to the sides. The one to the left carried a bow. The other two appeared unarmed, but David didn't like the sharp, hungry looks they were giving him.

"We're going to Gibeah," said the man in front. "Can you take us?"

Eliab waved them off. "Our cart is full."

"What have you got in there, anyway?"

"They mean to rob us," said Jesse.

A chill raced up David's spine. Eliab's sword was inside the cart with his brothers. The only weapon close to hand was the ox-prod.

He heard a noise behind them and noticed two more men sneaking up on the cart. "There are men behind us," he whispered, "and they have long knives."

"What have you got in there?" asked the first man again.

"That's not your business," said Eliab. He gripped the prod tight, but no matter how hard he hit the oxen, the animals wouldn't move fast enough to outrun the bandits.

"They'll rob us blind," hissed Jesse.

Abby's in the wagon, thought David. Who knows what men like this might do to her?

The cart rocked as Eliab stood up, hefting the cattle prod in front of his chest. "You would do well to let us pass."

The archer's bow creaked ominously as he drew back the cord. "Who should I kill first," he asked his companions, "the loud-mouth or the old man?"

The archer's hands were steady, the arrow trained on Jesse. The sun glinted off the bronze arrowhead as he pulled the cord all the way back to his ear. "Get down from the cart or the old man dies!"

"He's bluffing," whispered Eliab.

The archer smiled.

He's not bluffing, thought David. He's going to let that arrow fly!

David acted without thinking. He leapt from the wagon and landed lightly on his feet in the red dirt. The archer swung his bow, following him with the arrow's tip, but David rolled to the side, screaming as he went. The bowstring twanged, and he dove across the ground. The arrow whistled a hand's width over his shoulder.

David rolled directly into the path of the nearest rogue. The man reached for him but David bounced to his feet, elbowed him in the ribs, and spun away just before the bandit could grab him. Unable to look where he was going, he ran straight into a beefy thug the size of an ox who punched him in the head.

David saw stars and fell to the ground. Before he could see straight, the wide-chested man grabbed his hair, yanked him to his feet, and pressed the edge of a knife to his throat.

David felt the man's foul breath on the back of his neck.

"Struggle and I'll slit your throat."

Abinadab and Shimea piled out of the covered cart, swords drawn.

"Now we'll have a fair fight!" shouted Eliab.

But the bandits, who already outnumbered them, had allies of their own. A squad of four men on horseback broke through the palms at the side of the road. Heavily armed with longswords and shields, these men wore the dark tunics of Amalekite soldiers with the insignia torn off.

Jesse groaned.

David struggled to get free but the outlaw held him tight, the steel still pressed against his skin. The robbers outnumbered his brothers, had the advantage of riding horseback, and Abby was in danger. He had to do something, or they would all be killed.

Abinadab raised his sword to deflect a chop from an attacker on horseback but the height of his adversary left him at a severe disadvantage. He barely saved his head and the rider simply swirled around for another charge. Shimea also tried to stand his ground but was nearly run down by another Amalekite soldier whose horse sent him diving into the dirt.

The bandit still held David tight. At any moment his blade would slice David's neck. He had to do something.

An intense feeling of despair overcame him, and he remembered how that bear in the valley had been vaporized as it was about to lunge at him. If God had saved him that time, David prayed He would help again now.

The air crackled with energy. His vision blurred for a moment as something white passed before his eyes. Feeling a bit dizzy, he realized that something had come out of his chest, a weird white light in the shape of an orb.

He stared hard at it, worried for his sister and brothers and father. The light burned brighter and the air grew hotter until a scorching blast blew back against his face. Something burst from the orb as if he had somehow opened a portal to another place.

Something big. Something made out of light?

As it shot forward, he recognized the shape of a bird with a wing-span as wide across as a house. Only, it wasn't really a bird. It seemed oddly shaped, and longer than a normal bird, but he couldn't catch a good look at it. Its feathers burned in the hot sun like liquid fire.

The giant bird flew directly at the lead Amalekite soldier, wings flapping wildly. The man shrank back, his horse bucking and whickering.

The apparition nearly toppled the soldier from his mount. It swirled in the air, hovered above the horseman and broke apart into a flock of smaller birds that shimmered in every color of the rainbow. David had never seen anything so beautiful. They looped in the air, glittering like drops of dew in the morning sun, then flew at the attackers, soldiers and bandits alike, attacking in a silent frenzy, pecking and swirling about their heads. Some seemed to morph in front of David's eyes, growing talons long and sharp as steel and beaks that curved like daggers. Others changed in even weirder ways—one almost looked like it took a human head and another grew slender, stalk-like arms.

David felt the man behind him shudder. The bandit released his hold and toppled to the side.

Eliab had bashed the back of his head with the cattle prod.

Beneath the wave of luminous birds, the soldiers and bandits scattered, heading toward the hills. The flock streamed straight up in the air, making a column of rainbow-colored light. They streaked across the sky and disappeared in an explosion of color. David couldn't really believe that they'd been real.

Eliab kicked the man he knocked out in the stomach, and David grabbed his arm. "What?" he asked. "What did you see?"

"I saw a bunch of Amalekite cowards run away from some real fighting men."

"But those birds? All those birds?"

"Birds?" snickered Eliab. "Maybe this guy scrambled your brains when he punched you? We'd better get you out of the hot sun, David. I don't think you can handle any more excitement today."

David shook his head and scanned the sky for signs of the weird bird-like creatures. Finding none, he rubbed his sore temple and said, "I guess you're right."

Jesse marched toward him, each step an angry stomp. "David! You could have been killed! What were you thinking, going after that archer like that?"

"What did you want me to do? He was going to kill you!"

His father shot him one more sharp look before his face softened and he said, "Better me than you."

"Well, it worked anyway didn't it?"

"Yeah, it worked," said Eliab. "It took guts. I'll give you that, but you were just lucky. Try that on the battlefield and you'll get cut in half."

David grinned. That was as close as Eliab would ever come to giving him a compliment.

EIGHT

The rest of the trip to the city was uneventful and uphill, with the oxen struggling and lumbering along. The farms became larger and more developed as they neared Gibeah, and they passed terraced vineyards with striking views over the rocky farmlands of the tribe of Benjamin.

"Someday we'll have a vineyard like this," said Jesse.

Eliab cast his father a sidelong glance. Jesse had always wanted to plant a vineyard but never had time to build the retaining wall or money enough for the vine cuttings.

"Of course we will." David reassured his father although he didn't truly believe it. "Someday. Even better than these."

David's jaw dropped when he saw the great gate of Gibeah, which stood wide open as a variety of people and carts streamed in. It was huge, twenty cubits tall at least, built of stacked limestone blocks with an armed sentry posted at the top of each corner. A group of lepers milled about outside the walled city gate, many with dirty rags folded over their faces. They didn't approach, keeping instead to the shadows.

Eliab steered the cart clear, muttering, "Unclean."

"Stay away from them," Jesse warned.

David shrugged. "They're not allowed in the city."

"Many things happen in Gibeah, and not all of them are according to the rules. Wherever people gather together there is sinful behavior. Count on it."

"I am counting on it." Eliab winked at David.

Jesse pinched his ear. "And I expect you to stay out of trouble too. Remember you can't always tell if someone is unclean just by the way they look."

Eliab drove the cart through the gate.

David was amazed by all the strange and interesting people in the market square. Some were dressed in high turbans and elegant flowing robes of every color, while others wore torn rags. Snippets of music wafted toward them from the distance, a wild clash of drums and tambourines.

They didn't dare leave their goods untended. Abinadab and Shimea stayed behind in the shade to guard the cart.

Jesse handed David some small pieces of copper. "Go and buy that oil your mother wanted. Three pims should be enough for a full jug. And make sure it's full."

"You're trusting him with our money?" asked Eliab. "You might as well toss it in the street."

"I think he's earned the privilege." Jesse turned to David. "Three pims is a fair price. A full jug, I said. Remember. Meet me back here when you're done. If you can't make a good deal, come get me and I'll do it."

David watched his father and Eliab walk away.

Abby imitated Eliab's voice perfectly as she said, "I can't believe he's trusting you with our money."

David frowned at the pieces of copper in his hand. "That oil cost three and a half pims last year. I remember when he bought it."

The marketplace extended from the main plaza in every direction, a vast sea of wicker baskets, jugs and pots of all sizes, racks of dried meats, fruits and vegetables. They passed a wine shop, a butcher shop, a smithy, and an apothecary. The merchants hung colorful mats and rugs everywhere for buyers to see.

Abby flitted from place to place. She had to touch everything, running her fingers over each piece of exotic fabric and embroidered robe. She moved fast, but not fast enough. David yanked her out of the way of a tall man with a gigantic basket on his shoulder who nearly ran her over.

The sweet smell of fig honey stopped David in his tracks. His mouth watered as he hovered over basket after basket of date palms, fig cakes, and fresh grapes.

"Let's buy a fig cake," said Abby. "It only costs half a pim. I've never had one."

He weighed the copper in his hand, "We don't have enough for the oil as it is." He saw the disappointed look on Abby's face and added, "After I make some money playing the lyre, we'll come back. Until then, we can smell them for free."

A short time later, David and Abby headed back through Gibeah. David had a full jug of oil slung over his shoulder and Abby had a fig cake in her hand.

They had visited several shops. In each one Abby caused a distraction by carelessly handling some fragile item while David snuck a look behind the curtain in the back of the shop. When he found one that was obviously overstocked with jugs of oil, he offered only two pims.

"Two pims?" cried the shopkeeper. "Where's your knife? If you're going to rob me, you should at least have a knife."

As he had seen his father do many times, David shrugged and walked away. The frantic shopkeeper called him back and struck the deal—two and a half pims.

Abby handed David the last bit of fig cake. It tasted very sweet. They had only walked a little way before an approaching commotion caught their attention.

David grabbed Abby's arm, "What's that?"

Tambourines jangled and splashed. Hand drums pounded with a pulsating beat. "Look, it's a royal procession!" Abby practically hopped up and down.

David glanced across the street and noticed a strange man he could have sworn he had seen among the shops where he bought the oil. When their eyes met the man quickly looked away. He was dressed in a dingy gray tunic of coarse wool with a dark shawl thrown across his head and shoulders. He clutched the ratty cloth as if it were the only worldly possession he could claim as his own. Now that David looked closely at him, he was sure he had also seen that man when he'd bought the fig cake. *Who is he? Is he following us?*

Abby tugged at his arm. "Look David. Look!"

All thoughts of the strange man faded to the back of David's mind as he saw a splendid cart pulled by four mules. David had never seen anything like it before. The cart must have cost more than his family made in an entire year. Its gold-embossed sides and huge brass wheels sparkled in the sun. A slender steer horn, tipped in gold and silver, marked each of its corners.

The King stood at the front of the cart beneath an awning of fine linen. He looked down upon the crowd, stern and unsmiling. A thin band of gold circled his brow.

"King Saul's much taller than I thought he would be," said David.

Behind King Saul, the two royal daughters sat on a wooden bench. Flanking the cart on either side were two-wheeled chariots pulled by white stallions. Other carts followed, decorated with wild colors and banners, carrying people dressed in foreign clothes.

Eager to glimpse the royal daughters, David danced on the balls of his feet but the war chariot and its rider kept getting in the way. He could only steal a few glimpses as the cart rode by.

Even seated, the first daughter was taller. She wore a strapless gown of rich red fabric and a matching shawl across the top of her head. Her hair was elegantly coifed in tight ringlets that trailed down almost to her waist. Large shiny earrings dangled from her ears, a heavy necklace with a gold pendant circled her neck, and an elaborate headband of silver links rested on top of her curly hair. Exquisitely beautiful, she smiled and waved to the people.

But David barely noticed her. The second daughter wore a simple yellow dress with a red sash. Her earrings were much smaller and she had no other jewelry except for a plain gold necklace. Her shawl matched the yellow of her skirt, framing a face that had the same elegant proportions of her sister. Her hair wasn't quite so perfect. Although styled in the same fashion as her sister, it remained stubbornly unruly around the edges. She fidgeted in her seat, twisting the frills of her shawl in her hands.

"I love that red dress," Abby said.

David nodded, his voice temporarily stolen by the sight.

"She's the most beautiful girl I've ever seen!" shouted Abby.

She's picked the wrong daughter, thought David.

The girl in the yellow dress glanced across the street, but her eyes never met his. As the cart went past, David followed her for as long as he could. At last she smiled and waved at someone in the street, her face lighting up and her eyes shining.

And then she was gone.

David looked after the cart, feeling foolish. He wished she had smiled at him that way.

He saw a swirl of gray and spotted that same strange vagabond across the street. The man locked eyes with him for a heartbeat before he turned and melted into the crowd.

Who is he? I feel like I should know.

"Come, Abby." David grabbed his sister's arm and led her away.

NINE

David closed his eyes and lost himself in the music.

His battered old lyre fit so comfortably in his hands it almost played itself. By alternating a slow strumming with fast picking, he combined two folksongs into one. The fast passages felt like a heart dancing and the slow ones, a smoldering burn, like a heart aching. The two felt right together, and matched his mood perfectly.

Some lyrics came to mind and he sang them slowly in a low, soft voice.

"*My heart ignites within me*
And bright, the fire burns.
Tell me who I must be
And on what my future turns.
Surely every man is but one breath.

"*If I had the wings of a dove*
I would fly away, to heaven's nest.
If only I could carry your love
I'd fly away, and damn the rest.
Surely every man is but one breath."

He ended the song on a high, hopeful note. A dozen people had gathered on the street corner, but only a few took time to applaud and no one dropped copper in his bowl. These were not the well-dressed, fancy revelers of the festival. They were the simple people of Gibeah, dressed in drab, earth-toned robes. Music didn't come to their part of town very often and they favored him with only a smile or a nod before wandering away down the torch-lit street.

"How about something for the effort!" David rattled his bowl. A few pieces of copper jingled together. Four pims. Not much, but still better than he'd done last year.

He wondered whether he should stop for the night, when something dropped into the bowl with a solid clunk. It didn't sound like copper. He lifted the heavy piece of metal and twisted it in his fingers. It was gold.

"I liked your song very much. That melody is one of my favorites."

First, David noticed the fancy sandals—thick leather, with straps that wound themselves halfway up the ankles. When he looked up, he saw a young man with a strong face, and long, tawny hair that fell to his shoulders. He wore his beard cut neat and, like his hair, it was the color of ripe wheat. Dressed in a white tunic with fine golden embroidery along the edges, the stranger wore a red cloak over his broad shoulders.

"But I've never heard those lyrics before," added the stranger.

"I just thought of them today."

"Ah, sweet inspiration. Did you have anyone in particular in mind when you sang them? A girl from back home, perhaps?"

David paused for a heartbeat. He had been thinking of someone in particular when he'd sung those lines. He'd been thinking of the girl in the yellow dress, the king's daughter. But he couldn't tell that to this stranger so he settled on, "Something like that."

"Do you know the traditional songs?"

"Of course. I've played for some very important people." He

almost added "and sheep" without thinking because they were his usual audience, but he stopped himself.

"Even kings and princes?"

David shook his head. "No, but someday I will." He hurried to stand. Dirt from the street had settled on his rough wool tunic, but he didn't pat the dust away. He didn't want any of it to get on the stranger's fine clothes.

"That day may come sooner than you think. My name is Jonathan of the house of King Saul. There's a feast tomorrow."

David straightened his back and squared his shoulders. "Oh, I know."

"I mean a private meal in the palace. One of our musicians has taken ill, and he won't be able to play. I'd like you to come and play for the king. Would that be possible?"

"Of course."

Who wouldn't?

He tried to keep the excitement from his voice. "Will the entire royal family be there?" he asked without thinking. He imagined what Michal might look like at the feast, and his heart skipped a beat.

"You'll have a full audience. Come to the front gate first thing in the morning."

"I'll be there."

"Good. I look forward to it." Jonathan nodded and smiled before walking away.

David snatched the bowl with the gold piece before anyone else tried to get their hands on it, and secretly smiled at his good fortune. He had never held a gold piece before. He weighed it in his hand, keeping it well out of sight. It weighed at least two shekels. Two shekels of gold. That was half as much as they'd received for their whole cartload of wheat grain. His father would be impressed, and who knew how much more he might earn at the palace?

His father wanted him to return to the ox-cart when he finished playing. But his father and Abby were certainly already asleep, and he was much too excited to join them. Besides, he wanted to show off his good fortune to his brothers, so he tucked the bowl into the band at his waist and picked up his lyre.

His brothers hadn't stuck around to hear him play. Eliab had mentioned a place where they had an elephant on display though David thought he might have meant something else by the way he winked when he'd said it.

With only that to go on, David started out in the direction they had gone, away from the central marketplace, toward the outskirts of town. There were no houses or shops here, just tents. Most had been raised especially for the festival and lay half-obscured in the darkness. But while torches were few, many people mingled about. They shouted, laughed and argued. Several soldiers stumbled past, reeking of strong drink.

Entertainers of all types found their way to this part of town. A man dressed as a fool in a robe of brightly colored fabric juggled knives, five at a time. The wide blades glinted in the torchlight as they flew high in the air, spinning end over end. David held his breath watching, certain at least one finger would be sliced away. But the juggler's nimble fingers remained unharmed, not even a scratch. Incredibly, the man paid very little attention to the knives and preferred to look at the crowd which had gathered around him. He stuck out his tongue and made silly faces at them, even winking at David while the dangerous blades spun in the air. Many bits of silver found their way into this fool's basket.

David smirked. *Now, if I could throw blades like that, I wouldn't have to worry about bandits.*

He wandered past a few camels but saw no sign of an elephant. Now he was certain Eliab had been pulling his leg when he'd mentioned it. What did he really mean? Probably something to do with women, or drinking, or maybe both? Lost in thought, he almost bumped into a pair of men dragging another by his boots into an alley between the booths.

"Come inside, come inside! See wonders you've only dreamed

about!"

A tall man in a jeweled turban stood in front of a tent waving at people to enter. A short, thin man beside him played the flute. He might have been a child, but it was too dark for David to be sure.

A lively crowd stood outside the tent. David wedged his way through them to get a good look. The man in the turban lifted the flap halfway, offering a glimpse inside. A tall man stood just inside, naked except for a dingy loincloth, his hair bound up in a small red turban. His eyes bulged wildly as he slung a long, green cobra over each shoulder. He danced with slow sinewy motions as the hissing snakes dangled ominously, wrapping themselves in tight circles around the man's arms and neck.

On the other side was a woman who wore a yellow veil that completely covered her face. Honey smeared her entire body and locusts swarmed over the honey in a writhing mass. The woman gyrated slowly to the music of the little man's flute. Snippets of laughter came out from beneath the veil. The Bedouins cheered.

David wiped sweat from his eyes, not sure if he could trust what he had seen as the flap settled back down into place.

He rubbed his hand through his hair. Was that woman really naked underneath those bugs?

"Come in, son," said the barker. "Plenty more to see, if you've got a bit of silver for me, that is. Come on or move along."

As David walked away he heard his brother's voice a little farther down the row of tents. A group of men were arguing. One wore a leather vest and gray tunic. Was that Eliab? It was too dark to be sure.

One man pushed another and curses were exchanged but the argument didn't come to blows, and they both walked away.

"Eliab!" David called, but a loud cheer from the tent drowned out his voice.

David ran after the men.

"Eliab!" he called again. When he caught up to them, he tugged at his brother's shoulder.

Eliab spun with his fist balled and threw a looping, off-balanced punch.

David ducked. The punch sailed over his head and Eliab stumbled.

David caught his brother but struggled to support his weight. "It's David," he said. "David!"

"What?" Eliab squinted down at him. "What're you doing here?"

"I finished playing."

"So how did you do?" asked Shimae. "Did you get a few coppers in your beggar's bowl?"

"A few," said David. He was not eager to show his brothers the gold in their current state.

Eliab grabbed the front of his tunic. "A few pieces of copper," he muttered. "Is that all?" His breath smelled of sour wine. He pointed up at the palace on the hill. "You see that up there?"

David nodded and tried to wiggle free, but Eliab's hands held firm.

"The real festival is up there. Not down here among pickpockets and peddlers. That's all we ever get down here. Scraps from their table."

Abinadab shook Eliab's shoulder. "Shhh, brother. Don't say anything more."

"Well, why not? We're just as good as they are up there, behind their wall. Tossing over tidbits to the common people. To us! After they've already taken more than their share in taxes. So what did you get, little brother?"

Knots of people on either side of the street had started staring. David didn't want to show the gold piece right out in the open. He'd always felt safe with his brothers, but from their reddened faces, he was sure they'd all had too much to drink. Especially Eliab. "Not much."

"Not much," smirked Eliab, slurring the words. "That's not good enough for me, I'll tell you that. I should be in there. Up there!"

"Let's go." Shimae pulled on his arm. "Let's get away from here. You never know who's watching. Or listening."

Eliab grumbled and staggered down the row of tents.

David noticed a pair of eyes looking intently at them. A man stepped forward from the shadows. An old man. His hair, tucked haphazardly beneath a white linen cap, was the color of milk. He had mild features, a raggedy gray beard and blue-gray eyes. But those eyes startled David—so wild, so intense. He had seen them before! This was the man who had followed him and Abby through the town.

The old man reached out to them. He wore a tattered robe of white wool so worn it was little better than sackcloth. "Prophecy," he said. "I will tell all."

Abinadab paused. "Hey, how about it?"

Eliab shook his head. "He just wants our silver, like all the rest."

The old man whispered, "No payment is needed." He nodded curtly and waved them in. "Come inside."

Abinadab and Shimae glanced at each other, sly grins on their faces.

"Look at him. He's crazy," said Eliab.

David kept his gaze fixed on the stranger. Those blue-gray eyes burned through him.

Eliab grumbled. "He wants something. Let's go."

"Come on," said Abinadab. "If he doesn't charge us, what's the harm? I think it'll be fun." He stepped into the tent and the others followed.

The tent was as worn and ragged as its owner. A broad, flat wooden bowl sat on a mat in the center of the floor. That was all. The man had no possessions of any kind. He sat on the dirty floor and signaled for the others to join him. "Sit, boys. Sit. Rest easy."

Eliab leaned on David, nearly pulling him down as he eased himself to the floor.

"So many good, strong men," said the seer.

"Get on with it," said Eliab. "And remember, you said no payment."

The seer took one of Eliab's hands and laid it on the mat. He moved the flat bowl onto the open palm. From a pocket in his robe he produced a set of astralagi, the knucklebones of a sheep inscribed with symbols from the Torah. With a sharp flick, he tossed the five bones into the bowl.

The seer squinted at the bones. "A tall and strong man."

Eliab smiled.

The seer added, "Hmm, judge him by his heart, he is not the one."

"What d'you mean? Not the one? You promised me a divination."

"Yes. Yes." The old man glanced at the knucklebones. "You will find the inside of Saul's house, but it is a dark path you will tread."

"What's that supposed to mean?"

"A promotion."

"The house guard?"

The seer waved him off and reached next for Abinadab's hand. After shaking the bowl and rolling the bones, he said, "This one too the Lord has not chosen."

"Chosen for what?" asked Abinadab.

The seer looked him hard in the eye. "You will die on the field of Mount Gilboa, after a Philistine blade cuts your life's cord."

Abinadab jerked his hand away, scowling.

"Well, go ahead Shimea," said Eliab. "Put *your* hand down."

Shimea reluctantly lowered his hand.

"The Lord has not chosen these," said the seer. "Hmm, your end is in darkness. You will hang yourself from a crossbeam in the stable."

Shimea yanked his hand away, upsetting the bowl. "I've had enough," he said angrily.

David was worried he might hit the old man.

"Let's get out of here," said Shimea.

The seer looked down at his divination and mumbled, "Such dark portents for the house of Jesse."

The house of Jesse. How did he know that? wondered David.

The brothers had stood up and turned to leave when the man called out, "Have you forgotten the boy? Let me tumble the bones for David."

Eliab said, "David?"

"Sure," said Shimae. "Let David have a turn. I want to see what the old loon has to say about him."

The seer nodded gamely.

David sat back down, but a chill swept over him. The old man's eyes seemed to sparkle with unworldly light.

"Come on. Hurry up," urged Eliab.

David put his hand out, unafraid.

The seer placed the bowl on top and rolled the painted knucklebones into it.

The old man cackled. "Arise!" His wild, blue-gray eyes blazed hot. "Arise and anoint him, for this is the one."

"The one for what?" asked Eliab.

The seer scooped up his bones and stashed them into the folds of his robe. "This one will be the King of all Israel."

Shimea started laughing first, and it was contagious. Soon, the little tent shook with laughter.

"Well done," said Eliab, laughing so hard tears rolled down his cheeks. "Well done." He tossed a tiny piece of copper into the bowl. "That was worth half a pim after all."

"If David becomes king I guess I *would* hang myself," joked Shimea as he led his brothers down the street. "It all makes sense."

David ignored them. He thought about the weird fire that had consumed the bear in the valley and the orb and strange bird-like creatures only he'd seen during their fight on the trip to the festival. Still, he shook his head. It was late and his imagination had gotten the best of him. Of course the prophecy couldn't possibly be true.

He was nothing special, just a shepherd and lyre player. The seer was just an odd old man.

Halfway down the long row of tents, Abinadab stopped short. "Hey wait. I thought that crazy old man looked familiar. Do you think it could be him?"

"Who?"

"Samuel, the prophet."

"If it is, there's a price on his head," said Eliab. "The King has offered a generous reward for anyone who brings him in."

The men dashed back to the seer's tent. It was empty, the mat and bowl gone, the seer nowhere in sight.

"Damn," said Eliab. "Just my rotten luck."

Could it have been Samuel, wondered David. Samuel was a well-respected prophet among the Israelites. Years ago he'd been the one to anoint Saul in God's name. It probably wasn't him, though. How could it be? The old man looked ragged and wild, nothing the way Samuel had been described to him. His brothers must have been mistaken.

But if it had really been Samuel…

TEN

Michal swept her fingers against the arched limestone entranceway that led into the courtyard and struggled to swim through the feelings swirling through her mind.

The vast courtyard buzzed with preparations for the evening's feast. Servants hung tapestries from earthen walls. Others fussed over a raised wooden dais where her father, brothers, and the guests of honor would dine. A team of servants had cleared a large, square area for dancing and entertainment. Huge casks of wine stood at the ready with chest-high pyramids of wooden cups nearby. Each cask was decorated with a painting of a different battle King Saul had won. Soon the courtyard would be bursting with revelers and merry-makers, eating, drinking, and celebrating not only the wheat harvest but another year of prosperity under her father's rule.

Usually, she would be excited so close to an important feast, but that didn't describe how she felt today. Worried was more like it, though not quite right either. Hadi's talk of Molech and witches, and the ominous stranger Jonathan had captured yesterday worried her. She was also worried about her father's doubts and a potential betrothal for Merab among the many strange visitors sure to be attending the feast. Still, worried wasn't quite the right word for how she felt either. She felt as if she was poised to leap from a canyon and was unsure whether the water below was deep enough to receive her safely.

She turned and wandered down the hallway to look for her sister, when she heard lyre music coming from a nearby room. Odd, she thought. That doesn't sound like Calab playing.

The notes had a raw quality as if the fine polish from Calab's years of study had suddenly worn off. Michal peered into the practice room.

A young man her age sat on a stool with his back to the door. He strummed Calab's gilded lyre but seemed uncomfortable with its size and shape. An old, beaten up instrument leaned against the wall next to him.

Michal edged slowly into the doorway to get a better look at the musician. He had rich auburn hair with red highlights that flowed down to his shoulders in a shaggy mess. His face was tan, smooth, and pleasant looking. His beige tunic hung baggily over his shoulders as if he was wearing someone else's clothes. Thin, well-muscled arms moved under the loose-fitting fabric, and his fingers fluttered lithely over the strings. He wasn't trained, but the notes still sounded pleasant, the jaunty tune unique.

She turned to leave. It was improper for her to be in a room alone with a strange young man. But when he began to sing, she froze. His voice was sweet and strong. He sang an old love ballad, still unaware of her presence. She had heard this particular song before, many times in fact, but never like this. He sang with such sincerity, bringing the song's words and emotions to life in a way that caught her breath in her throat, and she swayed to the music. If he wrestled that messy hair into place, she thought, he might look quite handsome.

Just as he began the second verse, he lifted his eyes and spotted her. His hands fumbled over the strings awkwardly, creating an off-key twang, and his face reddened.

"I'm sorry if I startled you," Michal said.

"No, you didn't. My hand just slipped. I'm usually a lot better. It's just that they want me to use this lyre, but I prefer my own. This one is a little too fancy for me."

"Music is music, no matter what the instrument looks like."

"Then why bother putting all this gold trim on the lyre?"

Michal shrugged and backed toward the doorway. She'd get into trouble if her father or one of her brothers found her alone with a stranger, but it would be far worse for the young man. Her father had caught Merab alone with a servant boy two years ago. They weren't even doing anything except talking in a room not much different from this one. Merab had to work the kitchens for a month, and her father sent the boy away, never to be seen again. Some said he'd been whipped. She knew she should go, but she didn't want to leave just yet, so she lingered in the doorway. How much trouble could they get in if she was only in the doorway?

"Don't you want to hear the rest of the song?" David reached for his old careworn instrument, a confident smile lighting his face. "I'll use my own lyre and it'll be much better. I promise."

She returned the smile without thinking. She saw a rare earnestness in his eyes. Being the king's daughter, she was used to those around her always putting on masks to hide their true feelings. Not Hadi of course, but with so many others she rarely knew what to believe. So many false faces.

David lifted the lyre to his knee and cleared his throat.

He resumed playing, the notes stronger and more confident. When he sang, she lost herself in the truth in his voice, which was as honest as a young child's laughter. She looked deep within his hazel eyes, wondering where they might lead, when he looked up. It was her turn to blush as she quickly looked toward the floor.

When he finished, she said, "I have to go." She felt silly. This wasn't the first stranger she'd ever met and not the first musician either, but her tongue felt thick and she didn't know what to say. Her eyes flickered toward the hallway. Guests would be arriving at any moment.

"Do you like my playing? You didn't say anything."

She hesitated. She loved the song, but she couldn't tell that to him. She'd just met him, and he was too close to her in this room, alone where she shouldn't be. Her heart raced. "I thought it was fine."

David grinned. "Just fine? I could tell you liked it more than that."

"Really?" She crossed her arms against her chest. "How do you know? Can you read minds as well?"

David chuckled. "Of course I can. Don't you know that all musicians are really mind readers? All the good ones anyway. That's how we connect with our audience."

"I didn't know that. How about a test? What am I thinking right now?" As soon as the question left her lips she wished she could take it back. What if he really could read her mind?

"You're wondering what my name is."

Michal smiled, relieved that was all he said. "You are a seer! What shall I call you?"

"David," he said confidently. "That's my name. And one day everyone in the kingdom will know it."

"Why's that?" She was intrigued, but she was running out of time. She heard a noise from the hallway. A guest had arrived. She thought she heard Jonathan's voice greeting him. They were close.

"Well, let's just say that I have it on good authority."

"You seers and your secrets. How am I going to know if you really can see the future if you won't tell me?"

David hesitated. "I'm destined to be a famous warrior for King Saul."

"A famous musician turned warrior then." She pursed her lips. "It's going to be sort of hard to fight on the battlefield holding a lyre."

"This lyre is more dangerous than any sword." He swung the instrument in a broad loop, almost hitting himself in the head, and they both laughed.

"Why don't you join the house guard?" asked Michal. *If he's stationed at the palace, then I will see him again.* "You'd probably do yourself less damage that way."

"And just think, we'd see each other all the time. I'll compose scores of songs just for you."

"For me?" Michal looked away from his bright, penetrating eyes. *Has he seen right through me so easily? Am I so obvious?*

"Well, David, musician, warrior, and mind reader, I've got to go."

She stepped backward toward the door, but his eyes wouldn't let her go. He leaned over the top of his lyre, "I saw you yesterday, you know. In the procession through town."

"Oh, that."

"You seemed a little uncomfortable."

How had he noticed that?

"It was nothing," she shrugged. "I just don't like all that attention. All the people staring."

"You'll have to get used to it."

She leaned closer. "Used to what?"

David strummed a few notes on his lyre, letting the moment linger. "People staring." He smiled. "You're too beautiful for people not to stare."

Michal's face hardened. She didn't have much experience with men, but she knew he had crossed a line. "You shouldn't say that. If my father caught you saying something like that, you wouldn't like what would happen."

She turned and left the room. She should be furious with the brash young man, but she couldn't keep a smile from creeping onto her face.

When he finished practicing, David went for a walk on the grounds. His stomach growled. With all the commotion in the palace no one had remembered to offer him any food, and he'd been too embarrassed to ask. Even the servants were dressed in fine silks and did not look kindly on poorly dressed outsiders.

It didn't matter. The day had already been more exciting and more disappointing than he'd imagined. He hadn't gotten to see much of the palace, just the servant's quarters and the musicians' practice room, but he'd marveled at all the strange new sights and glimpses of how the King actually lived. The smallest of the rooms was larger than an entire floor of his house, the walls brightly painted in yellow and crimson. He was used to small dwellings with stained brown walls and dirt floors, eating the same food night after night. Everything in the palace was larger than life. He was sure the food would be extraordinary too, if only he'd managed a taste of it.

But the highlight of the day had been meeting the princess. Michal was more beautiful than he'd imagined, especially up close. And she hadn't seemed to look down on him at all. Her talk had been mostly playful and fun. And that smile...

He could almost believe that she might be interested in him. Almost. It would have helped if he hadn't acted like a fool or played so poorly. He'd tried to think of clever things to say, but how could he compete with all the educated men and witty philosophers she must meet every day? What could a poor shepherd say that she would find interesting?

As he replayed their conversation in his head for the hundredth time, he focused on her final warning. *If my father caught you saying something like that, you wouldn't like what would happen.* If my father caught *you*, she had said, not *us*. He felt hollow. He'd made a fool of himself. Flirting with Michal like an idiot. She'd never want him. She must have plenty of suitors from the best families all across Israel. How could he compare to them?

The evening feast looked as if it would be a great success. More food had been prepared and set out than at any other holiday Michal could remember. Platters full of roasted goat, feta cheese, freshly baked flat bread, figs, humus, raisins and honey covered the mat in front of her. Their varied smells mixed in the air and tickled her nose invitingly, but she couldn't take another bite. As it was, she hoped she'd left enough room for one of the sweet cakes.

She sat with her mother and sister on the edge of the courtyard not far from the dais. The open courtyard was filled with mingling guests dressed in colorful tunics, an odd mix of random colors that all blended together to make one vibrant picture. The room looked like a field of wild flowers. Women swathed in elaborate kaftans and beautiful gowns flowed throughout the hall while others sat on gilded cushions. Most of the women had worn their best jewelry for the occasion and the crowd glittered here and there with dazzling bits of gold and silver. One woman from Syria wore seven separate layers of clothing by Michal's count, her face completely covered with an embroidered veil.

In the broad, open space reserved for entertainment, three men from Judah danced an energetic folk dance, their high-stepping footwork perfectly timed to a frolicking tune played on the flute. Such happiness and wild energy radiated from their movements that she couldn't help but smile and clap along to the beat.

Even her father seemed to be in good spirits. He looked regal and oddly content, with a wine goblet held lightly in his hand and a knowing smile on his face. He sat, tall and confident, at the long dais at the head of the feast. He wore an elegantly embroidered green tunic and golden armbands and bracelets on both arms.

Now that dinner was over, the guests mingled around the room. Jonathan stood to her left. He leaned in close, sniffing suspiciously.

She stepped away. "What are you doing?"

"You're wearing jasmine perfume aren't you?"

"Maybe."

He scowled at her. "I've smelled that fragrance recently. Some place where it shouldn't have been. Michal, how could you?"

"How could I what?" she asked innocently, although she knew exactly what he was getting at. She'd been wearing jasmine perfume the night she'd snuck in to see the Ark.

"Never mind." Jonathan rubbed his hands through his sandy hair. "I don't want to know. One day you'll go too far, and I won't be able to help you."

"I don't know what you're talking about."

"Right," he muttered.

"I noticed that you and Father spent a lot of time talking with Gavriel yesterday. If I recall correctly, he has a son who isn't married yet. What's his name again?" She knew his name was Nathan, and she thought he'd make a good match for Merab.

"Are you looking for a husband already?" Jonathan grinned. "I can talk to Father, but I don't think he'll like marrying you off so soon. Although I did meet a Bedouin last night that said he'd part with a couple of camels if I found him a wife."

She stomped at Jonathan's foot, but he whisked it away just in time. "That's not why I'm asking and you know it."

"Oh?"

"Does Father want to marry Merab to Gavriel's son?"

"Don't worry about Merab. Just keep out of it," chuckled Jonathan, "if that's possible."

"You have to know something. Come on. It's not fair to keep Merab in the dark. You might as well tell me now. You'll tell me eventually."

"We'll see."

When the dancers finished, David emerged from the shadows, weaving among the wild flowers toward the empty space the dancers had vacated. She noticed the graceful, confident way he walked, his old lyre held in his hand. He sat on a small wooden stool and looked toward Michal. He smiled at her, and she quickly looked away.

Jonathan nudged her with his elbow. "I found this boy playing out on the street yesterday. He doesn't have half of Calab's skill with the instrument, but his voice is quite good."

David began playing.

"Who is he?" she asked, careful not to appear too interested.

"Just some shepherd boy from the country."

Michal noticed her father strolling toward them, a content smile on his face. He's pleased, she thought, and that made her happy. Perhaps his worries are behind him.

Just as he reached Jonathan's side, King Saul's eyes flickered toward the far side of the courtyard to where his cousin Abner, who served as general to his armies, had entered. An imposing figure, he wore a rich brown cloak strung across the typical gray tunic of Saul's army, his clothes smeared with dust from a hard ride. Michal thought he looked like a weed among the wild flowers.

King Saul signaled for David to stop playing and bent forward to listen to his general.

He needn't have bothered, for Abner never spoke in whispers. "The Philistines are massed along the mountain ridge above Elah. They're only a few days away from crossing into the valley."

"How many are they?" asked Saul.

"They number at least a thousand, but it was impossible to get an accurate count."

Her father scowled. "Who leads them?"

Abner looked uncertain, which was unusual for the confident general. "It was hard for the scouts to see at such a distance," he said. "But their commander… the man is said to be huge, at least half again as tall as an ordinary man. They say a giant leads them."

ELEVEN

Alzsheba detested the Ring of Sky. Long ago, a giant rock had fallen from the sky and smashed a vast crater into the earth. The rim of the circle was a jagged jumble of raised limestone, its base a flat expanse where the rock had been fused into a plain of glass so perfectly smooth it reflected the sky above.

She didn't despise the crater so much as the filthy bunch of Philistines crammed around it. They clogged the rim, perched along the ledges of stone, sitting atop crates and barrels and other assorted junk, or standing pressed together. She hated the smell of them — vile rabble, weak men, covered with the stink of their gender. She had nothing but disdain for all of them, their petty grievances and shifting loyalties, their base desires. So small, every one.

The soldiers gave her a wide berth. They sensed her contempt, and dared not sit too close. If any of them pressed his flesh against her, even by accident, it would be the last mistake he would ever make in this world. Maybe not instantly, but within a fortnight she always found a way to kill them. Strange sicknesses would overcome them, or weird accidents, even an unexpected suicide or two.

Torches circled the crater, changing the surface into a ring of fire as it reflected the bright red fames. A hundred different conversations fizzled away, merging into one ragged voice as the men began to chant:

"Goliath! Goliath! Goliath!"

Their champion stepped into the pit.

The men cheered.

Alzsheba's heart quickened.

Goliath was magnificent!

The giant towered above even the tallest of the Philistines, as broad at the shoulder as two men. She devoured him with her eyes.

How handsome he was. His pitch-black hair, a perfect match to her own, fell loose to his shoulders. A heavy brow overshadowed blue eyes that sparkled with a keen intelligence. He had a wide, flat nose and small ears, a jeweled earring dangling from the left. His powerful jaw was clean-shaven, his teeth white and straight and perfect.

Bare to the waist, Goliath wore only a steel shoulder-guard on one side and studded gauntlets of thick leather spanning from wrist to elbow. As the men cheered, he raised an immense sword in one hand, a heavy rectangular shield in the other. A long knife was tucked into his wide leather belt.

His proportions were more than human—his arms and legs so thick with muscle, his chest so huge it seemed almost as if the gods had chiseled him from stone. His entire body was massive, all the way down to his sandaled feet.

This, thought Alzsheba, is a man worthy to hold me in his arms.

Goliath tilted his head to the heavens and drank in the admiration of the soldiers. His only weaknesses, as far as she could tell, were vanity and overconfidence. She saw them clearly in the proud tilt of his head and the exaggerated forcefulness of his stride. *Is it weakness to be vain, or simply inevitable* when one is as superior as Goliath?

The giant thrust the sword into the ground, driving it like a wedge into the glassy plain. He stepped away, making it clear he had no intention of using it.

At the other side of the crater a pair of soldiers pulled on chains that lifted a door to a huge metal cage. A gigantic brown bear came tearing into the circle on all four legs. Blind with fury, the beast spun wildly around before it sighted Goliath.

With a terrific roar, the bear charged on all fours, froth pouring from its open mouth. It came fast upon Goliath. Rearing up on two legs, the beast stood as tall as the giant, flailing its claws in the air. Its sharp yellow teeth glistened in the torchlight. One bite from those savage jaws could snap a man's arm in half.

The bear lunged.

Goliath blocked the charge with his shield. The full weight of the animal crashed down on him and the muscles in his back strained as his thick legs were driven back into the dirt. Still, he held firm, grunting from the effort until he finally threw the bear to the side.

The Philistines cheered in a deafening frenzy.

The bear came at the giant again, jaw open, eyes blazing. This time Goliath not only blocked its charge, but struck its muzzle so hard with his shield, he knocked the animal to the ground. The giant kicked the beast as it rolled in the dirt and raised a fist to the adulation of the men.

The bear attacked again while Goliath played to the crowd. He pivoted just in time to block its charge, but the animal ripped away his shield. Bent in half, the twisted steel flew through the air, nearly cutting the head off of one of the bystanders.

Goliath drew his knife.

Alzsheba remembered the first time she'd seen the giant.

Ten years ago while fleeing Saul's purge of the Israelite towns, she'd sought refuge in the Canaanite city of Endor. After the

Israelites' treachery, she trusted no one and kept to herself, scratching out a living in a hut deep in the hills. She caught small game in her snares, coaxed vegetables from a little patch of red mud, and sold petty potions. Occasionally she traveled, always alone, in search of arcane knowledge, knowledge she could use to seek her revenge.

On her journeys she heard about the Nephilim, a race of giants who dwelled in the mountains outside of Garm. They were descendants of corrupted angels sent by Satan to taint the bloodlines of humanity. In time these superhuman giants would have dominated the earth, but the great flood thwarted Satan's plan—a global judgment meant to destroy the Nephilim and preserve the human race.

A few giants survived the flood. Relentlessly hunted by men, they were forced to hide in the caves and burial crypts under the town of Garm. The giants possessed a great knowledge of forbidden arts. Alzsheba wandered among the burial pits carved into the mountain, amid the bones and whispered voices of the dead, seeking Og-Sepher, the oldest and the wisest of the giants.

Deep within the maze of crypts a grotesque giant named Talnak seized her. He wanted to rip off her arms and legs and watch her wriggle on the floor like a worm, but as she had asked for Og-Sepher by name he brought her to him.

Hundreds of years old, Og-Sepher was taller and wider than Goliath, his body thick with massive rolls of pale flesh that hadn't seen the sun for many lifetimes. He sat hunched on a throne of bones below the mountains in a vast chamber lit by torchlight. Alzsheba proposed a trade, offering to share Molech's secrets in exchange for some of the giant's knowledge.

The giants held her in a cell until they determined her fate. She knew if they refused her, Og-Sepher would not let her live; she had discovered the entrance to their filthy little underground dwellings. One of her jailors was Goliath, grandson of Og-Sepher. His physical perfection and intellect intrigued her. Not content to remain hidden below the mountain, Goliath had secretly visited Canaan and a few neighboring towns. He told her of his ambitions and desire to explore the world.

She spoke softly in return, feeding his ego and aspirations of conquest. Among the Philistines, she said, he would no longer be hunted and reviled but treated with respect. He would become a hero.

Goliath scoffed at such a petty notion. He wanted to be a king among men. A king of all men. Why not? He was bigger and stronger and smarter than any of them.

Goliath enabled her escape, slaying three of his kinsmen in the process. Alzsheba raised a curtain of demon fire to cover their retreat, never knowing how many giants burned to death in her wake. Their screams echoed like thunder, and nearly brought the mountain crashing down. Goliath could never return to Garm. His path lay forward, not back. He would forge his future in the world and not scrabble among the rot and ruin beneath.

He called her his Ashtoreth, the Canaanite goddess of both war and sex, the consort of Ba'al, the god of storms. Alzsheba smiled at his grand and ridiculous romantic notions. She would use him in her plan of vengeance against the Israelites. He would lead the Philistines to attack Israel and destroy Saul. But he was much more to her than just a plaything. He was no sheep. He was magnificent.

Now, Alzsheba watched Goliath grapple the huge brown bear in the Ring of Sky. His keen eyes never left the animal, weighing its every move. He was confident and unafraid. The beast knew only blind ferocity, slashing and biting in a monstrous rage. Goliath blocked its raking claws with his leather gauntlets and met each open-jawed bite with a huge, balled fist before the bear could sink its teeth into him.

A score of claw marks had slashed the thick skin of Goliath's back before he made his first knife thrust. He sent his blade up under the jaw, pinning the bear's mouth shut. Then he lifted the massive beast from the ground by its neck, slowly twisting the head around. The muscles of his arms bulged with tremendous effort as the bear still flailed at him with its claws. But most of the fight had gone out of the beast by then, running down its neck in red rivulets from the knife wound. One last twist and the bear's neck snapped with a resounding crack.

The Philistines cheered as Goliath threw the carcass to the ground and stomped it with his foot.

Alzsheba's heart raced. *He is practically a god.*

She jumped over the rock ledge, slid down the slope and into the Ring of Sky and threw her arms around him. She was a tall woman but even reaching up as high as she could, her arms only circled his chest. She pressed her cheek against his sweaty flesh, breathing in his rich, animal smell.

"That was a good show," she said.

"I needed the exercise. No one here can give me a good fight."

"I'm glad you won."

"Was there ever any doubt?"

"Not for me. But I overheard Ahmad the Moabite placing bets against you."

"Did he?" Goliath grabbed a fistful of her long black hair and pulled it back, tilting her face up at him.

What does he see when he looks at me? she wondered. Does he see a beautiful plaything? Does he see only my sorcerous power? Or does he see his future queen?

He kissed Alzsheba full on the mouth, his lips rough as gravel, his passion hot like the blood that boiled in his veins.

"Let's go to our tent," she suggested.

Goliath glanced up at the night sky and took a deep breath as if tasting the air. "I'm not tired."

"Neither am I." She smiled and squeezed his hand.

He drank in her perfume. "You always smell so good."

She wore a spicy perfume of her own design, a mix of herbs

and scents specially created to drive Goliath crazy.

"You smell of blood," she said. "What a sticky mess you are."

She flicked her tongue playfully at a drop of blood clinging to his chin.

He pushed her away, leaving splotches of the bear's blood across the front of her leather bodice.

He grinned. "I just need to take care of a little something first."

She knew that look in his eye. The show wasn't over yet.

He strode to the edge of the crater where the men still lingered among the torches, settling their bets. He plucked Ahmad from the crowd, taking him by the neck and the seat of his tunic.

The man screamed in absolute terror.

Alzsheba smirked. *He'll never leer at me again.*

Goliath lifted Ahmad over his head, holding him by one leg and the opposite arm.

Ahmad pleaded for mercy in a high babble of indecipherable words.

Goliath ripped him in half like a piece of parchment and threw the pieces down into the Ring of Sky.

TWELVE

A week later, David walked among the flock again. His body was home, but his mind and heart were still back at the palace with Michal. It made him crazy. No matter what he did, or where he went, he only saw Michal: the dew that sparkled in the morning sun reminded him of her eyes; the sweet sound of the wind as it brushed through the tall grasses, her voice; the fresh scent of the wild flowers, her fragrance. Everything reminded him of Michal and nothing else mattered.

The goats slowly worked their way down the slope, nipping the tops of the buds with the sheep following along to take the rest. David paced nervously up and down the hill. The rocky terrain, the red dirt, the misty gray sky — none of it held much interest for him.

"What's bothering you?" asked Abby.

"Nothing."

She poked him in the back of the thigh with the stick she used to prod the goats. "It's not nothing. You've been moping around for more than a week, ever since we got back from Gibeah."

David sighed. "Leave it alone."

"I will not." She prodded him again.

"Stop poking me!"

"Then tell!"

"Why are you always so annoying?" He knew Abby wouldn't stop. All things considered, it would be less painful just to tell her, and he had to tell someone.

"I met this girl at the feast. I can't stop thinking about her."

Abby's eyes lit up. "What girl? Why didn't you tell me? What's she like?"

"She's amazing! She's more beautiful than the sunrise over the canyon. More lovely than—"

She poked him in the leg with her stick again. "Be serious."

"I *am* being serious!"

"Really tell me about her. I don't want to hear about canyons or sunrises or any other goofy stuff like that. Is she pretty? Is she nice?"

"I can't get her out of my mind. She has this way about her. Whenever I close my eyes, I see hers. People think her sister is the pretty one but they're wrong. She really is beautiful. Even more than her sister. She lights up the whole palace."

"Palace? Oh no, David. Are you talking about Michal? The princess?"

He smirked. "Well maybe, but I like to think of her as just… the king's daughter."

"Yeah. That's why everyone else calls her a princess. The King will never let you near her. They have all those big tall walls and guards at the palace just to keep her safe from boys like you. Besides, I'm sure she spends all her time with rich people with lots of land and gold and servants. You know - interesting people." She smiled and swiped her stick at him, but he stepped back before it smacked his leg.

"She's not like that. I bet she doesn't care about stuff like that. She's really nice, really."

"Oh, I'm sure. I bet you've never even talked to her."

"You'd be wrong then. We met in the practice room before I played for the King. She was nice. And smart too. We were just two people chatting as if I had met her at the well. It wasn't like she was a princess at all."

"Didn't you tell me that the royal family only marries for money and alliances?"

"That was before..." David paused. Before what?

"Before you met Michal," Abby said, finding the words for him.

"Yes, that's right. But I was just talking then, now it's different. Michal is different."

"Oh, brother, you'd better forget about her. You'll never be able to compete with rich landowners and princes."

"Can't I? Who says?"

One of the goats nipped a sheep and it bleated loudly.

"That's why," joked Abby. "There's your princess. Instead of lands and servants you wander empty fields and rule over goats."

David sighed. "Maybe you're right. All the way home, I just kept thinking that I won't ever see her again. And now I'm stuck here in this stupid field with you and she's all the way in Gibeah."

"You'll see her again. After the gold you made this year, Dad's sure to take you back next year."

"Next year's too late. If you'd met her, you'd understand. She has this wonderful smell, sort of like flowers."

"That's called perfume." Abby grinned, seeming happy to know something her older brother didn't. "I bet all the women at the palace use it."

"I guess so. The palace is full of fine things. All the walls are covered with tapestries. You should see them. Every color of the rainbow. When people first enter the place, priests anoint their feet with oil. And they make such a big deal out of it too."

"Wow. How did that feel?"

"I don't know. They didn't do it for me. I was just a musician, not a guest. The priests at the door wouldn't even look me in the eye."

"We're just farmers to them. They wouldn't waste any oil on

us." Abby frowned. "I wouldn't want some priest fussing over my feet anyway."

"We maybe farmers, but Eliab is right about one thing. We're just as good as they are. Even if we're poor and don't have the things they have. King Saul used to be just a farmer too."

David kicked up a puff of red dust. "We only met for a few moments, but I'm telling you there's something really special about Michal. I have to see her again."

"Sorry, brother. You'd need a miracle." Abby brushed some of her unruly hair from her eyes. "How about the miller's daughter, Rachel? She's cute and always smiles when she sees you."

"You don't understand! It has to be Michal."

The playful smirk fled from Abby's face. "You're really serious."

"Yes, I'm serious," he fumed. "Look at us, standing here. The same sheep, the same fields, the same dirt. Everything looks the same, but it's all different now. I can't go back to the way things were. Not now. Not after I met her. I've got to do something."

"What can you do? You'll never be a prince. At least you got to meet her."

"Yeah. I'll never be a prince." He took a few steps toward the flock then spun around. "But what if—"

Abby groaned. "Don't get any crazy ideas."

"What if I join Saul's army? Maybe I could get into the house guard and spend time in the palace? Why not?"

"The same reason as always. Dad won't let you go. You can't just think only about yourself. We need you around here. And besides, the Philistines are killers, David. I've heard they have some kind of a giant. That he's ten feet tall. I'm worried about Eliab and the others."

"Don't worry about Eliab. His skull's as hard as a helmet anyway. Maybe I can run away and join them. What's Dad going to do about it?"

"You wouldn't really do that," said Abby.

"Who says I won't? If that's the only way I can see her again, it's worth the risk. I just need a plan."

The next day, David had just coaxed the flock into their pens when he heard the braying of mules, a tinkling of bells and a shout from one of his brothers.

Three mules with riders had just passed the fence, bearing the silver and blue colors of the house of Saul. A tall man wearing a gray tunic and red cloak stepped down from his mount. David got there about the same time as his father.

Jesse greeted the man with a big, lopsided smile showing all of his missing teeth. "Welcome! Let me bring you a little bread so you may refresh yourself, and water to wash the dust from your feet."

"Do you have any meat?"

"None close to hand," said Jesse. "May I offer you some lentils?"

"Lentils? Do you think the messenger of King Saul is to be satisfied with some stale half-cooked lentils?" The messenger waved his hand imperially. "Never mind the food. Let us conduct our business and I'll be on my way."

"What business is that?" asked David.

"The King's musician has died."

A glint flashed in his father's eyes. "It just so happens that my son David plays the lyre, you know. He's quite good. Quite good. He even played once for the King."

"I know. I was there, though I have to say he didn't sound nearly as good as our usual man."

Jesse smiled thinly. "And you came all the way here to tell us that?"

"No," answered the messenger. "When your son played for King Saul, the King found something pleasing in his music. Though to tell you the truth I've heard many better all up and down the coast of Phoenicia."

Jesse smiled again. "But if the King likes it…"

"Then it must be good." The messenger grudgingly finished the sentence. "Yes. And the King requests that your son come and play for him in the evenings."

David's heart leapt. "At the palace?"

Jesse nudged him in the ribs, scowling at his enthusiasm. "Really, I'm not surprised the King is interested in my son's music. But such a thing is impossible. It's just impossible. I've three sons away at war already and not enough to see to the crops and the flock as it is."

"You could hire someone to look after the flock," suggested David. "There's only twenty sheep and a few goats."

"Could I?" Jesse's face flushed red. "Hired hands cost money. I'm not going to pay someone so the king can listen to you play. And hired hands are never as good as family. You have to watch them all the time. Am I going to follow some young kid around all day? You know how my back aches if I have to walk too much."

David turned toward the messenger. "I imagine there's a generous stipend?"

The messenger cleared his throat. "Two shekels of silver every month."

Jesse dismissively waved at the messenger, though David knew he could hire a new shepherd for half as much.

"Two shekels," said Jesse, as if mulling it over. "And he's to play for the King at night? You know there's talk in town." He lowered his voice to a whisper. "There are rumors the King is haunted by demons in the evenings. Demons, they say. You haven't heard anything?"

"Four shekels," said the messenger.

"My son is to risk life and limb, not to mention his immortal soul, for four shekels?" Jesse shook his head. "I won't have it. No, no it couldn't possibly be arranged. I'm sorry. You'll have to send my regrets to King Saul."

David couldn't believe his good fortune. A way back into the palace. He couldn't let his father ruin it. There was only one way to get him to agree.

"If the King wants me to go, I'll do my duty," he said. "But I can't leave my family in hardship. Six shekels."

"Five!" said the messenger as he crossed his arms against his chest.

"It sounds fair," said David.

Jesse gave David a half-wink and said, "I might agree on one condition. I have a young daughter named Abigail. If some position could be found for her in the house of Saul…"

The messenger nodded conspiratorially. "I'll arrange for it. We leave right away."

Five shekels was a steep price for a musician, thought David. Why pay so much? What are they really after? And what's all this talk about demons?

THIRTEEN

Michal sighed at the loosely stacked pile of wicker baskets at her feet. She hated weaving—the monotonous twisting of the fibers, the scratches the coarse flax strands left behind on her fingertips, the inevitable ache in her hands from hours of work. Well, hate was a strong word. Maybe she strongly disliked weaving baskets and trended toward hate. Still, weaving baskets provided her a convenient way to get Hadi away from the rest of the house servants. And she needed secrecy.

Hadi had only two baskets at her feet; two baskets were not enough. She tried to twist a long strand of hemp around the edge of a halfway completed basket, but her hands shook too much to complete the turn. Her eyes pinched together in concentration and she tried again.

Michal read the frustration in the tight line of her handmaid's lips. When Hadi tried to twist the strands again, her hands shook even more violently. Age and her failing health had left her too weak to work the fibers.

Every servant in the House of Saul was expected to pull his or her own weight. Michal's mother would make no exceptions for Hadi, especially now that they had so much to do because of the war with the Philistines. Hadi couldn't complete the tasks expected of her anymore. Hopefully when her health improved, things would change and the old Hadi would come back, but Michal had seen no sign of that happening. So she had volunteered herself and Hadi to weave baskets all day and stay out of sight.

Michal worked tirelessly to complete Hadi's share. She had worked well into the evening every night this week with nothing more than the light from her small lamp to brighten the hemp, but she still fell behind. She'd worried that her efforts would not be enough until Abby arrived at the palace this morning. No one knew what to do with the young girl, so Michal snapped her up. The weave of her baskets wasn't quite as tight or straight as Michal's or Hadi's, but she worked fast, and fast was what Michal needed most. Now, between the three of them, they had a chance to cover for Hadi. At least until someone else noticed Abby's skill at weaving.

The sun was near setting, its fading light barely enough to illuminate Michal's room. It would be time for dinner soon. Michal locked her eyes with Hadi's. The old woman's eyes were still sharp, but they were wide and sad. Michal knew what she was thinking and wanted none of it. "We've done enough today, Hadi. Put down that basket and rest while Abby and I finish these. Tomorrow will be another day. You'll feel better then."

Hadi said nothing, but shifted the shell of a basket off her lap, her thin shoulders folded down. Her gaze focused on the window.

Michal doubted she was interested in the sunset. More likely she didn't want Michal to see the sadness on her face.

Abby wore a simple gray shawl and skirt that ended by her ankles. When she'd first arrived she'd been so nervous her hands shook more than Hadi's, but those jitters dissolved away as the day wore on, and she completed several baskets. "So Abby, tell us a little bit about where you come from."

"We live south of here. About a day's ride. It's nothing like this. It's just a small house on a small farm in the middle of nowhere."

"Not long ago this place was just a small farm," said Michal.

When Abby's expression made it clear she didn't believe her, she added, "My father's only been king for ten years. Before that, we were farmers. I was young back then, younger than you, but I remember what it's like to live on a small farm with nothing much around."

"It's so boring," said Abby. "No one interesting ever comes calling."

Michal thought of her ordinary days. "Life isn't that much different here, except for the feasts."

"I was at the festival last week, but had to leave when the war started." Abby shifted her eyes between Michal and Hadi, "Do you think it's true?"

"What's true?" asked Michal.

Abby whispered, "That there's a giant who leads the Philistines. I hear he has two heads, is as tall as the palace wall, and can shoot fire out his eyes."

"I wouldn't believe everything you hear," said Michal. "What do you think, Hadi?" Hadi's turned toward them, her face gaunt, the skin stretched tightly against her cheeks. "I've never seen a giant myself, but I've heard they exist."

"Do you think they have two heads or shoot fire from their eyes?" asked Michal.

Hadi grinned. It was such a slight thing with only the ends of her lips, but just the small gesture made Michal feel better. The old Hadi still lived inside her. Once she started to feel better, maybe eat a little more and get her strength back, things would go back to the way they were. At least that's what she prayed would happen.

"No, I've never heard anything about shooting fire," said Hadi. "But it's said that giant blood burns all the time. Giants aren't just big-sized people, you know. They're different. Their skin is as thick as cowhide, their muscles like iron. And they're clever too. Much cleverer than people give them credit for."

"But how big are they?" asked Abby.

"Only the witches from the village where I was born had any

real knowledge of giants, and they were unreliable, as you can well imagine." Hadi shrugged. "They said most giants were twice as tall as men and as heavy as a full grown bull."

Abby turned white.

"Don't worry, Abby," said Michal. "Even if there is a giant, we have God on our side, and God will help us slay a thousand giants if need be."

Abby nodded.

Michal grinned. "So how does a farm girl from Bethlehem end up as a servant in the palace?"

"They came for my brother, so my father made sure I was part of the bargain." Abby's face reddened slightly as if she was embarrassed by the whole situation.

"Your brother?" teased Michal. "Is he some type of special giant slayer?"

"No," Abby chuckled. "He wouldn't know what to do if he saw a giant. He just plays the lyre."

Michal's heart skipped a beat. Plays the lyre. "What's his name?"

"I think you might have met him last time he was here." A sly smile snuck across Abby's face. "His name is David."

"David," repeated Michal. For a moment she forgot Abby and Hadi were in the room as she remembered the brash young man, the color of his hair, and the sincerity in his eyes. Then her wits returned. "I thought he wanted to be a warrior?"

"My father will never let him become a soldier. We already have three in the family and Dad needs him to do chores around the farm. Besides, I don't think he's ever swung a sword. He wouldn't know what to do with one. He told me he spoke to you, but I'm surprised you remember him."

"Oh, I only spoke with him a little, just before he played at the feast. He seemed very confident of himself." Michal resumed her weaving, making sure she looked at her hands.

"David doesn't lack confidence," chuckled Abby. "He'd face

down a mountain lion or a bear to save the sheep in his flock."

"Really," said Hadi. "A bear?"

"I saw him do it." Abby shuddered. "It still gives me a chill."

"Faced down a bear, huh?" Michal laughed. "I'm afraid someone like that might find the palace a little boring. Especially if there's someone special he's left behind at home."

"Oh, he doesn't have anyone special."

Michal tried her best to keep Abby from noticing the smile on her face. Having just finished the basket she was working on, she aimed the smile at her handiwork. "That's all we need to do tonight. Do you think you can find your way back to the servant's quarters by yourself?"

Abby nodded.

"Good, we'll see you first thing after morning meal."

Abby left and Michal shut the door behind her. When she turned, Hadi's gaze bore into her.

"So, is this the boy you've told me about? The one with the red hair?"

Michal shrugged. She never could keep secrets from Hadi. She had told her about his sweet voice, but left out his forwardness or that he was so good looking. "It's a shame that Caleb passed on so suddenly."

Hadi smirked, "Yes, Caleb did pass on unexpectedly. But we were talking about Abby's brother. I noticed that you asked a lot of questions about him?"

"I was just passing the time."

"Right. I see the same gleam in your eyes that you had when you couldn't stop talking about the Ark. You're much too quick to play with fire, child. You were lucky not to get caught looking upon the Ark."

"No one got hurt when I saw the Ark. You're the only one who even knows that I saw it."

"Yes, but you were just risking your own safety then Michal. You must be careful with this boy. His wellbeing is also at stake. It would not go well for either of you if you're caught alone together. But it would be especially bad for him."

"I understand the rules, Hadi." Michal leaned against her windowsill. "I won't break them."

Hadi joined her at the window. "The Philistines are close. Rules tighten when war rages. Your father and brother will act harshly."

"Father's won every war we've fought so far. With God on our side, we can't lose." Michal's voice trailed away. She remembered her father's doubts when he'd visited the Ark.

Had God turned His back on him?

Without God, how could they defeat a giant?

FOURTEEN

Two kitchen maids carried dinner into the servant's quarters, a large pot of plain couscous slathered with goat milk yoghurt. Another set down a small plate of boiled dumplings directly in front of David, but experienced hands grabbed them all before he had a chance to get any.

Just like home, David thought. Even at the palace, some things never change.

He wondered what the royal family was having for dinner in their fancy dining room. Not the entire royal family—only Michal appeared vivid in his mind's eye. Everyone else, including the King, was nothing but shadows. He'd spent the whole day wondering about Michal. What she was doing, what she was eating, who she might be spending time with...

He'd arrived the previous night too late for supper and had gone to bed hungry, settling down on one of the empty mats in the back of the servant's quarters. No one assigned him chores during the day, so he'd wandered freely inside the compound. He meandered aimlessly around the buildings—a full stable, a smithy, military barracks, a vegetable garden, a grove of fruit trees, shrines, kitchens, courtyards. All that and he hadn't even explored the whole place yet. But no Michal. He tried to sneak inside the palace a few times, but a member of the house guard stopped him and sent him away.

Well, at least I'm inside the front gate. I'll find some way to see her. Sooner or later.

The dozen men and boys in the barracks attacked the porridge in a frenzy as if this were their last meal. David was lucky to snatch a few scoops of porridge for his bread before they finished the pot. Afterward, a quiet gloom descended on the room. No lantern lit the inside of the building, which resembled the stables a little too closely for his tastes. Everyone seemed tired after their day of work and settled into their bed of rushes.

"So you're the new blacksmith apprentice, is that right?" asked the man on the mat next to him—a burly fellow with wild brown hair and an unkempt beard.

"No, I'm a musician." David nodded toward his lyre, wrapped in a gray oilcloth beside him.

"So that explains it, eh Harel?" The man nudged his son, who occupied the next pallet. "Not really built like a smith, is he?"

"He's built like a girl, I think," said Harel, who was not quite as big as his father but a good deal larger and taller than David.

"A musician, eh? Well," said the man, "what were you doing with the blacksmith this afternoon, then?"

David didn't like his sharp tone of voice. He thought he'd left his brothers back in Bethlehem. "He asked for a little help with the bellows that's all. It's none of your business."

"Not my business? Since you've got so much free time to help out, you'll start with me tomorrow in the stables. My son works too hard shoveling out all the shit. He'll be glad for your help."

"I'm not a stable boy. I'm a musician," said David. "Besides, from the looks of him, the dung suits him fine."

Harel scowled. "What's that supposed to mean? Is that some type of insult?"

"Some type." He rolled over and turned his back on them in

hopes of getting some sleep.

"Too good for the stables, eh?"

"Or not strong enough for the work?" asked Harel.

"You'll have to shovel the shit without me. I'll be in the fruit grove practicing. I want to sound my best when I play for the *King*." David placed quite a bit of emphasis on the word king.

"Well, I like music," said the stablemaster. "Why don't you practice now? Hey, get him his lyre, Harel. It's right over there."

"Where? I don't see it." Harel stumbled comically in the dark.

David sat up. He felt a nervous chill as the buffoon stepped close to his instrument.

"Hey! Get away from that!"

The young man stomped his foot onto the lyre. Wood cracked and a string snapped in a tortured squeal.

"Now that's music!" gloated the stablemaster.

"Oh how clumsy," said Harel. "I stepped on it. It's all broked..."

He laughed and so did several of the other men.

David balled his hands into fists as he stood up. "You'll regret that."

"Really?" sneered Harel. He kicked the broken lyre out of the way. "Maybe some stupid instrument's not all that's going to get broked tonight."

David knew he had to fight. And one thing he'd learned from fighting, it was always best to land the first punch. "Something's going to get broken all right. You're just too dumb to realize what."

He launched himself at the thug, driving his fist into Harel's flabby belly. When the bigger boy doubled over, David punched him hard on the point of his chin.

Harel staggered back a step, but as the shock of the blow wore off, he flew forward in a rage. Quicker than David could have guessed, Harel landed a right cross to his jaw that sent him sprawling to his knees.

The left side of his face felt like it had caught fire.

"Get up!" shouted Harel.

"Or better yet, stay down," said the stablemaster. "I'll expect you in the stables first thing in the morning."

David stood, rage powering his body. The servant's quarters had suddenly become noisy as the other men egged them on. They all cheered for Harel. And from the jeers aimed at David, he realized he had no friends here. He needed an advantage.

He spotted the broken lyre only a few feet away. David darted toward it and Harel rushed to meet him. David moved quicker. He reached the instrument before Harel could wrap his meaty hands around him. In one smooth motion, David snatched the instrument and swung it upward, smashing it into Harel's face.

Blood burst from the young man's nose, but it barely stopped him.

His head must be made of stone, thought David, just like his brain.

Harel grabbed David around the waist and tossed him over his shoulder like a sack of potatoes.

David crashed onto his back, groaned and saw stars flash in front of his eyes.

"Step back!"

The uproar in the barracks quickly died away.

"I've told you before, I don't want any fighting in the evenings."

David staggered to his feet, and Jonathan stepped between the two young men. He took a quick look at David's already swollen face and Harel's bloody nose.

"If this happens again, we'll find another stable boy, and stablemaster. And as for you..." Jonathan turned toward David. "It's time for you to earn your keep. Where's your lyre?"

Harel smirked.

"My old lyre broke on the ride here," said David. "It wasn't really good enough for the King anyway."

"Fair enough. We'll stop by the practice room and find you

another. Let's go. We don't have all night."

They stepped outside.

"You seem brave enough, but not very clever." Jonathan handed David a cloth to clean the blood from his face. "Harel's almost twice as wide as you and strong as an ox. You should be careful about fighting men who are that much bigger than you."

"I didn't really get a choice."

Jonathan nodded. "I see. Hazing for the new man. Most times we don't get to choose who we have to fight. But there are ways to defeat bigger opponents. I'll have to show you sometime."

"I'd like that."

As they entered the palace, Jonathan greeted the soldiers posted on either side of the front door and led David to the practice room.

"Where will I be playing?"

"The King's bedchamber. You have something soothing to play? He wants to sleep."

"Putting people to sleep is easy. It's getting them roused enough to dig in their pockets for some copper that's difficult."

"Not this time." Jonathan handed David the gilded lyre, then paused to look him earnestly in the eyes. "I have to warn you. There are some strange happenings here at night."

David's stomach turned. "Like what?" He followed Jonathan up a staircase to the second floor. They passed an open-air solarium and paused outside Saul's bedroom.

Jonathan's voice had lost some of its authority. "The King is... troubled at night. Sometimes he cries out. You're not to be alarmed if that happens. Just keep playing."

David remembered the rumors about demons his father had mentioned. The turn in his stomach tightened into a knot. "Is the queen inside?"

"She's sleeping somewhere else for now."

Jonathan opened the bedroom door. "You don't have to perform if you don't want to. I can send you back home."

"I'm not afraid."

"Good." Jonathan smiled kindly. "Let's go in."

The King's bedchamber was an immense, square room. David had never seen so much furniture in one place. Aside from the bed, there was a gigantic hardwood cabinet for clothes, and a table and chairs. Various small jars and urns cluttered the table, their rims stained with potions or medicines of various colors. Two large windows faced the rear courtyard. A thin slice of the garden and a stand of fruit trees could be seen between the fluttering draperies. A small cot, a stand with a washbasin and another small table loaded with fresh fruit stood near the door.

A pair of gilded pillars raised the large bed high off the floor. The oil in the two lamps on either side of the bed burned low but provided enough light to see the King covered in rich dyed-red blankets as he lay on the bed among the many pillows. He tossed and turned, looking much older than before. He moaned softly.

The King seems ill. Will he even hear me? Is he sleeping or awake?

David settled onto a low chair in front of the bed; Jonathan sat on the cot behind him. He knew a few traditional folksongs that were slow and melodic, but wasn't sure they were loud enough for the King to hear in his current agitated state.

He pushed the chair a little closer to the bed and began to strum his lyre. He played a song called "Simple Pasture" which was popular among the herders of southern Judah. It combined a slow melody with a rich texture. He used it sometimes to quiet an agitated flock of sheep when he camped out at night on the hillside.

Halfway through, the King moaned louder than before, tossing his blankets aside. David needed something more powerful, a strong melody that would reach into the king's nightmare. He remembered a song he had composed last year. He'd named it "Fire in the Sky", a song in praise of the Almighty. It had a sharp, pounding melody, an attention-getter to be sure, but depended on quick string work between the fingers of his left hand, a trick he could hardly manage with the big fancy lyre.

He fumbled with the tune for a few minutes. King Saul let out another anguished groan. David felt certain this song would work if he could only get the notes right. He tried harder. As the music took hold of him he sang from his soul. The world melted away, leaving nothing but the lyre and the notes and the music.

He felt dizzy and lightheaded.

And then, in the flickering lamplight, he saw them.

Three snakes hovered over the sleeping king. One was midnight blue, with a pair of leathery black wings flapping just behind its hissing face. Another was a fiery red cobra covered with small spikes and thorns. It writhed and twisted grotesquely in the air. A third, a black viper with broad yellow wings, turned its eyes toward him and snapped its mouth snapped open, showing monstrous fangs.

David didn't just see the snakes. He felt the waves of dark emotion that swirled around them, enveloping the king. Doubt. Indecision. Fear.

What are those things? Is that what demons look like?

His dizziness increased. Every breath became a struggle, but he kept playing. He focused only on the song, finding comfort and strength in the lyrics. Though he hardly had breath enough to sing them, the words rang from his mouth. Praise for the Lord.

He felt his chest fill with a wild energy that tingled down the length of his arms and coursed all the way down to his fingertips. He fumbled no longer. The strings became a part of him, as powerful and sure as the faith he felt in his heart. The song resonated from the lyre in perfect pitch.

The blue snake lunged for him, hissing and spitting. It circled David's head several times but couldn't harm him. If the King had doubts, David did not. He felt great certainty instead. He was right where he needed to be, doing just what he was called to do.

The other two snakes darted at him from the sides. But these were King Saul's demons and David stared them down. He had often been called impulsive, but never indecisive. Fear could be overcome as long as one had faith, and his faith was strong.

His music grew more forceful as the song took on a new dimension. A divine power flowed within him, speaking through his fingers. And that power was greater than doubt or petty suspicion or fear. As the music burst from his fingertips, the white orb he'd somehow conjured on the road to Gibeah appeared. The orb pulsed, releasing streams of multicolored light. The light whirled and spun and David recognized the many rainbow-colored birds that had fought the Amalekites. The shimmering figures were both beautiful and terrifying at the same time.

The birds swirled around the room in a frenzy as they attacked the winged demons with shimmering beaks and claws. The snakes coiled and hissed, writhing as if on fire. Let them burn, he thought. Let them burn in the Fire in the Sky.

And then, one by one, the demons vanished, leaving behind only puffs of acrid smoke. David continued playing, but his fingers were tired and his mind nearly exhausted. As he plucked the final notes the birds disappeared, for each one had been a note of his song, sharp and clear and true. The bright light in the room dimmed with the passage of each bird until David and the king were left alone in the darkened space.

The King rested peacefully, his brow no longer furrowed, the hard lines of his mouth relaxed and at peace.

Jonathan whispered, "Let's leave him now."

David turned, still breathing heavily. He'd completely forgotten about Jonathan.

Jonathan seemed to look upon him with fresh eyes. Where before his face had been colored by concern for his father and even fear, now he looked upon David with an expression of admiration and respect.

"Thank you."

"Did you see?"

"I never see them," Jonathan said grimly. "But I know when

they are there, tormenting him. I can feel them."

"But the light—you saw the light and the colors?"

"I heard…" Jonathan shook his head. "I heard your song."

David glanced back at the bed. He half expected the demon-snakes to have returned, but they were still gone.

"You've done very well, David. My father will be pleased in the morning."

"I didn't do anything. I just played a song."

"That's funny." Jonathan took the valuable, gold-trimmed lyre from him. "You didn't strike me as the modest type."

FIFTEEN

Michal tossed restlessly on her bed. Perhaps it was the full moon shining through the drapes that bothered her, or perhaps that Jonathan had returned from the front and hadn't spoken to her yet. She wanted news of the giant and she trusted him to tell her the truth. Or maybe it was the idea that David was nearby. David! After the festival she'd thought she'd never see him again, which would have been for the best, but now she was sure to run into him and she didn't know what to think, what to say or do, or how to act.

He's just a simple shepherd from a small farm. Our futures can't be entwined. It's just impossible.

She should forget about him, but she couldn't. She kept replaying their brief conversation in the practice room over and over in her mind until she felt dizzy.

She rose from her bed, bubbling with anxious energy. Since rest was out of reach, she decided to seek out Jonathan and discover the truth behind the giant. Surely he wasn't ten feet tall and couldn't shoot fire from his eyes? The stories must be exaggerated, but only Jonathan could confirm that for her. He must have seen the giant by now.

It was late, but he would still be awake. She slipped a simple shawl over her nightshirt and snuck out of her room. She'd get in trouble if found sneaking around the palace this late. Men could walk the halls at any time, but women were expected to stay in their rooms at night. She bristled at the injustice behind the double standard. Besides, she would stay in the royal family's wing, so who would spot her anyway?

Thin slices of moonlight slipped through the narrow window and lit the hallway. Jonathan's room was the one next to her father's corner room. She crept forward on the balls of her feet, careful not to make any noise. All the doors were closed except her father's door, which had been left slightly ajar.

As she raised her hand to knock on Jonathan's door, she heard music drifting from her father's bedchamber. Her heart skipped a beat and her hand froze. Someone was playing the lyre. The notes sounded slightly off, the rhythm uncertain, and she frowned. David must have been playing Caleb's lyre again.

Michal glanced at her father's open door. She should leave, but she couldn't leave. The song changed and the tempo sped up. This one sounded better, more confident. She brushed her fingers against the earthen wall, feeling the rough plaster as she stepped toward her father's room. The music grew louder and more pleasing. She hesitated at the doorway, but she had come this far. Why not peek inside?

She saw David sitting at the foot of her father's bed. His body swayed to the music as his fingers flew across the strings. His red hair glimmered in the flickering lamp light, the amber glow playing across his smooth features. His eyes shone with an unearthly brilliance. Her father tossed around on his bed, turning this way and that, a moan escaping his lips. A shadow swirled above his head.

She blinked her eyes. She thought she must have imagined the shape in the air, but she saw another shadow and then a third. They twisted above her father, menacing him.

The rumors about his troubled sleep and the demons that visit him at night are true.

She hadn't believed them before, but now she saw the horrible truth for herself.

Her breath froze in her throat when the shadowy shapes turned from her father and slithered toward David.

He continued to play, the music sweet. The menacing swirls darted toward him as if they might sink poisonous fangs into his flesh. He ignored them. The lamp must have started to burn brighter because she could have sworn that a sudden new light filled the room.

She wanted to call out to him, to warn him, but held back. She dared not disturb his song. The music seemed to shield him from the demons. Though the frightful clouds circled him, they did not harm him, and the strange light flared brighter and brighter.

Suddenly a burst of color joined the white light and the demons vanished.

David finished the song and lowered his lyre, looking exhausted.

Jonathan stood from the cot behind the bed and paused by her father's side. The king slept peacefully.

When Jonathan turned toward David, Michal hurried down the hallway. She slipped inside her bedroom and shut the door. Her mind whirled. *The demons are real!* She'd seen them! And somehow David had chased them away with his music.

How did he do that?

No sleep would come to her tonight.

SIXTEEN

Alzsheba peered into the swirling mists of the Third Eye. The scent of burning opium and poison hemlock filled her lungs. Her hand, burned when she'd pulled the demons from the fiery pit, still ached. Her mind swam with hatred.

The dirty gray mists parted; time and space fell away to reveal Saul lying on his bed. The snakes circled his head and she waited for them to attack but something was wrong. They didn't attack. He should be roiling in torment by now.

Why didn't they attack? Saul had a peaceful look on his face. Impossible! The demon snakes, which had a moment ago screamed with her hate, now grew fuzzy and weak. *What is that sound? Music?*

She watched in horror as colorful shards of light in the shape of birds attacked the snakes, their claws and beaks ripping at the demons until they disappeared.

She willed herself awake, slammed the Third Eye shut and opened her own eyes to the gloomy darkness of her crypt. The horrid music still rang in her head, splitting her skull in two, the pain excruciating. The walls of her little shrine in the cliff started closing in on her. *I have to get out, before I'm sealed alive in this stony grave.*

She gasped for air but the thick cloying incense only made her more lightheaded. She was drowning. Drowning. She knocked over the desecrated altar and stumbled through the crack in the cliff.

"What is it?" asked Goliath. "What's wrong?"

She gasped, still lost in the half-daze of the incense and the visions. A silent scream stuck in her throat. Goliath's face had become a hideous, grinning skull. Only for a moment, then the pale death mask disappeared, and he was her glorious, handsome Goliath again.

Alzsheba recovered herself, taking deep breaths. Fresh air chased the woozy feeling away. "There's someone there."

"Where?" Goliath leaned forward to look inside the crack.

"With the wretched Saul. Someone's protecting him."

"Who?"

"I couldn't see him clearly."

"You said the Third Eye sees everything."

"Not him. Not this one. But…"

Goliath's eyes glinted with scorn, as if he saw her weakness written plainly across her face.

Can't stand him looking at me like that. She straightened her back and lifted her head. "He's there, with Saul. In the shadows in the corner where the Eye can't see clearly. But I know he's there. He can't hide from me."

"Who? Who the hell is he?"

"A boy. He's just a young boy with red hair. A lyre player in the house. He's nothing, but somehow he's tapped into a great power to protect Saul."

"We'll have to kill him. That's all."

"Of course," she said, now speaking with confidence. "We'll kill him. We just have to decide how."

"I'll go there myself." Goliath grinned. "I'll march across the Valley and up the hill and straight into Gibeah. I'll tear down the front gate, brick by brick, and toss the guards aside like flies. I'll bring down the entire palace. And then I'll find him, this lyre player boy, and I'll drag him out of his hiding place and snap his neck."

She shook her head. "Sometimes a dagger in the dark can do things a war hammer can't. To kill a louse we need a louse of our own. Someone who can creep in the dark, someone a little bit less obvious than a giant. Someone who won't be noticed."

"There must be one among these dogs who can get the job done."

"Yes, I know the one. I just have to convince him to go."

"And how will you do that?"

She smiled. "I have my ways. He'll do anything I ask."

Goliath scowled. "I'll convince him. Just tell me who it is."

Was that a touch of jealousy on her dear giant's face?

"A man named Yarqon, a trader from Ashkelon. He's not much of a soldier but he's clever and good with a knife. He's perfect for this job. The boy won't stand a chance."

SEVENTEEN

The House of Saul rested on the Sabbath as priests performed religious services throughout the day. Michal spent the morning thinking about what had happened the night before. As impossible as it seemed, she was sure of what she'd seen. David's song had somehow raised spirits that had scared off the demons. She didn't know what to make of it. She knew good and bad spirits existed, but she'd never seen either before last night, and now she'd seen both!

Despite her unsettled mood, she left the palace and let the sun warm her face. She felt relieved. There would be no weaving today, no worries about the number of baskets she had to deliver, or the secrets she kept.

She spotted Abby walking toward her, a broad smile on her face.

"Happy there's no work today?"

Abby's smile grew even wider. "Yes, but I'm even happier about my trip to Gibeah. David said he'd take me right after I go to service."

Michal glanced over the young girl's shoulder. "I don't see him. Where are you going to meet him?'"

"He's down by the pear trees. I'll find him right after I finish with the service."

Michal stepped aside. "You'd better hurry. They should be starting any moment."

Abby sped past her.

Thoughts raced through Michal's mind. *David is down by the pear trees. I should at least thank him for helping Father. What would be the harm in that? But if someone sees us, how will I explain it?*

Most of the pears had been picked already, but some still hung on a few of the late developing trees. As she walked farther from the palace, the bustling sounds of the royal compound faded away. Few people wandered among the fruit trees on the Sabbath. Most men went into town and the women usually spent the day chatting in the courtyard or on the rooftop garden.

She swerved her way among the neat rows of trees as she looked for David. *What am I going to say to him?* Her chest tightened. She turned down a row and found him not more than ten feet away, leaning against a trunk, eating an almost-ripe pear.

She stopped. *There's still time to walk away. If I turn down another row, he might not see me.*

But then he turned, and it was too late to retreat.

"Hello, princess." David bowed, his bright eyes sharp and his smile honest. "I'm glad you found me."

"Who said I was looking for you? I might have just been wandering the grove looking for thieves." Michal pointed to the pear in his hand and her tone sounded much harder than she intended. "That fruit belongs to the House."

"Of course," said David as he took another confident bite. "But I found it on the ground and couldn't let it go to waste."

Michal chuckled, "I'll bet you did. I hear you're playing for my father."

"Yes. I guess he liked my music at the feast." He stepped closer to her, stopping only an arm's length away.

Michal noticed a sliver of pear clinging to his chin.

"Why aren't you using your own lyre?" she asked. "Don't let them make you use Caleb's."

"I don't really have much choice in instruments these days. Mine has a hole in it the shape of some idiot's foot. I don't imagine it would sound quite right." David took another chomp from the pear and grinned. "So you've been watching me. Did you see me play last night?"

"I haven't been stalking you or anything." The sun seemed to heat her face as if the day had suddenly gotten a lot warmer. "I went to talk to Jonathan last night and happened to see you through the open doorway. That racket you were making could have woken the dead."

"Oh." David tossed the pear core away. "It didn't wake your father. When I left he was sleeping like a baby, without a care in the world."

She studied his face, looking at the lines around his lips and eyes. She wanted to know what they meant, but they were mysteries. Women's lines were easy for her to read, but she had no experience with these. They could mean anything.

Is he just being polite, or is there more?

"I saw you play. But that wasn't all. I saw strange shadows that looked like swirls in the air, above my father's bed. Oh, it sounds stupid, but I don't know what else to call them."

"You saw the demons?" He was so close now she almost wiped away the bit of pear from his chin.

"Is that really what they were? They looked like smoke."

David moved closer still. He whispered, so she had to lean forward to hear him. "They looked like winged snakes with fangs. My song scared them off, I think."

Michal's heart raced as she felt his breath against her cheek. "I thought I saw light coming from the lyre."

David inched even closer. They were practically breathing the same air.

She noticed how the sun caressed the red highlights in his hair.

How his chin had only the slightest trace of stubble.

"I know this sounds crazy, but I felt a presence in me. Like God flowing through my fingers while I played."

Michal might not have been an expert on boys or men, but she knew he was being honest. "I don't think it's weird at all." She thought back to the strange feeling of strength she'd felt when she looked upon the Ark. "But I wouldn't tell anyone else about what happened if I were you."

"Why not?"

"It's just a bad idea. You never know how people will react. Some might feel threatened... or jealous. I doubt the priests would appreciate it."

David waved a bee away and his fingertips briefly brushed her shoulder.

She felt a shock. He'd touched her for less than a heartbeat, but she felt heat where his fingers brushed her skin. She pulled her shoulder back. "I've got to go."

He frowned, "Stay, I'll pick you a pear. There's a ripe one on top of that tree." He pointed to the highest branch on a nearby tree.

Michal scanned the grove, looking to see if anyone else was about. She had spent too much time with him as it was. "No, I've got things to do. I just wanted to thank you for helping my father." She turned, but David reached out and grabbed her hand. His fingers felt soft and warm.

"Come back next Sabbath. I'll play for you."

A voice inside her head shouted 'No', but she heard herself say, "Maybe" instead.

David watched Michal disappear down the row of fruit trees.

He smiled. He had been running himself ragged wandering the compound all day hoping to catch a glimpse of her, and she'd come looking for *him*. He had to thank Abby. She'd been in the courtyard all morning waiting to tell Michal that he was in the fruit grove.

That trip to Gibeah he'd promised her would be well deserved.

She came looking for me!

He'd felt heat when he touched her. He knew she felt it too. Now he had to find a way to see her before next week.

I can't go an entire week without being alone with her again.

A branch snapped close by and his heart froze. Had someone seen them together? The hair on the back of his neck stood on end.

"Is anyone there?" He felt stupid as soon as he said the words.

Another branch cracked and leaves rustled. He spun and found a squirrel racing down the path. *Look at me being silly, fearing squirrels.*

He turned to leave and realized the first sound he'd heard came from the opposite direction.

He turned. "Who's there?"

When no one answered, he walked briskly forward, cutting through the rows of pear and fig trees, but could find no one.

Yarqon melted back into the shadow of the pear trees. A few moments longer and he would have had the boy, but now was not the time. Two members of the house guard had strolled this way and would've happened upon them too soon. He had to stay hidden until the time was right. An assassin's blade preferred the shadow, not the light. He'd had to kill one of the house guards already. He knew they'd be keeping sharp eyes out for him.

But Saul's men could be avoided, fooled, outsmarted.

And Saul's men could only kill him, but the witch…

He dared not disappoint the witch. He'd heard tales of men who'd suffered at her hands. She played with their minds, it was said. Her favorite game was to douse men who displeased her with oil and set them on fire. While she watched them burn, the witch stretched their perception of time so that, in just one instant, they agonized the torments of an eternity.

No, he would not disappoint the witch. Today he had learned

exactly what he wanted to know. Now that he'd discovered their secret meeting place, among the branches and brambles and far from prying eyes—a place tailor-made for his dark purposes—he need only wait for the proper moment to strike.

So they were to meet again next week...

EIGHTEEN

David was so intent on playing his lyre he didn't hear Abby enter the practice room. He was strumming his song "Fire in the Sky", trying to understand how the notes changed when he played them for King Saul at night. But what he really wanted to know was how he conjured the orb and the spirits that drove the king's demons away. If he could learn to harness that ability, he'd use those spirits to defeat the Philistines and the rest of the Israelite's enemies. He'd be more than just a poor shepherd and musician. The king might even think he was a good match for Michal.

Abby interrupted his thoughts. "Your playing has gotten much better. You've been practicing. I'm impressed."

"Actually, I've gotten a little bit of help."

"What do you mean?"

David hesitated. He was uncertain whether he should say anything to Abby, but she was the only person he could confide in. "When I play for the king... a power comes over me and my fingers seem to move on their own." He lowered the lyre and looked at his sister. She might not be able to help, but at least he could trust her. "Do you believe in spirits? Demons and angels?"

Abby snickered. "Of course I do. What's that got to do with

anything?"

"I'll tell you, but you have to promise not to say anything to anyone else."

"Ohh. A secret. Sounds mysterious."

"I'm serious about this. If word got out, the king would be embarrassed and I'd be sent away forever, or maybe worse. I don't know for sure what he'd do but it wouldn't be good."

"Okay, I promise." She punched him on the arm. "But you'd better not be making this up just to scare me."

He lowered his voice. "Someone's put a curse on King Saul. When he sleeps, he's attacked by demons."

"Demons?" Abby scrunched her nose. "What demons? What do they look like?"

"Weird creatures. Flying snakes with huge fangs."

Abby shifted in place. "You're not making this up?"

"No, Abby. When I play for him my music turns into a strange light and then spirits pass through the light and into our world."

"So you summon spirit snakes and they fight the demon ones?"

"They're not snakes. They look like birds, made from light. Only they don't look like any birds I've ever seen. They're every color of the rainbow and they're beautiful. But they're also savage. When they fight the demons, they rip them to shreds."

Abby stared back at him with an uncertain expression, so he thought he'd try another way to describe it. "Remember that time when the bear attacked us in the mountain pass? That strange power crackling in the air right before it... vanished?"

"I'll never forget it."

"It's like that when I play, only it comes from inside me. I can't be sure what it is exactly, but I think it's some type of portal between our world and heaven. I used to think heaven was far away, but maybe it's not so far. Maybe it's just on the other side of that portal."

"You should ask the priests. They might know?"

He shook his head. "No, Michal warned me to stay away from

them. She said they might become jealous or think I'm lying. You're the only other person I can talk to about this. And you have to keep this secret. I've got to figure this out on my own."

"I'll help. We'll figure it out, together."

"Right. It happened once before, on the road to Gibeah. And I didn't even have the lyre that time. Abby, this power is coming from *inside me*. I have to find some way to control it—"

"David, this portal thing sounds dangerous. You don't know what you're doing or where those *spirits* come from. What if you get sucked away, and I never see you again?"

David smiled. "I don't think we have to worry too much about that. I won't get to heaven that easily, anyway. But if I can use this power—"

"That's not how it works. You don't use God's power, David. You let it use you."

"You don't know how it works. And stop finishing my sentences for me!"

"Just promise me you'll be careful. I don't like this. Why would God choose you to fight demons?"

"Who knows, but I'm going to find out."

NINETEEN

David spun the sling and let the stone go.

Zip. Plonk!

"That's not bad," said Jonathan. "But it's not too good either."

The small stone had hit the tree, but entirely missed the clay target that hung from the branch.

Jonathan handed him another stone. "You're generating a lot of speed, and that's good, but you've got to work on your accuracy."

"Okay." David loaded the stone into the sling's mesh pouch. He tested its weight. At the end of the two long leather straps the pouch dangled near the ground.

"You *are* aiming at the clay target? You can see that far, right?"

David frowned. "I can see as well as you."

Jonathan laughed and slapped him on the back. "I was just teasing you. Accuracy will come as you practice. It usually takes a couple of seasons before most men can reliably hit a target at thirty paces."

A small woodchat shrike perched on the branch above the

target. It tilted its red head as if daring David to try again.

Jonathan grabbed David's shoulders and turned him sideways.

"You twist the shoulder when you release the sling. And step toward the target. That'll give you better aim."

David frowned as he weighed the sling in his hands. "I really wanted you to teach me to use the sword."

"The sword's not right for you. Let the foot soldiers hack and slash. A strong right arm isn't the measure of a man. Foot soldiers have their uses, and the chariots too, but the slingers are also important. The slinger can strike, and kill, from a hundred paces away. A good slinger is worth a dozen infantry."

"I notice you've got a sword on your hip."

Jonathan laughed. "Yes, and a horse beneath me when I fight. That's different.

"How many men have you killed?" David had to look up at Jonathan. He was tall and had a deep chest and powerful shoulders and arms like Eliab. Unlike Eliab though, he moved gracefully.

"I've lost count. Dozens maybe? I fought in my first battle before I was your age. But I started as a slinger. You'll need to know how to handle a sword eventually, just in case the enemy breaks through the lines. But first you've got to master the sling."

"Okay." David centered the stone in the little mesh pouch. He spun the sling over his head twice, turned his shoulder, and let fly.

The shot went wide of both the target and tree.

The bird hopped up and down on the branch and stared back at him.

"Let me show you. Give it to me." Jonathan loaded the pouch, and the bird flew off as if it knew by instinct that he'd hit the mark. He swung the leather straps in a tight circle over his shoulder, as if the weapon was an extension of his arm, and let the stone fly. The clay target exploded.

"You'll get the hang of it. Just practice every chance you

get."

David nodded. "It won't take me long. I'll be hitting that target every time. You can count on it."

"I will."

Jonathan drew a leather coin purse from the folds of his tunic. "Oh, before I forget, I've got something for you."

He removed five shekels of silver and held them out to David.

"Your first month's pay."

"But it's only been five nights."

"Five nights, sure. But I've already seen the benefit you've provided to my father. And you'll need some coin to spend."

The demons returned every night, but David sent them away again. Each time the task seemed easier, the demons less dangerous. And after a few good nights of rest King Saul *had* started to look better. He never said anything to David or even acknowledged him at all, except for a polite nod when he entered the room.

"I don't want the silver," David said. "Not now, anyway."

Jonathan arched his eyebrows upward. "Why not? What do you want?"

"I want extra food to take to my brothers in the field."

"Food?"

"Barley cakes and figs. And ten loaves of bread. I want to make sure they have enough to eat."

"All right, but that's not a fair bargain. They'll get the food and you can have four shekels besides." Jonathan handed him four pieces of silver.

"And I want to bring it to them," added David.

Jonathan nodded, a sly smile on his face. "You do, do you? This isn't just a scheme to see the front line, is it?"

"Of course not."

"Right. I'm going to Elah this afternoon. Let's take a ride."

TWENTY

David had never ridden a horse before. Jonathan's white steed was much taller than a mule and flew across the plain, kicking up a long tail of red dust in its wake. David felt as if he were flying. The wind whipped his hair wildly as he tried to find a place to hold on. He didn't want to grab Jonathan's fancy red cloak for fear he might tear it, so he clutched at the ends of the saddle with his fingertips. When they reached the southern hills of Elah, the horse slowed and lumbered its way up the slope.

David heard something whiz past his head, buzzing in his ear like a giant mosquito. The small stone struck Jonathan's left shoulder and turned his entire body, knocking him from the horse. His leg swung around as he fell, toppling David with him.

David hit the ground with a painful thump.

Jonathan rolled to the side and drew his sword in one smooth motion. A pair of riders darted from behind the thick trunks of juniper trees on either side of the path.

David recognized the dark rust-colored tunics and square-plated hauberks of the Philistine army. He dodged quickly aside and narrowly avoided being trampled by one of the horses as it galloped past. Neither soldier paid him any attention. They were only concerned with Jonathan.

Jonathan raised his sword to block a powerful downward slash from one of the riders. The driving force of the blow, backed by the horse's momentum, staggered him but he tore off his cloak and flung it upward like a whip. The cloak wrapped around the scout's neck and Jonathan ripped him from his saddle with a fierce pull.

When he hit the ground, the Philistine quickly regained his feet, drew his sword, and met Jonathan's charge. As their two swords clanged and slashed, the other rider swung down off his mount to join the fight.

Jonathan moved faster and more confidently than either of the two Philistines. His swordplay was the best David had ever seen but he still labored to outfight two men at the same time.

I've got to help, thought David. But he only had his sling for a weapon. He loaded a small stone into the pouch, kept low to the ground, and tried to find a target among the moving men. When he thought he saw his chance, he spun the sling and let fly. The stone sailed above the heads of all three men.

Jonathan spun like a dervish, concentrating his assault on the smaller adversary. He parried the thrusts of the larger man, but sent his own attacks only at the smaller man.

David loaded another stone.

Jonathan's judgement proved correct. The smaller man was the weaker swordsman and earned a thrust through the belly for his clumsiness. Jonathan tried to yank his sword from the man's stomach, but the Philistine twisted and the blade stuck.

The taller scout had a deadly opening. He came at Jonathan swinging, a savage battle cry on his lips.

David let another stone fly. His second shot missed his target as well, but it came close, barely zipping past the attacker's face, delaying him just enough for Jonathan to wrench his sword free and turn away a decapitating blow.

Jonathan went at the man hard, his long sword splashing

blood as it slashed at the scout again and again.

The Philistine fell back from the onslaught. In desperation, he swept up Jonathan's fancy cloak and threw it back at him. Jonathan slashed the cloak in half. But the scout used the diversion to swing up onto his mount and spur his horse away.

Jonathan whistled for his own horse, but the scout was gone.

"Ruined a good cloak." Jonathan tore a strip of gold-edged linen off his cloak and wrapped it around his forearm. His arm was bleeding, but the wound didn't look too serious.

Jonathan cinched the knot with his teeth.

"You did well, David."

"I missed, both times."

"You came close enough. You kept your head. That's important in a fight."

"Shouldn't we go after him?"

Jonathan looked back down the rugged hill path. "We'll never catch him."

He kicked the scout he'd stabbed in the ribs, but the man did not stir. He was already dead.

Jonathan approached the fallen man's horse slowly, making low cooing sounds. Eventually it let him take the reins.
He glanced back at David. "A good time for you to learn to ride."

The Israelite army concealed their camp among the redbuds and pines that grew near the top of the slope of one of the hills of Elah. Three rows of tents housed the bulk of the army. Since it was late in the day, most of the men bustled in and around the tents.

"I have to tell General Abner about those scouts," said Jonathan as he scanned the row of tents. "You'll find your eldest brother in one of those. His name is Eliab, isn't it?"

David nodded.

Jonathan strode toward the huge command tent, leaving him in the middle of the camp.

He'd deliver the extra food to his brothers soon enough, but they could wait a few moments. He'd dreamed of being a soldier for so long, he wanted to explore the camp.

David drank in the smell of meat roasting over the small cooking fires and the pungent oils the soldiers used to soften their leather. Saul's warriors clamored everywhere, going about their tasks with methodical precision. The clink of metal on metal rang out as some practiced with swords and shields.

David slung his sack of food over his shoulder. He couldn't pass up a chance like this. He strolled toward the smith, who bent over his anvil, pounding bronze blades into shape. A vast array of weapons lay spread out on a woven mat before his crucible, some for repair, some for sharpening.

David studied the size and shape of each sword, trying to decide which one he might wield someday.

He wanted to maybe catch a glimpse of this giant everyone was talking about, so he walked farther on, passing through a lightly wooded area at the outskirts of camp. Nobody noticed or said anything to him; he was just a peasant boy in a dusty tunic.

At the edge of the ridge, he studied the expanse of the valley of Elah laid out below. Stones and scrub brush littered the broad, flat plain of red dirt that separated the hills. And that was all he could see. The Philistines carefully hid their camps among the trees and bushes on the opposite slope, out of reach of arrows and slings. Only a few wisps of smoke from their campfires swirled above the trees. The wind gusted and David thought he heard men chanting. He paused to listen carefully and when the wind blew again he was sure he heard it. The Philistines were chanting, "Goliath. Goliath. Goliath."

He stepped back. He thought it too far for an arrow to reach across the gap, but he wasn't sure how far an arrow shot by a giant might fly.

He returned to the camp and entered the tent Jonathan had pointed out to him. Two of his brothers were inside, along with a few other men sitting on long rows of reed mats.

"Oh, look what the cat dragged in," said Eliab.

"David!" shouted Shimea. At least someone was pleased to see him. "What are you doing here?"

David opened the linen sack and took out a loaf of bread. "I brought some food."

Eliab snatched the loaf from his hand and tore into it.

"Ah, you're a good soul, David," said Shimea. "They hardly feed us here. We go to bed hungry half the time."

David laid out some cheese and fig cakes.

Shimea passed them out to the other men.

"You're a good boy," said Eliab through a mouthful of bread.

"How are things back home?" asked Shimea.

"I wouldn't know. I've been staying at the palace."

"The palace?" scowled Eliab.

"I've replaced the royal lyre player."

Eliab laughed. Half-chewed bits of bread sputtered down the front of his tunic.

"It's not funny. I play for the king. Otherwise he can't sleep."

Eliab chewed and swallowed. "Okay, David. It's good to know you're doing your part. I wouldn't want the king staying up too late at night."

"I'm learning to use the sling... and the sword."

"That's great. Try not to hurt yourself. Pass me some of that cheese."

"Where's Abinadab?" David asked.

"He was hurt yesterday in a skirmish along the western ridge. His arm was cut pretty badly."

"Will he be all right?" David felt wobbly, as if he stood on shifting sand. None of his brothers had ever been hurt before. He sat down on the mat beside Shimea.

"He'll live, which is more than I can say for most of the patrol," explained Eliab. "They were ambushed by the Philistines. It wouldn't have been so bad except that damned giant was there."

"Goliath?"

"Is there another one?" said Shimea.

"I could almost believe there are two," added a sour looking man on the other side of the tent. "Yesterday he attacked a scouting party on the eastern side. He moves faster than lightning, that one."

"How bad was Abinadab hurt?"

"He was lucky, like I said. It could have gone worse. The giant and his men caught them by surprise."

"The other Philistines had little to do with it, the way I heard it. Goliath came running at them. He's faster than a war horse, even on foot. The ground shakes when he runs—I've felt it. It's like thunder.

"He went at our men with that gigantic sword of his. The blade is as tall and as wide as any man here. There were ten men in that patrol. They didn't stand a chance. I heard he skewered two men on the sword and was still swinging it as they screamed their last."

The man shuddered. "When Goliath knocks men down, he stomps them like they're grapes, laughing all the while."

"How did Abinadab survive?" asked David.

"He rode away with a few of the others. Fell off his mule, that's how he hurt his arm."

"The hero of the western slopes," said Eliab in a mocking tone.

"At least he's still alive," added Shimea.

"Not for long with that giant running around," said a thin man across the tent. "Mark my words, with that devil spawn at their helm, the Philistines will break us. They'll roll right over us and march into Shephelah and then Hebron, Bethlehem and Gibeah itself."

"Don't let my father hear you say that." Jonathan stood at the entrance to the tent.

The soldiers immediately jumped to their feet.

"I didn't mean anything by it," the man quickly added.

"The Philistines may have a monster," said Jonathan. "But we have the power of the true God on our side. As long as we keep faith, we'll win."

"Yes, my lord," said the men, roughly in unison.

Jonathan looked Eliab up and down. "You're the eldest son of Jesse?"

"Yes, my lord."

"Good news then. A promotion. King Saul wants you to join the house guard back at Gibeah. Hurry and pack your things. David and I are leaving right away."

Jonathan gave David a little wink.

Eliab rushed to bundle up his few possessions.

David smiled. *You can thank me later, brother, but you won't.*

David followed Jonathan out of the tent. The prince walked with an easy confidence, his shoulders straight, his head held high. David wondered how the prince would fare against Goliath, if it should come to that.

He pictured the monster, swinging his massive sword. Then he imagined what Jonathan's face might look like as he was cut in two at the waist. Better not to think about it.

TWENTY-ONE

Thump-thump-thump.

Michal's heart raced as she paced across her bedroom. She was being ridiculous, stupid, silly, dumb, childish. Five nights had passed since she'd talked with David among the pear trees and she hadn't slept a wink since. Every night she paced nervously in her bedroom and pictured him facing those horrible demons—winged snakes with snapping jaws. She couldn't get the image out of her mind. *What if the music stopped working? Could they kill her father? Or David?*

He was only down the hall just now, playing for her father, not more than a hundred feet away. So close.

She'd caught glimpses of him around the compound: in the courtyard, by the stables, in the kitchen. Once she went to find Jonathan by the olive trees and saw David practicing the sling and Jonathan grinning as if they were the best of friends.

After a dozen throws and misses, she'd walked away. She didn't want to talk to Jonathan with David so close. Her brother knew her too well. He'd hear something in her voice or see it in her face. She didn't know what she felt for David, but she certainly didn't want Jonathan to figure it out before she did.

She continued to pace across her bedroom. He was just a shepherd from a small farm. She was the king's daughter. Their paths could never twist together, but still, he intrigued her—his handsome face with the honest lines, the way the light caressed the red highlights in his hair, that sweet voice he used when he sang her a love ballad and...

She shook her head. Silly thoughts. Silly fantasies. There was no place for them in the real world.

She pressed her ear against the wooden door and listened intently, hoping to hear David's lyre. She imagined his slender fingers flying over the strings and the bright light shining from his eyes. But her father's room was too far to hear the music—through the closed door, anyway.

What if I crack it open? What would be the harm? At least I could hear the music. Her heart quickened as she pushed the door open a sliver—not enough to see out, but enough for air to breeze in from the hallway.

She tried to quiet the sound of her own heart thumping and hear the music, but the door was still not open enough. She inched it just a little bit farther. It took a moment for her eyes to adjust to the dim lamp light in the hall. She blinked and saw David. He sauntered down the hallway, head high, chest out. She held her breath. He strolled so confidently, the lyre held lightly in his hand.

He approached quickly—twenty paces, ten, five.

Her breath came hard and fast.

His eyes flickered to her open door, and he smiled.

She quickly shut it, but was it too late? Had he seen her through the narrow opening in the darkness? Did she want him to see her?

Michal strode into Hadi's room, surprised to find her handmaid sitting comfortably on a mat, baskets piled up around her. The old woman had been feeling better the last couple of days, her hands faster and stronger. With Abby's help, she finished her chores without drawing unwanted attention.

Michal smiled. Hadi still wasn't as strong as she used to be, but every sign of improvement lifted Michal's spirits. Hopefully, the old Hadi had returned to stay.

"Where's Abby?" she asked.

"I let her go for the night. We've done more than enough weaving for now. She wanted to find her brother."

"She went to find David? Well, she deserves a little free time, I guess, but I could use her help carrying these baskets to the stables."

"I'll help." Hadi groaned slightly as she stood.

"No, you needn't bother," replied Michal hastily. "You've just started to feel better. I'll go look for Abby. I'm sure I'll find her around here somewhere. You take some rest."

Michal gathered up a pile of baskets.

"It's almost dark. I'm sure those baskets can wait until the morning."

Michal shook her head. "I should take them to the stables tonight. Yes, tonight is better. Who knows? Maybe someone's going to fill them with supplies and deliver them to Elah tonight. You don't know how important those supplies might be."

Hadi frowned. "So you'll be right back? I don't like you wandering around the compound. Not after they found that house guard murdered the other day."

"Jonathan thinks it's probably just a gambling thing. As much as he tries to discourage it, the men still play dice. The one they found murdered was famous for losing and had a hard time paying his debts."

"Maybe, but they still haven't found who killed him. And I've heard he'd been in a good mood lately. Usually when someone loses at dice, everybody knows about it."

"So what do you think happened?"

"I don't know, but it seems suspicious enough that you should be careful."

"As soon as I find Abby, I'll be right back. It shouldn't take long at all."

She turned and hurried from the room.

Abby could be anywhere in the vast palace, but there were only a few places David could be. *Where should I look? The practice room.* If he was anywhere in the house he was likely there.

Michal flew down the staircase, through the courtyard, and into the hallway. When she reached the open doorway she glanced inside. Abby sat across a table from her brother, a wooden game board between them. Abby said something and David laughed. It was a beautiful laugh—free, easy, genuine.

Michal hesitated. She wanted to go inside and talk to him, to test what she felt for him. But at the same time, she didn't know what might happen if she spent time with him. Something special might happen. She feared that almost as much as she feared her father's wrath. Almost, but not quite as much.

Butterflies swirling in her stomach, she pushed past the doorway and walked into the room.

Both David and Abby stood.

"Princess." David nodded, a small smile across his face.

"Is something wrong?" asked Abby. "Hadi said I could go for the night."

"Nothing's wrong. I need your help, that's all." She avoided looking at David straight on. She felt much more comfortable stealing glances of him out of the corner of her eyes.

"Abby's just taught me how to play this game," said David.

"Well, she has to go now," said Michal, hating how stuffy she sounded. "We need to deliver these baskets to the stables, and I want her help."

"I'll help. It will be my honor." David did his best impression of a courtly bow.

"No, we can manage. I just need Abby."

"How about a game first?" He nodded at the game board. "Abby's explained the rules to me. I'm sure the baskets can wait while I win a game or two."

"You win?" She smirked. "I don't think so."

"There's only one way to find out." David sounded light and confident. "Why don't we play?"

Michal glanced at the open doorway. "I can't be in here alone with you, that's why."

"You're not alone," said Abby. "I'm here."

"And I'm allowed to be here," said David. "It is my practice room after all."

"How come I never see you practicing then?"

"My fingers get tired." He waggled them at her. "Sit down. Let's have a game, unless you're afraid to play me."

Michal smiled. *One game couldn't hurt.* "You'll be sorry. I never lose."

She sat opposite David with the cedar game board between them. She took her pieces—five infantry, two chariots, and one king—and considered where best to place them. They had to start in the back two rows on the square board. The pieces were turned so only the person placing them could see the markings on the back which identified their rank.

David had already set his pieces on the board. He seemed to be studying Michal rather than the game, staring at her face and her eyes.

She smiled again. David had put one piece in the corner and the other pieces in the middle of the second row. His placement was aggressive and simplistic. The piece in the corner was obviously his king. The king was the target; to win she had to capture his king by moving one of her pieces to the same square.

She used a bit more guile. She placed one piece in the corner, but that was an infantry piece. A bluff. She placed her king in the middle on the second row.

"Shall we start?" she asked.

"Of course, ladies first." David handed her the die and their fingers touched, his hand lingering on hers for a moment.

Heat flushed her face, even though she tried to stop it. She held his gaze for a heartbeat before she pulled her hand away, clutching the die. "That's very gallant of you."

"It's the least I can do. You being a princess and all."

"You can stop calling me that, you know."

"Stop calling you what?"

"Princess. All of my friends call me Michal." *Well, if I had friends they'd call me Michal.*

"All right. Michal it is, princess." He laughed and she joined him.

"I hope your spirit won't be crushed when a girl beats you."

She tossed the die and moved a chariot. Chariots moved two squares for each number on the die while infantry and the king moved only the number that showed. Once a player moved a piece, the opponent might guess the nature of the piece by how many spaces it traveled.

David tossed the die.

They moved a few times in silence. David played aggressively, sliding his chariots out front. Michal played more defensively, leaving a few pieces behind for strategy, while her infantry worked their way toward the corner.

"I hope my playing at night isn't keeping you awake," said David.

She thought she saw a playful glimmer in his eyes. Had he seen her the other night?

"No, my room is far from my father's. I sleep like a baby at night." She felt foolish about lying, but she didn't want to be discovered, and there was still a chance that he hadn't seen her in the candlelight. "I hope you're finding enough to do during the day to keep busy?"

"David's learning how to use the sling," said Abby.

For a moment Michal had forgotten that Abby was in the room with them. She was so consumed with David's presence, wondering what he was thinking, whether he was having as much fun as she.

"How's the slinging coming, then?"

"It looks a lot easier than it is." David smiled. "But soon I'll be an expert. Then Jonathan will drill me with the sword."

"Oh," said Michal as she tossed the die. "So you hit the target regularly then?"

"Not every time, but I've almost got the hang of it." David moved a chariot close to the piece Michal had placed in the corner. The game was almost over. She rolled the die and moved a chariot four spaces closer to David's king.

He held the die in his hand and grinned. "We don't have to finish the game if you don't want to. We can call it a draw."

"Are you afraid to lose to a girl?"

"No. If she's smart enough to win, what does it matter?"

She saw nothing but honesty in his eyes. Most men would be embarrassed to lose to a woman, but it really didn't matter to him. Even Jonathan became surly when she bested him at something. "I heard about what you did yesterday in the kitchen. How you stood up for Rebecca."

"It wasn't her fault in the first place. The stablemaster bumped into her. He's a clumsy oaf. I'm glad that soup spilled on him."

Michal chuckled. "I agree. A clumsy oaf with a temper. The way I heard it, he would have beaten her if you hadn't stepped in between them. He's done that before."

"She looked angry to me. I think she wanted to tell him off but she couldn't."

"Rebecca has a temper too. It's gotten her into trouble before. If she spoke her mind, she would have gotten a whipping. God forbid a woman should be allowed to speak up for herself. I'm glad you spoke for her. She's a pretty one. Don't you think?"

"I really hadn't noticed."

"I'm sure." Michal grinned. "Still, that was a brave thing you did. Not many men would have protected her."

David shrugged. "It was the right thing to do, that's all."

He returned his attention to the game. "I still think you should take the draw. No matter what I roll, I'll take your king. I just thought that maybe—"

She smirked. "Well, roll then."

David rolled a four, which was more than enough to capture the piece she'd placed in the corner. "Sorry," he said as he lifted it from the board. When he turned it over his confident smile faded and his eyes widened. "But I thought that was your king. You've tricked me."

Michal tossed the die. "That's why the game has strategy." She took David's corner piece and turned it over. It was the king. She had won.

"Well played," he said, nodding thoughtfully. "There's a lot more to it than I realized. I'll get the hang of it sooner or later. How about a rematch?"

Michal glanced at Abby. She wanted to stay, but she'd spent too much time already. Hadi would ask questions if she lingered too long, and she didn't want to answer them—she didn't know how to answer them.

"I've really got to go. Those baskets…"

"Perhaps some other time?"

"Maybe." Michal took Abby's hand and hurried from the room.

There was that word 'maybe' again. Every time she should say 'no', the word 'maybe' seemed to tumble out of her mouth. Maybe was going to get them both into a whole mess of trouble.

TWENTY-TWO

The huge command tent of the Philistines was empty except for the general, the giant and the witch. Alzsheba frowned as General Bulgossa bent his head to study the maps spread across the table. He stank of stale sweat and human weakness. A burly man, heavy with the weight of middle-age, he braided his long beard at the ends, each strand tipped with little eyelets of silver. A thin circlet of ivory rested on his brow, bearing his emblem of rank. Other signs of his gross vanity were abundant. Armbands of silver and bronze covered his upper arms, with rolls of thick skin bulging between them. And he wore a huge silver necklace half as broad as his chest, emblazoned with the winged lion of the Philistines.

My Goliath would never wear such silly trinkets, thought Alzsheba. *His perfection needs no adornments, except perhaps a crown.*

Goliath towered over the general, his head brushing against the canvas roof of the tent. Alzsheba stood beside him, careful to keep herself between the giant and the general.

"Look here." Bulgossa stabbed the map and left a greasy smudge on the parchment. "What good is it, having our army sitting idle, just staring across the ravine at the Israelites? How are we supposed to win like that? With dirty looks and insults? We'll have to make a charge. I can't stand waiting here any longer. King Farrah expects results and I'm going to deliver them to him."

Goliath shook his massive head. "Any army that goes charging down into that valley will face very high losses, probably as many as half the men. With the Israelites holding high ground on the other side, they'll rain arrows and spears down on us. The men will be completely exposed while crossing the valley and then climbing the other side. It will be a slaughter."

Bulgossa wiped the stain with thick fingers, smudging the map even worse. "I don't care. We have more men than the Israelites. We can afford to lose half and still win on the other side."

"And still have enough to take the Israelite towns and hold them? I don't think so."

The general ran his fingers through his thinning brown hair and stared down at the map for a long moment, as if willing it to change. "We might not have enough men to take all we want, but we'll have enough to take the palace and hold Gibeah. King Farrah will be happy with that," he said at last, but his voice had lost the conviction it held only a few moments earlier.

Goliath's jaw clenched and his back stiffened. "That's a good plan if all you can think to do is bludgeon straight ahead."

"Well, what would you do? There's no alternative."

"There are several. I can lead a party of men the long way around." Goliath pointed to the northern hills above Elah. "The Hebrews have sentries here and here. I can take those sentries out before they raise an alarm."

"Can you?"

"Of course. I can spear a man at a hundred paces."

Bulgossa scoffed. "Maybe. If you could get a clear shot. But I don't expect they'll expose themselves."

"They can be drawn out," said Alzsheba. *The fool has no imagination at all.*

"Oh, so the viper is willing to step out of the shadows at last," said Bulgossa. "And what would you be willing to do to distract them?"

"That's my business." She wanted to slap that pathetic leer off his face, but she stayed her hand.

"And after they've seen you? What then?"

"They won't live to tell about it." Alzsheba grinned.

"It might work," said Bulgossa.

"It *will* work," said Goliath. "Once we've broken their ranks at the flank, the main force will run right over them."

"It's an excellent plan but premature," said Alzsheba. "And we can't spare Goliath yet. He must continue his daily challenges, at least for now."

"Those damned challenges," whined Bulgossa. "That's one idea of yours I should never have agreed to, Alzsheba. It's all a complete waste of time. Every day he goes down there and repeats the same challenge. They aren't going to take him up on it. No one dares fight him. They're not total fools."

"You're right about that," said Goliath. "But the challenges…" He glanced sidelong at Alzsheba.

She continued for him, "They serve a vital purpose. Every time Goliath enters the pass and they refuse to meet him, every day they have to cower in fear at the sight of him, they lose hope. They lose faith. They wonder if their God will see them through. They doubt. They begin to believe that they are just another army. One led by King Saul instead of their God. King Saul…" She laughed. "A spineless, weak leader who they neither respect nor trust. Every time they back down, they become weaker and weaker, in their hearts, where it counts the most."

Bulgossa grumbled.

"She's right," observed Goliath. "My spies say their morale is breaking down a little more each day. We have good supply lines. We can wait them out a little longer. When the time is right, I will strike."

"I'll think about it," allowed Bulgossa as he returned his attention to the remaining roasted lamb on his plate.

"That's all we ask. We have every faith in you, General." Alzsheba bowed slightly and stepped out of the tent.

Goliath followed. "That man is an idiot!" he hissed.

"He is," returned Alzsheba, "But a useful idiot."

"What if I go back and stuff that lamb down his throat until he chokes on it? Do you think the men will follow me?"

"I'm sure they would, but King Farrah won't be very pleased. General Bulgossa is his cousin."

A grim smile crossed Goliath's lips. "And if I turn this army around and attack his capital? If I squash Farrah like the worthless little bug that he is? What then?"

"Turning the Philistine army against each other is not the best of ideas. Better just to play along. Once you've broken the Israelites and conquered Judah, a suitable accident will happen to Bulgossa and then you'll be the rightful commander. It will be your boot heel that crushes Gibeah, and my blade that slays Saul. This way, when you return to Ashkelon with the Israelites as slaves, King Farrah will greet you as a true hero. Bulgossa will be nothing more than a pathetic memory. Just stay the course and everything will fall in line just as I've promised."

"Just do as you say, you mean." Goliath drew aside the entrance flap to his tent and they stepped inside.

"I give counsel. You don't have to take it. But mark my words. I'll be the queen of the Philistines one day. And you their king. Together, we'll rule Gaza, Ashkelon, and Gath and that will be just the start."

Goliath's tent was empty except for his weapons and armor. He has no possessions, Alzsheba noted. *He's really still an outcast. He seeks nothing except power.*

She lifted his bronze helmet. "Come, let's get you dressed so you can go forth and humiliate our enemies some more."

Goliath pushed the helm aside. "A man can't fight on an empty stomach."

"You want food?"

"I want you."

He grabbed her by the arm and pulled her toward him. He towered over her.

She parted his tunic and kissed his chest. His musky animal smell had the same effect on her as her perfume had on him. She ran the tips of her fingers across the gigantic muscles of his chest.

"Not now," she laughed. "We have to get you into your armor, not out of your clothes. We'll have plenty of time when you get back."

"Now!"

Goliath squeezed her tight. One arm encircled her so completely she couldn't move. He grabbed her hair with the other hand and pulled it down to angle her face upward. He kissed her fiercely, biting her lower lip.

She fell into the kiss, losing herself completely in his monstrous passion.

As soon as he pulled back, she raked her fingernails across his shoulder.

"When you get back," she said. "But first you go and make your challenge. Stick to the plan." She licked a drop of blood seeping from her torn lip. Salty. Sweet.

"We'll have plenty of time," she assured him, "when you get back."

"Then let me get it over with," he said, annoyed. "It bores me, threatening a bunch of scared children again and again."

"Fine. Be bored. So long as you go down into the valley and make them cower." The Witch of Endor bent to one knee. She caressed the giant's massive calves as she strapped bronze shin guards across the front of his legs.

"Now put on your war shirt."

"Why bother?" Goliath grumbled. "I could go out there naked and it wouldn't matter."

She stepped toward the tunic, which lay strewn across a heavy table. The shirt was made of an elaborate weave of overlapping bronze scales. "When you go down there, dressed for battle, it excites me. The way the sun glints off your shoulders, you look like a god."

She tugged at the tunic but it was much too heavy for her to lift.

Goliath snatched it up. "All right."

He flung the tunic over his head. The armor plates jangled as they settled in place. "But I *am* a god. And I'm not wearing that helmet. I want them to see my face."

Goliath stormed down the rocky slope toward the ravine, trampling through the scrub brush in his path, flinging aside stones that ordinary men couldn't budge. Dirt and rocks trailed behind him in a small-scale avalanche. He wanted to get this over with. Every day it was the same. But Alzsheba was right. It served a purpose.

He plunged lower and lower. The heavy tunic of scale armor, the bronze greaves and shoulder plate weighed more than five thousand shekels, but it didn't bother him. He had strung an iron-tipped war spear across his back. Wide as a tent post, the spear shaft and its iron point weighed as much as a full-grown mule. Most men couldn't even hope to lift it. It was a toy to him.

His reckless charge down the steep decline ended with a leap that took him out onto the floor of the ravine. The ground shook as he landed square on both feet. He took a few gargantuan strides forward, then stood motionless as the dust settled around him. He raked his gaze across the opposite side of the valley, scouring the incline for tell-tale signs of his foes. He knew the Israelites camped there, hidden among the rocks, peering down at him, pissing themselves. Afraid to face him.

The Philistine army cheered their champion.

Yes, thought Goliath, among these puny men I am a god.

Their cheers did not impress him; the Philistines were little more than animals to him. *Let them cower behind the rocks. Let them watch as I step out, unopposed and unafraid, to offer battle to their enemies.*

This whole ordeal was a nuisance, a minor obstacle on his way to greater things. Once he conquered the Israelites he would rip the crown from King Farrah's head or rip his head off, from under the crown. Either way, the crown would be his, and he'd rule the Philistines.

But first, the tedious business at hand.

Goliath roared, "Israelites! Who will fight me in single combat? Who will come forth to battle?"

He waited. The Philistines grew quiet above him and on the other side the Israelites made no sound.

"Choose a man and send him down to me! If he is able to strike me down, we will become your subjects and we shall be slaves to you. But if I slay your champion, you will become our subjects and be slaves to us."

There was no response from the silent, cowering hillside.

"Why not?" He spun in a slow circle and raged. "You are slaves already. Slaves to Saul, a weak-willed king who sends you to the battle lines half-starved and full of fear. I spit on the armies of Israel! I defy your God! Give me a man and let us fight each other."

Of course there was no response.

"Cowards! Dogs!"

He roared with laughter.

He turned and stomped back up the slope, where he found another figure waiting among the rocks at the bottom of the crag.

Alzsheba laughed as well. Her laugh was a high laugh, a rasping sound, like fingernails clawing at your face, like the screams of the damned.

"These Hebrews are so afraid, I can smell their fear from all the way down here. Soon they will be ripe for the picking," she said.

"I waste my time and my breath," grumbled Goliath.

"Who knows? Maybe someday someone will fight you.

You'll come back with Israelite blood smeared across your war shirt and their flag beneath your feet."

"That's never going to happen," he said, weighing his war spear in his hand. "Who would ever be stupid enough to fight *me*?"

TWENTY-THREE

Michal peeled back a low hanging tree branch and muttered to herself. When she woke this morning, she'd been sure she wouldn't look for David in the grove among the fruit trees. When she attended religious service, she had no intention of searching for him afterward. When she went outside to see the sun, she just wanted to feel the warmth against her face. But she started to wander toward the grove and all of a sudden she found herself swerving through the rows of trees, trying to remember where exactly she'd found him last week.

She told herself she merely wanted to avoid the gossiping women who sat on the rooftop garden all morning on the Sabbath. All they talked about was the war and the giant who spat in the face of God while the entire Israelite army sat powerless to do anything about it. She knew the situation at the front was bad. The stalemate continued and morale among the troops was plummeting beneath the taunts of the Philistines. Some even suggested her father should face the challenge himself. With God on his side, they reasoned, what did he have to fear from the pagan giant?

She knew things weren't as easy as that. Her father had doubts, and those doubts would never let him face a giant in single combat.

At least she hoped he would never try and fight the monster. The idea sent a shiver down her spine.

She swerved between another row of trees and found David sitting on a wide rock with a lyre at his feet. Moist dirt caked his sandals, and his face was turned to the sky, his eyes closed as if he were dozing. The pear trees formed a canopy of branches, with leaves and fruit dangling over his head. Sun filtered through, splashing his face with light.

She stepped on a branch and it crunched under her foot.

He smiled and stood as she approached.

All thoughts about the war and the other women on the rooftop garden flew from her mind. She smiled back at him. Goosebumps tickled the back of her neck.

"I'm happy you've come, Michal. I was a little worried that you wouldn't."

She liked the way her name rolled off his lips. "Really, why?"

"You beat me so easily in that game, I thought you wouldn't want anything else to do with me." He hung his head.

"You just need to learn the strategy, that's all. I've been playing for years, so you shouldn't feel—"

He lifted his face and the sun brightened it. His eyes smiled back at her.

"Oh," she said, "I get it. You aren't serious are you?"

He chuckled, "I've been called many things, but never serious."

She laughed with him. The air smelled sweet, scented by ripe pears.

"I met your brother, Eliab, yesterday. You two don't really..."

"Seem like brothers."

"Not really," she smiled. "He doesn't share your... outlook on life."

"That and he's an ugly brute. And he can be nastier than a goat that hasn't eaten all day. He's not like me. Still, he's my brother. Has been, all my life. I hope he didn't say anything too offensive."

Michal thought the two men couldn't be any more different—

except for the eyes. Their eyes shared the same color, but David's burned brighter. "No. Jonathan just introduced us. We only exchanged greetings."

"Good. I'd hate to have to beat him up again." David smirked as he leaned against a tree.

"Oh really? I have a hard time picturing that."

"So do I." David chuckled and she joined him. His laughter was contagious.

She reached just beyond his face and twisted a ripe pear from the tree.

"I wish we had fruit trees where I live. We've tried to grow some, but the soil isn't rich enough."

"I'm sure you grow other things that are just as important. What's it like? Tell me about your home."

David gestured toward the rock.

She sat beside him, close together but not touching.

"There's not much to say. We have a small farm where we grow mostly wheat, but I get to roam the hills with the sheep. I'd love to show you the canyon pass sometime. When the morning sun first strikes the rock formations, it feels like God's woken for the day and graced us with His beauty. It's impossible to describe, really."

His almond-colored eyes sparkled in the sun. She noticed small silver swirls that twisted with the brown. "It sounds beautiful."

"It is when it's not raining." He paused and stared beyond her eyes to some place deep within her.

She shifted uncomfortably. *What does he see?*

Awkward silence filled the distance between them for a moment, until he broke the connection and said, "Dad's a dreamer though. He wants to start a vineyard, but we'll never really do it."

"Why not? It's good to have dreams."

"My dad comes up with all kinds of plans, but he never follows through. So how can he ever achieve them? I think it's important to go after your dreams. Make them happen. How about you? What are your dreams? Do you want to live in a palace, surrounded by servants?"

What are my dreams? Nobody had ever asked her that question before. Men assumed women didn't have dreams. They could only be good wives and mothers. Anything more was forbidden. "I just want to be happy. To share my life with someone I love." The words poured out of her, before she'd even had time to think.

"It seems like we want the same thing." His lips were so close, moist and inviting. She had never been this close to a man before. She could almost feel his heart beating.

She felt drawn toward him, but she fought hard against it and pushed him lightly on the chest to break the mood. "I thought you wanted to be a great warrior. For everyone to know your name. Isn't that what you said when we first met?"

"I'm hoping both things are possible, but if I had to choose only one, I'd choose happiness and the one special person to share my life. What could be more important than that? How about I play you a song."

He lifted the lyre and started strumming. He sang an old love ballad, slow and melodic, sensual and honest. When he reached the second verse, Michal joined her voice with his. She sang tentatively at first, her voice higher pitched than his. He raised his an octave and she lowered hers a little to meet him. The music took her away and she sang louder and more confidently as their voices twisted together. The lyre provided the melody, but her heart provided the percussion. It raced along with the tune. The song sped toward its conclusion, and they sang the sweet, tender lyrics of the love song in perfect harmony.

She didn't want the song to end, but when it did, he placed the lyre at their feet. "Wow, you have such a lovely voice. I'd be happy playing for you all the time. You should sing more often." He placed his hand on top of hers.

She glanced at their hands. Time stood still. Touching between unmarried men and women was very much forbidden, yet she didn't move her hand away—she couldn't move it away. When she looked up she saw beyond his unruly hair, old tunic, and coarse ways. She saw his passion for life, his confidence, his fierce goodness. The man who stood up for a female house servant, and who didn't care about losing a game to a woman. He asked about her dreams, and his song summoned angels to defeat demons. She had never met anyone like him. *But can I trust him?*

She slipped her fingers among his, lacing them with each other, their hands twining together. His heat flooded her body, burning through her, melting her. She didn't know what would happen next, whether anything could happen next. She leaned in close. Desperate to break the rules and explore.

"What are you doing!"

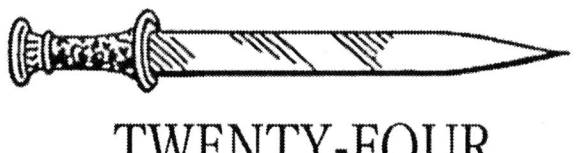

TWENTY-FOUR

David recognized Michal's sister, Merab, right away. She glared at them as she stomped forward, her long curly hair trailing behind her.

Michal released David's hand and whirled around. "We were just singing."

From the angry look on Merab's face, David doubted she'd let the matter go so easily, and he didn't want Michal to get in trouble. "It's my fault," he said. "I surprised her among the fruit trees. I shouldn't have stayed."

"Right, *lyre player*, you'd better leave right now or I'm getting my father!" Merab jabbed her finger at him. "I don't want to see you around her again."

He cast a hesitant glance at Michal and locked eyes with her. He hoped she'd stand up to her sister, tell her this was none of her business, but she looked away.

What did I expect? I'm just a lowly farmer.

"You'd better go," she whispered.

He felt angry and hollow at the same time.

He tried to keep his voice light but couldn't keep the anger from burning through. "I'm sorry for any misunderstanding, *princess*," he said to both of them.

As he turned to leave, a flash of movement and color caught his eye. A thin, wiry man sprang from between the pear trees. Slightly taller than David, the man wore the grimy red tunic of a trader from the southlands cinched tightly around his waist, the sleeves cut short. A black balaclava covered the lower half of his face, revealing only a sharp nose and dangerous onyx-colored eyes.

Merab stood closest to the stranger. "Who... who are you?"

A sly grin sparkled in his eyes. "Definitely not a friend, princess." He slapped her hard across the cheek, and sent her spinning to the ground. Her foot caught on a tree root, twisting her ankle as she went down.

"You're the murderer," said Michal. "The one who killed that house guard."

David jumped between the killer and the sisters. "Leave them alone!"

The assassin drew a short curved blade from the back of his tunic. "You're a fool. You'd sacrifice your life to protect them?"

David stood taller. "You'll have to go through me to get to them."

The assassin sneered. "This is my lucky day. You're nothing but a *musician*. Let's see how well you sing after I cut your throat."

"Run!" David shouted to Michal.

Michal tried to help her sister to her feet, but Merab couldn't stand and fell back to the ground, clutching her ankle.

Merab pushed her away. "Go," she cried, but Michal wouldn't budge. She lifted her head high and glared defiantly back at the assassin.

"Fools." The assassin slashed at David.

David danced backward and the blade just missed his stomach. *What rotten luck. My first knife fight and I don't even have a knife.*

As the assassin crept forward, David circled to his back and left, hoping to draw him away from the princesses. The killer flicked with his blade, but it was only a feint. When David darted to the side, the assassin punched him in the face with his opposite hand. The blow connected full on David's jaw. He stumbled backward and saw stars.

The assassin chuckled. "Musicians are so easy to kill."

"David!" Michal tossed him a branch.

He caught it. Similar in size and weight to the staff he used back home, he felt a little of his confidence return. At least he had a weapon. "Shepherds are a little tougher to kill than musicians."

"I'm done playing," growled the assassin.

David twirled the branch in his hand. "Good, because I've got to play for the king tonight."

The assassin weaved the knife in a threatening dance, its blade glinting in the sunlight. He half-stepped to the left and then shuffled to the right.

David didn't flinch. He kept watch on the killer's cold, merciless eyes. The eyes, he thought, would tell him which way the attack would come.

The assassin lunged forward and tried to carve a hole in his stomach.

David swung the branch down hard on the assassin's wrist. The wood snapped in half, but not before the knife went skittering from the assassin's hand.

The killer grunted, grabbed David's waist, lifted him off his feet, and drove him to the ground.

David saw stars again.

The assassin jumped on top of him and bore his full weight down on his chest. David tried to push him off, but the killer was too strong. He punched David in the head, but David twisted at the last moment and the blow glanced off his temple. David swung his strong legs, locked them around the killer's shoulders and managed to pry him off.

David staggered to his feet, but the assassin moved faster. He punched David hard in the stomach and blew all the air from his lungs. David gasped for breath but before he could suck in any oxygen, the assassin clamped his hands around his throat. He squeezed and David's world began to turn gray. All he saw where the assassin's onyx eyes filled with hate.

David reached for the killer's hands, but he had no strength left to fight. Stars burst in front of his face, and then he thought of Michal. If the murderer killed him, she would be next. He felt a surge of renewed strength, dug his fingers into the man's hands and struggled to pry them off.

Clunk!

The onyx eyes rolled inside his head, and the assassin fell to the ground.

David gasped for air. When he could see clearly again, both Michal and Merab stood over him. Michal held a sturdy tree branch in her hand.

"Don't think this changes anything," said Merab, a purple bruise blooming on her face.

"Merab!" said Michal. "He saved our lives. That man was sent here to kill us!"

"Well, of course. Who else could he be after? The musician?"

"If David wasn't here, that monster could have gotten both of us."

"*Please.* We'd never have been out here in the first place if it weren't for your little tryst among the fruit trees. Anyway, you were the one who saved us. If you hadn't hit him on the head, he would have killed all three of us."

"Don't worry about me. I'm all right," grumbled David as he rubbed his sore neck.

"You'll live. And don't think you're in the clear, *lyre player.*" Merab pointed at the two house guards rushing toward the grove. "They can arrest two just as easily as one."

The two house guards dragged the would-be assassin from the grove and left the two princesses by themselves.

Merab stepped closer to Michal, limping on her sore ankle. "Are you crazy? What were you doing with him?"

Michal put her hands on her hips. "Why did *you* show up? Were you following me?"

"No, of course not. I was on the rooftop garden and noticed you walking this way toward the grove. I thought I'd see what you were up to. And good thing I did!"

"I'm not up to anything." Michal turned away to hide the lie in her eyes.

"You were holding his hand!"

"Shhh! Someone might hear you." Michal spun to face her sister. "I just got caught up in the song, that's all."

Merab grabbed her shoulders and leaned close. "Are you insane? You can't be alone with that boy. He's not right for you. He's only a poor farmer. Father will never match you with him. You shame the entire House by touching him. You are the king's daughter!"

Michal shook free. "And what about my happiness? Why is that not important? Why do men get to decide who they marry and women have no voice? It isn't right."

"Why do you always think that the rules don't apply to you?" Merab crossed her arms against her chest. "Well, guess what? They do. Just like they do for me. Father's going to pick my husband, just like he'll pick yours, and there's nothing either of us can do about it. So stop thinking you're better than everyone else or you're going to get hurt."

"It's not fair. We should have rights too. Why does Jonathan get to choose his bride, and we suffer with whoever they throw at us? Like we don't count. Like we aren't even human."

"That's just the way it is."

"What about love?" As soon as the words passed her lips, Michal blushed.

"Love? Forget about love. You're too old for this foolishness. You're a woman now. You have responsibilities and obligations."

"There has to be more to life than that. I want more."

"There is more, Michal. There are traditions and rules and punishment. You will not shame this House. If Father knew you were alone with that *lyre player* he would punish you both. Your little suitor could get ten lashes just for being near you unchaperoned. And if anyone saw you holding hands with him, who knows what he'd do? He could lock him up or exile him, or maybe send him to the front as fodder for the giant and the Philistines."

"He wouldn't send him to the war." Michal's voice lost steam as doubt crept in. "Would he?"

"You hear the whispers around the palace. Things are not going well at the battlefield. Father's under a lot of pressure. You see how it bothers him. He could easily decide he needs all the men he can get and send your precious lyre player to the front."

Michal forced herself to appear calm. "I know, sister. I just got caught up in the moment. I won't let it happen again."

"That's not good enough. And that's why I'm going to Father. It's time this lyre player left the palace for good. He can't be trusted."

"No, don't do that! Please, Merab. He helps Father sleep. He chases away his demons at night."

Merab's eyes nearly jumped out of her head. "What's this nonsense about demons? Don't tell me you believe those rumors."

Michal hesitated. She couldn't tell Merab that she'd peeked into her father's room at night. She was in enough trouble as it was and that might push her sister over the edge. "I don't know for sure, but Father's been much better since David started playing for him. Jonathan says David helps him."

"We can find another lyre player. This has to stop. Now. Tell me you won't see him again."

Michal bristled, her jaw clenched tight.

"Promise me!"

Merab was right. She was being selfish. David was in real

danger if she kept seeing him. She would have to be stronger than that. She would have to put him first. "I promise."

"If I catch you with him again, I'm telling Father everything — that I found you with him alone and that you were touching him. And then David will wish he was just sent away."

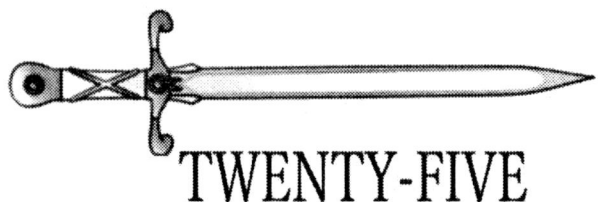

TWENTY-FIVE

Saul studied the prisoner's eyes. *What's in there? Fear. Doubt. Indecision. I might as well look in a mirror.*

Those same demons plagued him every night until David chased them away with his music. The King didn't know how or why, and he didn't care. At least he could sleep. Still, the demons always hovered about him, even during the day. Inside him. Part of him. Gnawing on his soul.

He stared hard at the prisoner but kept his expression carefully neutral, so General Abner and the others would not see his own weakness.

The prisoner tried to turn away but Jonathan held him steady.

"Why were you running?" Saul asked.

The man shook his head, his eyes glued to the ground.

"What's his name?"

"Ezrom," said Jonathan. "He's from the high country outside of Ephraim."

Saul nodded slowly. "And how many deserters today?"

"Six in all. The others escaped. We caught this one when he fell and hurt his leg."

"Have mercy on me," pleaded Ezrom.

"I will," said Saul. "More than you deserve. I promise you that. But I want to hear it from your own lips. Why were you running?"

"Please, I have a wife and three children."

"Tell me why."

Sweat coated Ezrom's long stringy brown hair. He tossed his head to flick the wet strands from his eyes. "Because... I don't want to... die."

General Abner stood behind the king and glowered. "That's not it. The penalty for desertion is death. You knew we'd kill you when we caught you."

"It's that monster, that abomination. The giant. They say if he kills a man, his soul is damned forever. I think it's true. He's a..."

"Yes?"

"He's a demon. He can't be stopped. I saw him bite a man, taking him by the back of his neck just like a dog. He drank the blood and laughed. It's too much. I'm just a miller. I grind wheat into flour. I'm not meant for..." The man hung his head.

King Saul frowned. "I see. But you understand, we need to maintain order. The penalty for desertion is death if you get caught."

"Please—"

"You got caught."

"Mercy! I have a wife and three... three children. You promised me mercy."

"I did." Saul nodded at Jonathan. "Make it quick. But do it where all the men can see."

Jonathan and another soldier dragged Ezrom from the tent, leaving Saul and General Abner alone.

"It's a problem," remarked Abner. Not nearly as tall as Saul, he was much broader at the hip. He wore the typical gray tunic of Saul's army, with a heavy brown cloak slung across his shoulders. He was Saul's first cousin, and a few years older as well. His hair and beard were curly, cut short, and speckled with gray.

"Every day we lose a few more," continued Abner. "Every day

that miserable giant makes his challenge, and the men see him in the valley, and they hear his words. You've heard the things he says, the way he insults you, the way he defames our Lord God."

"He's… quite a sight. But the Philistines won't win by parading around one ugly beast, no matter how fearsome he is. They won't attack through the valley while we hold the mountains."

"He rallies them. The sight of him gives them confidence."

"And I don't?" snapped Saul.

Abner stayed quiet.

He knows better than to answer truthfully, or to try and lie to me, thought Saul. *He believes I've lost the army. Maybe he's right.*

"Why don't we bring out the Ark?" suggested Abner. "The Philistines fear it. If that heathen monster rattles our ranks, the Ark will do the same to them."

Saul shook his head. "Because…"

He couldn't bring himself to finish the sentence. He wouldn't use the Ark because he feared what would happen. The Ark of the Covenant could make an army invincible, but it was only as reliable as its commander. And if he, a man so riddled with doubts, should put the Ark before him, something terrible might happen.

Twenty years ago, Eli used the Ark to bolster his crumbling battle lines against the Philistines. As a result, the Philistines routed the army of Israel, captured the Ark and paraded their prize through the Philistine towns. They brought it from town to town, from Ashdod to Gath and Ekron, but everywhere it went, the pagan statues tumbled and the people suffered tumors and panic and death. Babies were born misshapen. The hair and teeth fell from people's heads. Eventually the Philistines returned the Ark to Israel, just to be rid of its destructive power.

"We can't use the Ark," said Saul, "because Goliath does not fear it. The Philistines might cower before its power, but that beast will not quail before it. Who knows what he'll do? We can't take the chance."

"Then we must answer his challenge. Every day he calls for

single combat. If someone were to kill Goliath, we would win this war."

"If the Philistines keep to the bargain."

"Even if they break their word, it won't matter. When their men see their champion defeated, their spirit will break. And think of our troops. If they see the giant killed, our men will rally to the cause and fight like never before."

Saul smiled sadly. "You make it all sound so simple, cousin. But we have no such champion. The men are all afraid."

"Not all. Jonathan approached me again today. He wants to answer the challenge. He's not afraid. And he's the best fighter we have. The men will rally behind him. If he should win…"

"No! I won't hear of it." The King shook his head but couldn't shake clear the image of Goliath holding Jonathan's severed head high in triumph. "It can't be Jonathan."

"Then someone from the outside. We need a righteous champion of our own."

"Or an angel of the Lord."

"I'd settle for either."

"So would I," admitted Saul. "But what else can I do? I've already offered a small fortune as reward."

"It's not enough. You'll have to do better. And soon. We're running out of time."

"Perhaps," said Saul. "Perhaps I can do better."

A roar rose from the valley below. The Philistines cheered as Goliath made his challenge once again.

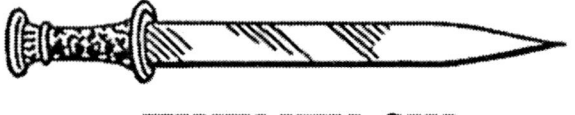

TWENTY-SIX

David strummed his lyre until his hands ached, one slow love ballad after another, the notes heavy with longing and sadness. The ache in his hands matched the ache in his heart. He sat on the rock in the fruit grove where he last met Michal. He'd started to think of this spot as *their place*, even though that was totally ridiculous. It wasn't their place at all, just a desperate place that he wished was their place.

He was trying to command God's power, to make the portal and the spirits appear, but he had no luck. He heard footsteps and looked up expectantly, but those steps belonged to Abby, not Michal.

"You've spent all Sabbath here in the grove waiting for Michal?"

David shrugged. "Maybe."

"She's on the rooftop garden with her sister and mother and the other ladies of the House."

"I figured as much, but there's still a chance she'd come."

"Not very likely." Abby shook her head. "Your playing has gotten much better. But do you have to play such a sad song? It's kind of pathetic."

David smirked. "Yeah. I guess it is."

Abby tugged at his sleeve. "Never mind that. Come on, David. Eliab has a letter from home. He's in the house guard barracks and wants us to come to him."

"Of course he does," muttered David.

"What's the news, brother?" David asked.

"What does it say?" Abby grabbed for the letter, nearly ripping it from Eliab's hand before he yanked it out of reach.

"Hey, careful." Eliab brushed imaginary dirt from his new tunic, which had the deep blue color of the house guard rather than the dull army gray. Ever since he'd been promoted, he strutted around the compound like a peacock. Of course he'd never once bothered to thank David for the assignment. "I don't want any stains on my new uniform."

Abby's eyes were wide with anticipation for news from home.

David hadn't realized she was so homesick. He'd thought all the excitement of the palace would be enough for her, but she practically hopped in place. "Come on. What's it say?"

"What do you *think* it says?" teased Eliab as he leaned against a table. As it was Sabbath and a light work day, the three of them were alone on the second floor of the house guard barracks.

"Probably how much he misses us," suggested Abby.

"Well, he misses David." Eliab glanced again at the note. "He says the boy he hired to be shepherd quit on him. He has to walk the sheep himself, so his back is aching day and night. And his feet aren't feeling too good either. Everyone else is too busy with the fields to help. If he can't hire someone new, he wants David to come home."

David crossed his arms over his chest. "I'm not going back."

"If Dad wants you, you're going back. I'll tie you onto a wagon and haul you there myself. What's so important? Playing music for the king? He can get another minstrel, I'm sure."

"There's a lot more to it than that."

"Like what?"

David looked out the window. The sun blazed hot as it sank below the towering walls of Gibeah, looking as if God had set the town on fire.

"There's a girl," whispered Abby.

David scowled at her. *Great, this is the last thing I want to talk to Eliab about.*

"Oh?" A lecherous grin spread across Eliab's blocky face. "And what girl is this?"

"Mind your own business. You don't need to know."

"Oh but I do, I do," said Eliab with glee. "Let's see. There aren't too many servant girls here. The only good looking one is that Rebecca who works in the kitchen. Don't tell me you've spent time alone with her?"

David shook his head.

"Didn't think so. I wouldn't have believed you if you said you had. But I can't think of anyone else who doesn't have wrinkles covering half her face. Is it that old washer-woman that does the linens? Or maybe someone inside the palace? Why, aside from Abby, there isn't a handmaid younger than a hundred years old. Is it that ancient pagan woman that Abby's learning from? I bet she could teach you a few things." Eliab started laughing. "I know you're desperate but—"

"I'm not desperate. And it's none of your business. Leave it alone."

A strange light broke over Eliab's eyes.

David cringed. *Not now!* It was a miracle he had witnessed only a few times before. His brother was getting an idea. And at the worst possible moment.

"You're not talking about the king's—"

"You can't say anything!"

Eliab smirked. "Just what have you been doing, little brother?"

"Nothing really, I play music for Michal sometimes as well as the king. Now you know, so keep your big mouth shut."

"Well of course you do," snickered Eliab. "They pay you five shekels a month to play your lyre. And that's all. Don't think that stunt with that crazy trader means anything, either. The way I hear it, she had to save *you*! If you think she has any romantic interest in you, you must be completely nuts. You're nothing more than the hired help, no better than a pet bird that sings a pleasant tune."

Eliab's tone and smug face so irritated David. He wanted to stuff his brother's words down his throat so he started talking anyway, although he knew he shouldn't say anything more.

"It means more than that, you stupid oaf. A lot more. We meet every Sabbath in the fruit grove. Alone."

"You're lying."

"No he isn't," said Abby.

Eliab grinned. "You met today?"

"No. Not today. She didn't show up. I haven't seen her for a whole week. Whenever I get near her she turns the other way. It's making me crazy."

"I know what's going on," said Eliab.

"Really?"

"How would you know?" asked Abby.

"Sure, it's obvious." Eliab shook his head knowingly. "I've heard about this sort of thing before. Sometimes princesses and rich women like to toy with the hired help. They treat them like playthings. It's fun for them. When they get bored, they toss them away."

"She's not like that. You don't know anything!"

Eliab chuckled. "You're probably right. Why would a princess want a puny guy like you? Maybe I should talk to her sometime and offer her my services. I'm sure I can scratch her itch."

David charged forward and barreled into his brother. He caught Eliab off guard, but Eliab outweighed him by so much it was like wrestling a bear.

Eliab grabbed David's wrist and swung him around. When he

let go, David flew halfway across the room.

He would've made another charge but Abby jumped between them.

"Stop fighting! Don't you see? We've only got each other." Tears brimmed in her eyes.

"I don't care what he says about me, but he can't talk about her like that!"

"Grow up, David! You're nothing more to the princess than the stable boy or some performing fool. Maybe she has bad taste and actually likes your music, but she's not interested in you. Be certain of that. You will only make a fool out of yourself and get whipped in the process."

David bit his lip. He almost told them how he had held Michal's hand—the way their fingers had laced together, even if it was just for a moment. That had to mean something. But he couldn't tell Eliab about that. He would never understand.

"It's because of her sister, Merab," he said. "She's keeping Michal from me. It has to be. She caught us together last Sabbath. It must be her. Abby, can't you find out?"

Abby clicked her tongue. "That's not exactly something I can ask, is it?"

"Has Michal said anything about me? She must have."

"She doesn't say much of anything lately. She just sighs a lot and keeps looking out the windows."

Looking out the windows, thought David, what does that mean? *Is she looking for me? If I can just talk to her. There has to be someplace where her sister won't find us. Maybe...*

"Don't you get mixed up in this, Abby," said Eliab. "Dad didn't send you here to get on the wrong side of King Saul."

David grinned. "I'll send her a note. She'll meet me on the rooftop garden, you'll see. After I play for her father. No one will be around then."

"You'll do no such thing," said Eliab. "Don't think your new best friend, Jonathan, will save you from King Saul. He'll be the one using the whip to lash you bloody. I've seen him use it before! Maybe it really is time for you to go home. You can tell the goats all about your romantic adventures and any other wild stories you've been dreaming up when you get back. I hear they're good listeners."

"I'm not going back." David turned toward his sister. "If I write a note, will you give it to her?"

Abby hesitated, her face uncertain.

Eliab stepped between them. "No she won't. David, I'm warning you. You always think about what you want, and the hell with everyone else. Well, keep her out of your crazy schemes. You're old enough to make your own mistakes. I won't lose any sleep if you get strung up and gutted as a traitor, but I won't let that happen to Abby!"

TWENTY-SEVEN

Murder!

Alzsheba awoke from a dreamless sleep.

The scent of murder poisoned the air. She could smell its foul, rotten stench.

She glanced over at Goliath, who slept on the floor of the tent beside her, the rough wool blanket so small in proportion to his huge frame it covered only his groin and thighs. She thought perhaps she might have caught a whiff of his dreaming, which was almost always about somebody's death and destruction. No. Not tonight. Goliath slept peacefully, his mind untroubled and relaxed.

But murder hung in the air. She could taste it.

The witch rose and cast a black silken robe around her naked body. Trouble had found the Philistine camp this night. Normally she'd let the foul deed play out. What did she care if one sheep killed another? But she believed it was coming from Bulgossa's tent, so she slipped into the gloom.

She passed quickly through the camp, her raven hair and black robe smothering her silhouette in the inky darkness. She flung open the flap of the General's tent. Bulgossa lay on his bed of soft pillows like some disgusting pig collapsed in its sty. A filthy animal. His snoring was thick with drink, his mouth gaped open, his every breath a wretched drunken rasp. The bones of a roasted lamb lay scattered among his bedsheets, the grease still smeared on his hands and face. In his gross nakedness, rolls of disgusting pale flesh peeked from the edges of his gilded nightshirt. *He looks like a blind, bloated worm. A mindless slug!*

One of his wives stood over him, a dagger in her hand. A lithe girl, not yet out of her teenaged years.

"What are you doing?"

The girl turned. In the pale lamplight, her face was littered with purple bruises. Caught in the act, her jaw dropped open but she said nothing.

"You're going to kill him?" Alzsheba asked.

"He deserves it."

"I'm sure he does," she agreed. "How many wives did he bring from Ashkelon? Three? He keeps you cooped up in his harem tent, shut away from everyone else. He calls you to him when he wants to paw at you, using you like playthings whenever he wants."

"He beats us. For no reason."

"Does he need a reason? You're his property, aren't you? Your father sold you for a bride price of some silver pieces." Alzsheba crossed her arms over her chest. "And what about you? Did you object? Were you lured by all his gold and trinkets? The fine silks and food you imagined he would shower on you? Were you happy? Tell me!"

The girl shook the blade. "I was young. I didn't know better. Now I do. And here it is." She jerked the dagger at Bulgossa. "This is what he'll get."

"Not tonight. I can't let you kill him."

"He deserves it. You said so."

"True. He deserves that blade and worse, but I still need him."

"*You* need?" The girl stared at Alzsheba in confusion for a moment, and then the answer dawned in her eyes. "You're Goliath's woman. You're that witch!"

Alzsheba was amused. "You say that as if it's a bad thing."

The girl kissed the ceremonial figurehead embossed on the hilt of her dagger. She began to chant, her voice rising in pitch to a near-panic. "Great Dagon protect me. Great Dagon protect me." She spat on the ground by Alzsheba's feet. "Foul creature. Unclean. Witch!"

"Be quiet you idiot or you'll wake him! Who are you to talk, anyway? Poor little defenseless girl, sold off to the general. Helpless thing. Did you even think you had the nerve to shove that knife in his flesh? What would you do—cut his throat or stab him in the heart? I saw your hand shaking. You couldn't do it. No matter what he does to you, how badly he treats you, you won't. Because you're weak."

The girl swung the tip of the knife at the witch, her hand shaking worse than ever.

"Now *that is* a mistake," purred Alzsheba.

The girl opened her mouth to raise an alarm, but Alzsheba lashed her with her eyes.

The girl's mouth opened wide but no sound escaped her lips.

Alzsheba stared into the girl's soul, feeling her blood chill. The girl shuddered violently, but could not move.

"Helpless little thing." Alzsheba slapped the knife from her hand.

Unclean! She dares to call me unclean!

"You spit at my feet? Why? Because I won't bow down to men? Because I'm powerful? You want to call for help? Who do you think is going to help *you*?"

For a moment she pitied the girl. Many years ago in Tekoa, after the death of her parents, her sisters had been used by men in the same way. Still, it wouldn't do to be found here like this. The girl knew too much. She must silence her.

Alzsheba stretched a long slender finger and tapped the thin gold necklace around the girl's throat. She whispered an appeal to Molech under her breath. The golden necklace twitched. *Yes, that's it! Grant me this boon, my glorious dark Lord. Grant me this.*

The necklace opened its gilded jaws and a slender forked tongue flicked out. The elegant links in the chain blurred and changed, resolving themselves finally into a mesh of shimmering scales. The delicate golden serpent, still circling the girl's throat, slithered tighter and tighter. Tighter and tighter it coiled until its golden scales cut into the flesh at the girl's neck. *You should not have called me unclean.*

The girl collapsed to the floor, unable to scream. She tried to pry the serpent from her neck, but it continued to coil until its scales cut into her flesh. In a moment she lay dead.

Alzsheba clenched her fists. *What a waste!* The young girl dead at her feet while that fat bastard Bulgossa slept drunkenly away. *He'll get what's coming to him, though. I'll see to it.*

She saw a flash in her mind's eye, as she occasionally did, a brief prophetic vison of the future — General Bulgossa's decapitated head hoisted high on an iron spike, black flies circling his gaping mouth. Just a flash and then gone.

Yes, that day would certainly come to pass. And she smiled at the notion, not knowing who had mounted the head on the spike. Maybe she would hang it there. Or perhaps it would be Goliath. Either way, she would enjoy the sight even more the second time.

TWENTY-EIGHT

Michal stared at her bedroom wall, but she didn't see anything. Lost in her own dark thoughts, she felt isolated from everyone she knew and loved. She felt as if she had squandered a precious gift on something much less valuable, much less important. Having lost all interest in life's daily routine, she made sure only to cover for Hadi's failing health. She needed to keep Hadi safe, but other than that, she wanted to crawl into a pitch-black cellar and stay there until the light returned, if the light ever returned.

Hadi sat on the bed beside her. "What's wrong, child? You haven't been yourself in a week."

Michal heard concern in Hadi's voice, and it sparked the smallest trace of life in her. She didn't want Hadi to worry about her. The old woman needed all her strength to get better.

"I'm just tired. Tired of being the king's daughter, tired of the palace, tired of war and giants, and tired of all these rules and responsibilities."

"I know life as a princess can be hard."

"I never wanted to be the king's daughter. I was happy being the daughter of a simple farmer."

She remembered when her father told her that he had been

named king. As a young girl, she'd understood what the words meant and delighted at the small golden crown that rested on her father's brow, but she had no idea what it really meant.

Merab realized it right away. When they were alone, she whispered that nothing would be the same again. Michal hadn't believed her then, she hadn't understood. Now she knew the truth in her sister's words. They had been transformed from simple farm girls to princesses. She could call herself the king's daughter all she wanted, but everyone else thought of her as a princess. No one could undo that now.

Hadi squeezed her hand. "I know you never asked for your father to become king. But I never asked to be a servant either. These changes are thrust upon us. The Fates twist the strings of our lives. They decide many things for us. We can only deal with the aftermath of their choices. But I know one thing for certain. You are strong enough to be the king's daughter."

She didn't feel strong enough. "The Fates decide these things, or God?"

"What does it matter? Your priests say God. My people say the Fates. In the end, we must be clever enough to deal with whatever life sends our way."

"Can't we carve out our own fate? What if we don't like the one we're stuck with? Who do we appeal to? How do we change it?" She glanced at Hadi, but only for the briefest moment. If she lingered too long, tears would come.

"That's the essence of life, sweet child. One can't swim too long against the tides. The Fates create waves that will drag us down. It's up to us to realize which ones we can swim under and which we must accept. My husband was fated to die. I could not change that. Still, his death led me to Gibeah and here with you in this room. Perhaps the Fates needed me to be here with you now? Who can know?"

"Merab doesn't seem to have any problems being a princess. She's embraced her fate and all the rules and responsibilities that come along with it."

"You could learn a little something from your sister."

"She'll marry whomever they say, whenever they say."

"As it must be."

"Why? Why must it be? Tell me about your husband. How did you feel when you were in love with him?" She turned to face Hadi, tears just below the surface of her eyes.

"Oh." Hadi clucked her tongue and smiled. "This is about that boy with the red hair, the one who protected you and Merab in the grove?"

"He was brave when he faced that killer with the knife. But he's so much more than that. He's also smart and clever and kind. He asked me about *my* dreams. And when he sings, he sounds like an angel."

"Merab warned you away from him, didn't she?"

"Yes but I... never meant to..."

"Fall in love? We never mean to fall in love, child. It just happens." A wistful look settled in Hadi's eyes. "Sometimes I think the gods give men red hair just to tempt us. My husband had red hair. When the light hit it just right, it looked like smoldering embers from a fire. I loved that hair."

"If I wasn't the king's daughter then maybe..."

"Maybe the poor musician would be right for you? Perhaps, perhaps. But you are a princess. Your God made that choice for you. You cannot go back and change Samuel's mind. That fate is sealed."

"But David's fate isn't. He's a poor farmer and musician now, but who knows what he might become?" A whisper of life echoed in her heart, and she raised her voice. "Who knows what he might become? Father was a farmer before he became king. If he could change his fate, then David might do the same. It's possible!"

"Anything is possible, Michal, but while he's still a poor farmer you cannot see him. It's far too dangerous. If his love for you is strong enough, he must seek change on his own. Love between two people often finds its own way. Not always. Sometimes the Fates have ice in their hearts."

"And if the Fates allow it, what then?"

"This is no small task. I'm afraid the road would be long and difficult and unlikely to result in happiness."

"But love is worth it, right? You wouldn't change your time with your husband."

"No, sweet child, I would not change my brief time with my husband. We had a short life together and that was all. But it was worth it. Sometimes I think we are here on this world solely because we have the ability to love. That's not something easy to cast aside, I know. Luckily I found love in my life again." Hadi gave Michal's hand one last squeeze and released her. "I will pray that the Fates grant you love with this boy. That this particular fate can be changed. But it must be his doing, not yours."

Hadi left the room.

Michal thought of David's fate. How could he ever change into an acceptable match? One that her father might approve?

She reached into the folds of her shawl and pulled out the note David had sent. 'Meet me at the rooftop garden after I play for your father tonight — David.'

She stared at the neat block letters, uncertain what she should do. *Is there a chance I can be with him? Is ours a fate we can change?*

Michal pressed her fingertips against the door. She'd spent a lot of time by the door listening lately. Too much time. Too many hours holding her breath, hoping to hear music or footsteps or worrying about demons. The door had become just another barrier in the way of her happiness, blocking her path, stopping her, preventing her from making her own decisions, finding her own way.

Her mind whirled, and for a moment her thoughts sang with joys and possibilities, then the next it threatened to spin totally out of control as she struggled to corral her ramblings and create order from the chaos. *How come my thoughts turn fuzzy whenever I think about him?* She groaned. Simple decisions became complicated puzzles whenever they involved him.

She was so preoccupied she almost didn't hear the footsteps in the hallway, but David made such a ruckus, scuffing his sandals as he passed her room, she couldn't miss them.

She sighed and leaned her forehead against the door. Time slowly ticked away. She traced the rough edges of the crumpled note with a fingertip. *What should I do?* Indecision wasn't like her. She hated this feeling of uncertainty.

I need to see him, if only to tell him that we can never be together. I owe him that much. Besides, he's much too persistent to simply ignore. If I don't meet him tonight, he'll just send another note and another, taking more and more risks until I finally give in. Or worse, until Father catches him.

Tonight was as good a time as any to do what she must. She pushed open the door and crept down the long hallway. She didn't dare wake Merab or her brother, and she certainly didn't want to answer questions from a house guard. She reached the staircase and descended to the first floor and into the courtyard. No one walked the shadowed palace halls this night. No one was looking for a wandering princess, who should be safely sleeping in her room.

When she reached the ladder that stretched to the rooftop, she turned and glanced around the courtyard. The almost-full moon cast silvery light across the open space. Out of the corner of her eye she noticed movement among the shadows. She held her breath. Her heart raced. Someone was watching her.

The shadow shifted, and she saw him. Tall and wide, he wore the blue tunic of a house guard. David's brother, Eliab, stood in the shadows. She couldn't make out his expression in the pale moonlight, but he seemed to smirk and turn his back.

She exhaled, steadied her nerves, and climbed the ladder to the rooftop. When she reached the top, she saw David's silhouette outlined at the edge of the roof with his back to her as he gazed out at Gibeah. He stood in the same spot where she had chatted with

Merab only a few weeks earlier—when Merab had been worried about a future husband. When she'd resolved to marry whomever Father chose for her, to do the right thing, the necessary thing, to be brave.

Michal almost retreated down the ladder, but no one else was on the rooftop. This was a good opportunity, perhaps the best chance she would get to talk to him alone. She trudged forward, each step a chore as if she waded through drifts of deep sand.

The moonlight danced on David's hair. Strange how she had met him only a few weeks ago, but she could spot him in the darkness or in a crowd at a far distance. She knew every inch of him—his thin but strong build and well-muscled legs. The way his hair tumbled toward his shoulders but fell just a little short. The way his bright eyes glowed when he spoke passionately about beauty or love or his faith.

She shook her head. She couldn't lose herself in his details. She needed to keep a distance. To keep her head clear. To be a princess.

Without turning, he said, "Gibeah is really beautiful at night. The fires in the hearths look like lights in the night sky." He pointed toward the towering palisade that protected the city. "Those walls look as sturdy as any mountain. I can't imagine anyone breaching those walls. Not even a giant."

"Stronger walls than those have fallen. They look permanent and secure, but they can be torn down just like everything else we build."

He turned to face her, his lips only a few inches from hers. "You sound afraid."

Her mouth went dry. "Afraid of what?"

"Of the war? The Philistines?"

She shook her head. "No, not them. With God on our side, we have nothing to fear from them." She was afraid of so many things lately she couldn't hide the worry from her eyes—not from David, not tonight under the moonlight.

He gently placed his hand on top of hers.

Heat spread throughout her body as if his touch had set her ablaze.

His eyes glittered in the quiet darkness. "Are you afraid of your sister, or what your father might do if he finds us together?"

Her hand suddenly turned cold and she pulled it away. "Yes," she whispered. "You know I shouldn't be here with you."

"I'm not afraid." He lifted his eyes to the star-filled night sky. "We're really so small when compared to the rest of the world. Just two people on a rooftop. Look around. The lights in the sky, Gibeah down below, the mountains in the distance. It's as if all this was meant for us to see, tonight, together."

Michal felt it too. The world *was* vast, and they *were* small, and if they were small then her worries must be tiny. Maybe she had less to fear than she thought.

"When I tend to my sheep and spend the night out in the open, I get this feeling that God has plans for us. He shows us what we're supposed to do. He doesn't speak to us directly. That would be too easy, I guess. The trick is to recognize the signs He gives us. To understand His message. He's sent me here to chase those demons away from your father. And he's brought me to you."

He leaned closer.

She stared at his lips. She wanted to touch him, to taste him, to feel a closeness that she'd never felt with anyone else. She could share that bond with him. She could trust him. He was so close.

"I think God wants us to be together," he whispered.

Michal felt as if she were falling, plunging from the rooftop and diving into the passion and honesty of his eyes. She so wanted him to be right, and he sounded so sure. The stars and the night sky and his closeness overwhelmed her. She gave in and leaned toward him, pressing her lips against his. They felt soft and inviting. She melted into them and pushed harder and kissed him again. His lips parted and so did hers. She pushed her body against his and felt dizzy.

She lost herself as David's hands caressed her back and roamed downward to rest against her hips. She felt connected to him as if they shared the same body and spirit. The feeling so intense it left her completely breathless. Gasping for breath, she pushed him away.

Cool air flooded her lungs with a chill that brought troubling thoughts. Thoughts about her sister and her father and Hadi crowded out her passion. She found the strength to push him back as he tried to kiss her again.

A vision of David tied to a tree, bare backed, her father holding a bloodied whip, burned in her mind. She could see the blood, his blood dripping from the leather straps. He'd risk that for her, but she couldn't let him. She had to be strong for his sake.

"What's wrong?" he asked.

She tore her eyes from him, and looked back toward Gibeah and its formidable walls. Walls were made for reasons, and not all walls were made with stone.

"It's no good. This can't be."

"But it is! If I work another few months, I'll save enough silver to buy a half dozen sheep and start my own flock. We can run away together. We can go north and keep going. The flock will grow, and no one will ever find us. You won't have all this, but we'll have a life together. It might be a simple life, but we'll know happiness. I promise you."

She wanted to say yes. Happiness could find them among the hills with a few sheep. She could imagine it. They would have children together, grow old together, live on a small farm or in a bare shack in the woods. It didn't matter. They would share a life—one life—together. She wanted to leave right now, this very night, but she knew it was a child's fantasy. She was a grown woman now. Wherever they went, her father would find them. They would never be safe. David's head would find its way into a noose. They could never be together like that.

"That's not a life for me."

David's face reddened. "But you said you just wanted to be happy. That you didn't care about lands and servants."

She hardened her heart and her voice. "I don't want to be a poor shepherd's wife. I want more. You're not right for me." She tore her gaze away. She couldn't bear to see the pain in his eyes, and she was too worried he would see the lie in hers. "I don't want to see you again. I'm not going to run away with you."

She moved to leave, but he grabbed her arm. "There must be another way then. Something we can do…?"

"It's not possible. That's what I came here to tell you." She shook her arm free and left him alone on the rooftop.

She could say no more. Her voice would crack and that would betray her. They could not change this fate. He would never be worthy in her father's eyes. If he kept pursuing her, he would end up swinging at the end of a rope.

She walked unsteadily toward the ladder, feeling shattered. A black hole ripped open in her heart and threatened to overwhelm her. Tears flowed freely down her cheeks. Every inch of her wanted to go back to him, to tell him the truth—*yes, yes, I love you*—but she needed to keep him safe. She waded through air as thick as soup and walked in slow motion down the empty corridor. The whirlwind of emotion was almost too much, the taste of David's kiss still on her lips, the heat in her heart, the tears on her cheeks.

When she opened the door to her room, she found Merab standing by the window with her arms crossed against her chest. "So. Is it over?"

She couldn't speak. All she could do was nod. The tears had stolen her voice away.

TWENTY-NINE

David tensed his shoulders and swung the sling over his head. He stepped forward and let go.

Thunk!

The stone struck the high branch of the olive tree, far above the clay target. The little shrike appeared unimpressed. It didn't stir from its perch on the branch.

Small wonder I can't hit anything. All I can think about is Michal. He glanced up at the rooftop garden as if she might still be there. No sooner had he looked away than his eyes found the roof again. Each time, he felt a jolt of energy, hoping to catch a glimpse of her, but she was gone.

He loaded another stone. *What should I do? I could send her another note, but she won't meet me again. I just know she won't. I could spend the next month or two wandering the palace grounds, playing for the amusement of the king, and never see her again. There must be some way to get her alone. Some way to change her mind, convince her that we're meant to be together.*

He knew how strong-minded she could be. He liked that about her. He'd have a hard time getting her to change her mind. David spun the mesh cup faster — two, three, four revolutions and let fly again. The throw missed the tree entirely and the shrike cawed at the stone as it sailed past.

"What are you trying to hit?" asked a deep rumble of a voice, the mocking tone unmistakable.

Eliab sauntered beneath the olive tree. "This clay target?"

Resplendent in his house guard uniform, he smashed the clay into pieces with his sword. The shards flew in all directions, the shrike taking flight with them.

"That's how you do it. It's all very simple if you've got a strong right arm. Put away that sling and take up a man's weapon."

"Okay," said David. "Why don't you show me how it's done since you're such a mighty swordsman?" He picked up a short training sword from an assortment of weapons braced against a marble plinth. It had a leather handle and a hammered bronze blade with a dull edge. The sword was light and easy to handle compared to his brother's iron war sword.

"That's right," said Eliab. "Hold it straight up."

David did as he was told.

Eliab stood three paces away. "Eyes sharp. You look at me and nothing else. You want to block my thrust."

David tried to concentrate, but his gaze flickered again to the rooftop. *She's bound to visit the garden sometime today.*

"Eyes!" barked Eliab. "What are you looking at? Are you fighting me or the palace wall? The eyes tell you where the next strike will come."

David forced his gaze to his brother's eyes but his mind would not follow. Having Michal avoid him was one thing, but what had happened on that rooftop was another, hearing the words from her own lips, saying they couldn't be together, that she never wanted to see him again. Every word felt like a stab in the gut. *Did she really mean it? Why avoid me, if I mean nothing to her?*

Eliab looked left, and his sword followed. David just managed to swing his blade in the way. Eliab's stroke clanged against the bronze blade and a shudder of pain shot up David's arm.

"A little slow but at least you blocked the thrust," said Eliab, "You have to get the sword back to the center again right away. Don't just sit there gawking like an imbecile who can't believe he's blocked the strike."

David raised his sword again. Eliab roared and attacked to the right. Eyes first, sword second. David blocked the thrust more easily this time, but Eliab spun around and swung back the other way. His blade stopped just short of slicing David's neck.

"Are you paying attention at all? Once you block, you have to strike back. Otherwise you're no better than the clay target."

David tried to clear his head, but it was useless. He'd held her in his arms. She'd even kissed him first. That had to mean something.

"Come on," said Eliab. "Come at me."

David charged, swinging his sword at Eliab's head. He held nothing back, his anger and frustration boiling out of him. Eliab blocked the stroke with a short powerful chop that sent David sprawling to his knees.

"That's the way to block," Eliab laughed. "Hit like you mean it."

David dusted the dirt from his tunic and waited for the next attack.

Eliab weaved from side to side to conceal his intent.

Maybe Eliab is right. Maybe she can't stand to be a poor shepherd's wife. Maybe all of this was just a silly dalliance for her? All a game? Like that game with the chariots and the pieces that moved on the board? A game she knows how to play while I'm helplessly lost?

David had forgotten about Eliab until the sword came whistling toward his neck. He blocked the strike only part way, his sword glancing off his brother's heavier blade. The war sword stopped at his neck, its iron pressed against David's flesh. If his brother hadn't held back, his head would've gone flying.

"Useless idiot!" said Eliab. "Forget about battle, you won't even survive the practice."

David charged, swinging his sword wildly, hacking at his brother over and over and over. The blows fell in an unbalanced torrent.

Eliab easily parried every swing, a broad smile on his face.

David was lost. Just like with Michal.

She kissed me. She kissed me and that kiss was real, not just some part of a silly game.

Eliab kicked him in the chest and he fell backward again, tumbling into the red dust of the courtyard.

She was everything he ever wanted. It was all right there, in that moment. *Real, not some rich girl's game.* He'd felt things he had only imagined before, only to have it all ripped away.

"Get up!" thundered Eliab. "I'm trying to show you something. Now watch here."

David stood and braced himself for another attack, sword held upright and ready.

Eliab feinted to the left but stopped short and reversed himself. David saw the move in his brother's eyes and met his blade early. Before Eliab could react, he slashed his sword at Eliab's stomach. His brother partially deflected the swipe, but the edge grazed his uniform.

"You idiot!" Eliab raged, as he stared wide-eyed at the rip in the blue cloth.

He stomped down hard on David's foot. Distracted, David didn't see his next swing until Eliab punched him in the face with the hilt of his sword. It wasn't a full shot, but it was hard enough to send him spinning. Eliab laughed and swung his sword at David's side. Still off-balance, David tried to parry but Eliab turned his sword, slipped it under the block and struck him hard across the thigh with the flat of the blade.

David stared at his brother, but he didn't really see him. All he saw was Michal. It was no good. He tossed the practice sword on the ground. Everything was crashing down around him, all his hopes dashed. He had lost her. She had told him to go away. Told him never to talk to her again. She had meant it. Meant every word. There was no way to turn this around, no hope.

"What's that?" said Eliab. "Are you crying, David? From the flat of the blade?"

David brushed a tear from his eye and shook Michal from his thoughts. He had hardly felt the slap of the blade.

"Oh, you're hopeless. Totally hopeless," Eliab said and then he lowered his voice. "No wonder the princess will have nothing to do with you. Women like strong men who can protect them."

David rubbed away the tears in his eyes. "What do you know about it?"

"I was in the palace last night, you idiot. I wanted to make sure no one saw you on the rooftop. I know the princess met with you, and I know she came running down a few moments later. From her hurry, it looked as if she couldn't get away from you fast enough. Time to grow up, David. She was just playing with you."

When David didn't say anything in response, Eliab waved his sword in the air in mock surrender.at him. "You'd better go practice with that lyre." He stalked away to join the other house guardsmen practicing in the field. "You'll never be a warrior."

David groaned. Once all he wanted was to be a warrior, and his brother's words would have hurt him. Now he didn't care what Eliab had to say. All he wanted was Michal and she wouldn't have him.

He looked up at the rooftop garden again, but when he saw no one, he forced his eyes away. No more. He had lost everything.

Why even stay?

THIRTY

Every breath hurt—not a stabbing pain, but a dull ache that filled Michal's whole body. The blackness she felt had started to consume her, fill her head, her heart, her lungs. She could hardly breathe. She had done what she thought right, what she had to do, but knowing that did nothing to lessen the pain. She stared straight ahead, looking at a tapestry that hung on the opposite wall. It depicted a simple farm, with a small house, wheat fields, and sheep grazing in the distance. The house looked much like their little family farm had looked, before her father became the king, before she became a princess.

She suddenly realized the room had turned quiet and everyone was staring at her.

She sat on the floor between her mother and Merab. Aunt Tamar and Aunt Sara sat across the rectangular rug upon which their plates, water goblets, and wine glasses rested. Just women dined this evening. Her father, brother, and uncles had all gone to the front at the Valley of Elah.

"Aren't you going to answer?" said the Queen.

Michal glanced at her mother. For the countless time, she noticed the similarity between her mother and Merab. They shared the same lush curly hair, wide eyes, and round face. She felt a pang of jealousy as she glanced at her mother now. Queen Ahinoam still looked stunning. A few more lines around her eyes and streaks of gray mingled in her dark brown locks perhaps, but she possessed a timeless beauty. Merab would age the same way. Michal was certain she would not.

"I'm sorry Mother, I wasn't paying attention. What did you say?"

"Your aunt asked why you weren't eating." The Queen nodded toward Aunt Sara, whose face wrinkled in a sour expression.

Michal peered down at her wooden plate. A small scoop of humus, a few pieces of roasted lamb, and a slice of flat bread stared back at her. "I guess I'm just not that hungry."

"I hope she's not catching something," Aunt Sara said.

"Maybe we should send a priest to look at her," said Aunt Tamar.

"What do you think, Noami?" added Aunt Tamar. She alone used the shortened version of the Queen's name. As the eldest sister, Tamar carried an air of authority over the Queen, who was the youngest of the three. Michal couldn't imagine anyone else calling her mother by the nickname. Even her father used her full name, Ahinoam.

The Queen glanced at Michal, but said nothing. Instead, she folded her cloth napkin precisely into a neat square and placed it by her plate.

The small dining room was Michal's favorite room in the palace. It reminded her of good times, simple pleasures, laughter and a feeling of closeness shared by her family. It usually brought a smile to her face, but not tonight. Nothing could drag a smile from her tonight.

Only one oil lamp hung beside the arched entrance of the small chamber. No more than six people could eat comfortably on the floor without bumping into each other. Two small, square windows permitted light and cool air to filter in from the courtyard.

Though her aunts wore colorful dresses of flax linen, her mother was rarely seen without a gown of fine Egyptian silk. She wore a full-length yellow robe with broad, finely embroidered shoulder straps that wrapped snugly around her trim waist. Her head never went uncovered, even at an informal dinner like this one. An elegant, wrap-style headdress of matching yellow silk concealed her hair and neckline. She wore no necklace tonight, only a pair of glittering gold earrings.

"It's important to drink plenty of water when there's so much stress," said Aunt Sara. "Please pass the wine, Ahinoam."

The Queen frowned and handled the jug to her sister. Aunt Sara was married to Uncle Abner. He was a hard man. Abner lived for war, going from one battle to the next. From the Ammonites to the Amalekites to the Philistines. Aunt Sara knew a lot about stress.

"Aunt Sara is right. Merab, your water goblet is empty. You should drink more," said the Queen. "Pass the pitcher to your sister when you're done."

Typical, thought Michal. *She always thinks about Merab first.*

"Have some too, Michal," said Aunt Sara. "You look so pale, dear. We don't need any sicknesses with this war going on."

"I'm sure she just has a lot on her mind," said the Queen.

Michal glanced at her mother. *Has Merab told her about David? What does she know?* She tried to read the lines on her mother's face, but they were fuzzy. Did her slight smile mean more than simple motherly concern, or was that just her imagination?

"She's fine," said Merab. "She ate a pear before dinner, that's all. Isn't that right Michal?" Her sister elbowed her in the ribs.

"Yes, Merab's right. She's always right." Michal muttered under her breath just loud enough so only her sister could hear, which brought another elbow to her ribs.

"You know better than to spoil dinner with fruit," said the Queen. "There's a proper order to things for a good reason." The Queen locked eyes on her, and Michal's heart jumped. *Is she talking about food or David? How much danger is he in?*

"Yes, Mother." Michal tried to hide the anxiety in her voice. A sharp knock at the door shattered her thoughts.

"Enter," said the Queen.

David strolled through the open archway and into the room, his hands wrapped tightly around his lyre.

Michal's jaw dropped. The little food she had eaten threatened to revolt in her stomach.

"What's he doing here?" Merab asked sharply.

The Queen smiled. "Since your father and the men are away tonight, I thought it would be fun to have some music. We could all use a little entertainment to brighten the mood. Perhaps put our problems in the proper perspective."

Michal gazed at him. *He's so angry.*

David's jaw was clenched tight and he held the lyre in a death grip. He cast his eyes downward as he sat on the floor against the far wall, the lyre braced between his legs.

He won't even look at me.

"Well," said Merab, "play us something."

David bowed his head in a short courteous nod and began raking his fingers across the strings. Michal recognized the song immediately. He had played the same piece when they had sung together in the fruit grove. Only now he played it slowly, mournfully, converting the love song into a sad ballad.

She bit her lip and tears welled in her eyes, but she fought to keep them back. She couldn't reveal her true feelings in front of her mother. She started to think of a reasonable excuse to leave when Merab said, "I don't understand why Father likes his playing so much. Do you, Mother?"

Merab spoke loud enough that David could hear her over the song.

"He's very talented." The words sputtered out of Michal's mouth. She didn't have to look at Merab to feel the heat behind her glare, so she kept her gaze glued to her plate.

"You shouldn't be so critical, Merab. I agree with Michal," said the Queen. "He's quite good for someone without formal training. He'll do for now, but I'll send him back to his farm when I've found a better musician. I've already sent a messenger to Judea to look for a more suitable replacement."

A more suitable replacement... send him back. These were not just loose words. Her mother must already know the truth. David was in a lot more danger than she'd thought. *Mother knows everything that goes on at the palace. He has to leave tonight.*

She chanced a quick glance at David. She had to warn him, but he kept his eyes focused on the lyre as he began another slow melody.

The Queen cleared her throat and raised her braceleted hand to stop him. "I have news from the king that we must discuss."

"Shall we send away the musician?" asked Aunt Sara.

The Queen gave David an appraising look, lingering over him for a short moment. "No. This news will be public tomorrow. I'm sure we can count on his discretion until then. Isn't that right, musician?"

He nodded.

"Good. The king has made a proclamation. I wanted you to hear about it before it gets announced in the square. Whoever slays the giant in a battle of champions will marry one of you two."

Michal felt the world spin. "How can he do this? We're not prizes to be auctioned off like a purse full of silver."

"What are you worried about?" spat Merab. "I'm the oldest. Any suitor will choose me to marry, not you!"

"They treat us like slaves, Mother!" Michal crossed her arms. "Why can't we have a say in our own lives?"

"Is that what you think?" answered the Queen with a sly smile. "That men are in control?" She chuckled softly. "Men believe they make all the decisions, but it's our job to guide them, so they make the *right* decisions. We have many ways to influence them. Who do you think persuaded your father to accept the kingship in the first place?"

Michal's eyes widened.

"Don't be so surprised. In time you'll learn how to influence them and understand."

"So you agree with this plan?" asked Merab. "That we have to marry whoever bests this giant?"

Queen Ahinoam frowned. "As I understand it, the only way to rid ourselves of these Philistines is to defeat this giant of theirs. To do that we need the best champion, and what better way to ensure that we get the best, than to offer a royal marriage? If the Philistines win this war, we're all lost. Everything will be gone." She indicated the palace with a broad sweep of her arm that finally came to rest directly in front of her two daughters. "Everything."

"I don't want to marry some grubby soldier," said Merab.

"I would think a champion who bests a giant would be a good match," answered Aunt Tamar.

"He'll be some big, smelly brute," said Michal.

The Queen smiled. "I wouldn't be so sure of that. We don't have a giant to face this Philistine, so it seems to me that our champion will have to be different. Brute force and muscle won't get the job done. He'll need to be a favorite of God, and the Lord treasures those with hearts that are true. That would be a man worth marrying. Either way, your father has spoken. Our responsibility is to live out this decree."

Michal glanced toward the far wall to see David, but he was gone. She hadn't noticed him leaving.

Strange that he left his lyre behind.

THIRTY-ONE

David rubbed his bleary eyes. Noise filled the servants' quarters: the hay rustled, the old men talked endlessly, others gambled and argued over the dice. The stablemaster, who slept on the next mat, snored louder than most and his idiot son Harel worst of all. He muttered in his sleep *and* snored. It sounded as if he tortured dogs all night and gave a running commentary while he did it. None of this was new, but David had a hard time ignoring it. He wrapped a spare tunic around his head to drown out the noise and muffle Harel's terrible stench. He reeked of the stables, stale sweat, and horse dung.

But tonight, none of that mattered. He wouldn't have been able to sleep even if he were alone in a quiet room. His mind raced in circles, refusing to stop on any one idea. He needed a horse, and he needed to get to the Valley of Elah. He wanted to start right away but he had to wait until first light. Without daylight he had no hope of finding his way to the front. He remembered most of the landmarks he'd seen during his previous visit with Jonathan, but couldn't possibly make them out by moonlight. He had to wait until morning.

What if King Saul has already chosen someone else as his champion before I get there?

He closed his eyes and visions of Michal filled his mind—her penetrating gaze, her sweet smile, her beautiful laugh, the taste of her lips. Why had she pushed him away? Was it because she didn't want to marry a poor farm boy? Who could blame her for that? Once he killed the giant, everything would change. Saul had offered a small fortune as a reward and his blessing for the marriage. All his problems would be solved at once.

All he had to do was get to the front in time to answer the giant's challenge. He had to be first. He couldn't think about what would happen if someone else claimed the prize. *What if the champion chooses to marry Michal instead of Merab? I can't let that happen. This is my chance. The only chance a poor shepherd could ever get to marry a princess. I can't miss it. I won't miss it...*

The bottom of a sandal crunched David's hand.

"Oh sorry about that," snickered the stablemaster. "I didn't see you sleeping there."

David rubbed sleep from his eyes. The servants' quarters were empty. *What time is it?*

He jumped to his feet and ran to the open doorway. The sun hovered just barely above the horizon. He had to move fast! The stables were on the opposite side of the compound. He raced from the servants' quarters, avoided the house guard outposts on either side of the main gate, and cut across the small garden in front of the palace. As he crossed the cobbled pathway he nearly bumped into the blacksmith.

"Sorry." David skipped around the burly old man.

The blacksmith grumbled, but David didn't pause to listen.

He slipped inside the stables, stepping lightly on the straw-matted floor. The cedar building was long and narrow with a row of stalls on either side. Warm morning light streamed in from two rows of square windows set high among the rafters above the stalls.

He kept a careful eye out for the stablemaster, but saw no one as he threaded his way behind a pair of broken ox-carts along the wall. With any luck, the stablemaster had gone for breakfast.

The heavy farm animals were all kept to one side. Grumpy, weather beaten oxen stood quietly in their places as they waited for their morning feed. Along the other side of the stable, a row of narrow stalls held a donkey, two mules and the few horses that hadn't already been taken to the front.

He needed a horse, and a fast one at that. He spotted one of Jonathan's steeds peeking over its stall door. The Prince had already taken his favorite white stallion to the valley; this horse was slightly smaller with a dusky, red-brown hide. Perfect!

He hurried along the line of stalls, but stopped short when he heard a familiar off-tune humming. Harel pitched hay in the empty stall next to the brown horse.

David cursed to himself. He couldn't ask to borrow one of Jonathan's horses. Harel would never let him.

Watching carefully, he waited for his chance. If he wanted to escape without being seen, he'd need a head start before anyone knew he'd stolen a horse. Sweat dripped down his face. Time was not on his side. David ducked into an empty stall.

The pitchfork scraped against the floor as Harel swept the hay into the stalls, coming closer and closer. He could smell Harel's stink now, even above the odor of dung and horse-sweat that filled the stables.

The top of Harel's granite head loomed above the wooden stall door.

David silently cursed his bad luck as the latch rattled, then ducked under one of the slats separating the stalls and into the next stall.

The pitchfork followed him along the row of stalls, scraping the hay from the corridor. David ducked under the next slat, and into the last stall in the row. He had nowhere else to hide. Another moment and Harel would find him.

The latch rattled and David readied himself. He'd charge Harel when he stepped into the stall and hope to catch him by surprise.

Snap!

Harel cursed. He'd broken his pitchfork in two. He threw the broken pieces against the stall and stomped away, muttering to himself.

David breathed easy, but did not hesitate. He slid silently from the stall and crossed the gap. Jonathan's favorite charger was kept in a stall secured by two bolts, a crossbar at the top and a drive bolt at the bottom. He pulled the drive bolt out of the ground and reached for the upper latch.

"What are you doing?"

David whirled to find Harel glaring at him, a new pitchfork in his hand.

"I asked you what're you doing there?"

Great. David straightened his back and tried to act confident. Everyone, including Harel, knew Jonathan spent time with him. Maybe the dumb block of wood would think the prince had given him a task. "Jonathan wanted me to check his horses."

A sly grin spread across Harel's wide-lipped mouth. "No you weren't. The prince is gone since early this morning. You were looking to steal one of his horses."

"I'm not a thief."

Harel stabbed the pitch into the ground. "Oho," he laughed. "Oh yes you are. You'll hang for this!" His face lit with malicious glee.

"Only if you can stop me. I guess we'll just have to finish that fight you started the other day!"

The big oaf lumbered toward him and lunged with both arms in an attempt to wrestle him to the ground.

David ducked under and punched Harel's flabby belly.

"Oof!"

David smiled.

As red-faced as a beet, the huge boy shook off the blow and

straightened himself. "Forget the hanging! Now I'm going to kill you myself!"

Harel swung his meaty fist in a wild roundhouse.

David couldn't avoid it. He turned at the last minute so the punch only glanced off the side of his head instead of knocking it clean off his shoulders. He stumbled backward, a sharp pain shooting up his neck and shoulders.

Harel advanced on him again.

David scrambled toward the stall door and kicked the broken pitchfork Harel had tossed aside.

"You idiot!" said Harel. "Now you're trapped."

David grabbed the pitchfork's handle and smashed it against Harel's block head.

Thud!

The wood snapped and Harel fell to his knees.

David knocked open the crossbolt latch.

Harel staggered to his feet and closed the gap. He rammed a beefy fist into David's stomach and David doubled over, all the breath knocked out of him.

Harel glanced at him and then at the open carriage doors, fully expecting him to run. But David didn't move. He needed that horse!

"You like that?" sneered Harel. "Oh, there's plenty more."

He charged at David again.

David had to end this now. Otherwise the stablemaster might return and he would be lost. He stood his ground, half-crouched, and waited for the exact moment to make his move. When Harel thundered toward him, he swept his leg out and tripped the burly stablemaster's son. Harel stumbled to one knee.

David jumped, caught the top of the stall door, and swung his legs over it. As he cleared the top of the door, he swung it wide and bashed it right into Harel's face.

He cleared the stall door and landed on the horse's back with a jarring thump.

The horse reared up and nearly toppled him over.

"Oh no you don't!" raged Harel. Blood flowed from his nose in two thin, red streams.

Breathless, David kicked the horse in the side. The animal bolted through the open stall door and headed straight at Harel. The stable boy reached for the horse's bridle but David turned it aside. As he passed the stable boy, he kicked Harel in the back of the head using the full force of the horse's charge to strengthen the blow.

Harel's eyes rolled to the back of his head as he plunged face-first into the dung-strewn floor of the stable.

"Hey, don't let your father catch you sleeping on the job." David grinned, gripped the braided leather bridle with both hands and leaned forward to guide the horse out of the building.

House guard posts flanked both sides of the front gate. Too many soldiers . He'd never be able to bluff his way through. He pulled on the reins and maneuvered the horse toward the rear of the compound, passing the smithy and the kitchen building. A wide carriage lane ran between the fruit trees and the vegetable garden at the rear gate. The horse's hooves clattered against the cobblestones.

The gate was open, with only one guard posted.

The guard hailed David. "You there! Stop!"

"Stand aside!" yelled David. He spurred the horse faster.

The guard waved both arms. "What are you doing?"

"Taking supplies to the valley."

"What supplies?"

No bags were attached to the horse, not even a blanket beneath him. It didn't matter. He kicked the horse's ribs again and urged it past the guard and out the gate.

The horse flew down the path, and it was all he could do to keep from falling off. He refused to look over his shoulder. Whatever lay behind him was not important. Even if someone decided to pursue, they'd never catch him.

Everything would be fine, just as long as he found his way to the Israelite camp in time. Just as long as he reached King Saul before he chose another champion.

THIRTY-TWO

Michal surveyed the palace grounds from the rooftop garden. The dew-moistened grass glistened in the early morning light. The gardeners were already at work, the cooks busy in the kitchen, but Abby hadn't arrived yet. Michal wanted to give the girl a message for David—needed to get him a message. She'd spent all night considering her mother's unusual behavior from every angle, circling it as she would a flowering cactus. The flower stood on top, but those stinging nettles looked dangerous all around.

Does Mother know about David and me?

Merab swore she hadn't said anything, but if that were true, why had Mother acted so strangely? She'd never sent for a musician during dinner before, and all those statements with double meanings...

They could all be harmless, mere coincidences, but she didn't think so. A tingle crept up her back. She knows. *She knows about us.*

He had to leave right away.

Michal noticed movement on the trail outside the palace walls. A blur on a brown horse raced through the back gate. *Odd that a messenger would leave in such a hurry so early in the day.* She squinted into the sunlight and caught sight of his back and his hair—*long, curly red hair.* The breath froze in her throat. The rider wobbled on the back of the steed as he tore down the trail.

It's David! He must have figured it out for himself.

She watched him grow smaller and smaller.

She felt all the energy drain from her body as she thought she'd never see him again.

The tower bell shattered her thoughts. *Clang! Clang! Clang!* Three rings—the alarm when something was wrong. She instinctively glanced over the horizon toward Gibeah and beyond. If the Philistines were coming they'd march from that direction.

Nothing.

She looked again at the dusty trail and the wobbly rider speeding away.

Michal's heart jumped.

"Oh no," she breathed. "David, what have you done?"

Michal raced to the front gate. A large group of the house guard had already assembled along the stone palisade.

"He couldn't have gotten too far." The captain of the guard's booming voice addressed the gathering crowd from the top of the wall. He was a heavyset man, with a long jagged scar that ran from his left eye to the base of his neck.

"We'll find him. Don't worry about that. No one steals a horse from our stables and gets away with it. Two shekels of silver to the man who brings him back—dead or alive!"

A dozen guards cheered and stomped their feet. Michal saw Eliab cheering as well, his fist pumping in the air.

The crowd broke out into dozens of excited conversations all at once until the captain bellowed, "Listen up, this is important."

A hush settled over the group.

"I don't care about the thief, but I want the Prince's horse brought back alive!"

The stablemaster led four horses from the stables. The house guard began to jostle each other as they rushed to get to the horses. They nearly trampled the burly stablemaster and a couple of fist fights broke out.

Where is Abby? Michal needed to find her before anyone realized she was David's sister. She spun in a circle and found the young girl standing by herself between the stables and the small shrine in front of the palace. Tears rolled down the girl's face.

Michal grabbed her arm and pulled her away from the crowd. "Come with me."

Abby looked up at Michal, red-faced and sobbing. "David would never steal a horse. There must be some mistake. He's never stolen anything in his whole life! You have to believe me!"

"I know, Abby. He's no thief. I think there's another reason for this mess. And it's all my fault."

"What?"

Michal whispered, "We'll talk in a moment. Keep your head down. Don't look anyone in the eyes and get behind me."

She took Abby's hand and led her across the cobbled path toward the kitchen building.

A nearby guard spotted Abby, his bushy eyebrows high on his forehead.

Michal didn't like his suspicious expression, so she threw her shoulders back and glared at the man. Hard. "Shouldn't you be looking for the thief? My brother will want that horse back. What does my father pay you for?"

The guard averted his eyes and turned away.

I need to find Hadi. Michal scanned the palace grounds, looking through the knots of people who were all talking excitedly about the thief.

She has to be here somewhere.

Just then, she spotted Hadi on the edge of the crowd, talking to one of the older servants who worked in the kitchen.

Michal approached Hadi with Abby in tow. When Hadi saw them, she turned to the kitchen servant. "I've got to go now, Delara.

We can talk later."

Delara nodded respectfully at Michal and hurried back toward the kitchen.

Michal opened her mouth to start talking, but the serious look in Hadi's eyes silenced her.

"This is a horrible shame that we had a thief in our midst." Hadi spoke loud enough for anyone nearby to hear. "Let's go pray that justice will be delivered."

Abby started to protest, but Michal squeezed her arm tight and followed Hadi to the fruit grove where they could be safely alone.

"This is all a mistake," said Abby. "David would never have stolen that horse."

"He took it, that's for certain," said the old woman, "but I never saw a thief in him."

"He's no thief," added Abby.

"I know, child," said Hadi. "But I just don't see why he would take it."

"Not to run away," said Michal.

"Why then?"

"Oh, don't you see?" Michal tried her best to whisper, but her voice wouldn't cooperate. "He's going to the front! He's going to volunteer to face the giant!"

"What's this about the giant?" Abby's face had gone from red to bone white.

"My father's decided that whoever defeats the giant as our champion can marry one of his daughters. The decree was going to be announced at midday today in the courtyard."

"Fight the giant. Th-th-that's crazy," sputtered Abby. "David wouldn't have a chance."

"I have to find him before he sees my father. I have to talk him out of this craziness. He'll get himself killed."

Hadi stared deep into Michal's eyes for a long moment. "Perhaps this is the work of the Fates. You asked them for a chance to be with him. This might be that chance."

"But it's no chance, Hadi. He's no soldier. What chance does he have against a giant?"

"Only the Fates know for certain what type of web they weave."

"I don't care. It's too dangerous! I need to see him. I've got to get to the valley."

"And how are you going to do that?"

Michal glanced back toward the stables. "I'll get a mule from the stables. I'll say that I need to go to Gibeah. From there I'll just keep going."

"You're going to Gibeah unescorted?" Hadi shook her head. "They'd never let you past the gate."

"I'll sneak out, then."

"Child, you don't even know how to get to the Valley of Elah. You'll need my help."

"Will you help me, then? I have to do this. I won't be able to live with myself if he dies because of me. I have to stop him. One way or another, I'm going."

"The front is a dangerous place for a princess."

Michal glared at Hadi until she relented. "Are you certain this is what you want? Even if you see him, it doesn't mean he won't still try to face the giant. The Fates may have already decided. It might be impossible for you to change this."

"I don't care about the danger or the Fates or my mother or sister or father. I just need to be with him."

"You are as stubborn as a mule." Hadi smiled. "And I'm crazy as a goat left in the hot sun all day. Let's see if I can't persuade the stablemaster to give me a cart. Go put on your plainest travel robe. Make sure it has a hood and meet me behind the blacksmith's shop."

"I'm coming too." Abby's lips formed a thin, determined line.

Michal draped her arm over Abby's shoulders. "She has to come, Hadi. Someone's bound to realize she's David's sister. If we're not here to protect her and the house guard gets their hands on her, I don't know what they'll do."

Hadi glanced between the two and nodded.

"Once we get to Gibeah, you two can get off the cart and stay in the city." Michal didn't say the rest—that she was concerned about Hadi, that the front was a long way for her to go in her condition.

"Don't worry about me, child. I'll be fine. There's life in these old bones yet. Get going. Both of you. Hurry! We don't have much time."

Michal met Abby behind the blacksmith's building. "Any sign of Hadi yet?"

Abby shook her head.

Thoughts about David fighting the giant caused her heart to hammer in her chest. The giant must be twice his size. If half the stories Jonathan told her were true, he was a fearsome killer who could wipe out a score of ordinary soldiers without breaking a sweat. What chance could a shepherd have?

The clatter of hooves roused her from her thoughts. Hadi arrived on top of a wooden cart pulled by two strong mules. The old woman flicked the thick leather reins and whispered, "Climb up. Michal, you'll need to go in the back and hide under the woolen blanket. Abby, you can sit up here next to me."

Michal climbed on top of the cart and jumped into the back. The cart was packed with flat bread, barrels of wine and humus, and a couple of crates of pears and olives. She spotted the blanket and ducked underneath, squeezing herself into a ball with her knees to her chin.

"Come on." Hadi encouraged the mules with a snap of the leather straps and the cart lurched forward.

At the front gate, the cart stopped and a rough voice called out, "Where are you going, Hadi?"

Michal's heart lumped in her throat.

"I've got to deliver these supplies to the front." Hadi's words sounded clipped and hard as if she were annoyed.

"That's no job for an old woman. Where's Isaac? He usually makes the deliveries."

"He went to look for that thief. Two shekels is a lot of silver."

The guard huffed. "Everyone else gets to go, but I've got to guard this stinking gate."

"You should talk! I've a long ride ahead in the hot sun, while you sit in the shade."

She tossed the guard a fresh pear.

He took a bite and smiled.

Hadi made a clucking sound with her tongue and the cart started to turn.

The leather straps snapped and the cart rolled out of the palace.

After a few moments, Michal joined Hadi and Abby on the front seat. The lush farmlands on the outskirts of Gibeah rolled by on both sides of the trail.

"How did you get the stablemaster to give you the cart?" asked Michal.

"He's been carrying on with one of the Queen's handmaidens. That's how come he gets extra rations and special treatment. He doesn't want the Queen to find out."

Michal glanced back over her shoulder at her home.

The wheels creaked.

The mules brayed.

And the cart rolled away from the palace, away from her family and toward the war and a giant and David.

THIRTY-THREE

Sweat soaked David's back as he rode past farmlands and featureless plains of scrub brush and red dirt. Everything looked the same. He searched the steep mountain trails for landmarks he remembered. Anything that might mean he was headed in the right direction. But he didn't recognize anything.

He was hopelessly lost, but he still believed he would find his way to Elah. God had led him this far and would see him through. Time and again he strayed from the path, but each time, the horse stopped and changed course and David found himself back on the correct trail. After a while, he realized the answer was a lot less mystical than all that. The horse simply knew the way to Elah better than he did.

By the time he reached the Israelite camp, it was late afternoon. David didn't know what time the giant came out to make his challenge. *What if I'm too late? I can't be too late!*

The horse bolted forward as soon as it spotted the tents, and David nearly fell off. He had never figured out how to stop the thing.

"Look out! Runaway horse!" he shouted at a small knot of soldiers, but he should have known better. His capable steed stopped on its own before it plowed into anybody.

"If you can't control the horse, you shouldn't ride one!" An angry soldier with a narrow face grabbed the bridle. "Who are you anyway?"

David swung down from the horse and eyed the soldiers cautiously. He had to be careful. If he told the soldiers he wanted to fight the giant, they'd never let him through.

"I'm David, son of Jesse. I've come from the palace. I have an urgent message for King Saul."

"We don't know you," said the narrow faced soldier, eyeing David suspiciously. Three more moved in, surrounding him.

"You know my brother Eliab."

The soldier poked him hard in the chest. "So why didn't they send him?"

David stood firm. "They sent *me*."

"Tell us the message," said one of the others. "We'll see that the king gets it."

"I won't. It's for the king only. Step aside or you'll regret it."

Two men grabbed David from behind. Their hands twisted his arms behind his back.

"He's either crazy or a Philistine spy," said one of the men.

David twisted, but the soldiers gripped him too tightly. Pain shot up his arms. "Let me go, and I'll show you how crazy I am."

A hard-faced soldier laughed, "Stop it, you're frightening us!"

"We'll take you to the king," said the first soldier, "But you'll be roped and tied, and maybe a little worse for wear."

"What's this all about?" Jonathan stepped between the men. "That's one of my horses. David, what are you doing with it?"

David shook loose from the soldiers' grip. "I have to see the king."

"What for? What's happened?"

David glanced at the ring of suspicious faces. Two of the men had already reached for the hilts of their swords. He sighed. *I don't have any choice now. It's all or nothing anyway.*

"It's about the giant."

"Goliath? What about him?"

"Has he made his challenge yet?"

"Not yet. But David, don't tell me you've just come here to gawk at the giant? We don't have time for games."

He stepped close to Jonathan. "No, it's more than that. I have to speak to your father. It's important. You have to trust me."

Jonathan stared hard into his eyes.

David unflinchingly returned the look.

Whatever Jonathan looked for he must have found because he finally said, "All right but this had better be important." He waved off his men. "Move aside. Let's go, move aside."

Jonathan marched him across the encampment. Most of the soldiers milled aimlessly about, their faces downcast. A few leaned wearily against trees or sat together in small groups in quiet conversation. Three men arguing around a campfire turned quiet when they saw Jonathan coming. David noticed the change in the men's mood from his visit only a few days earlier. All energy had been sapped from the Israelite forces.

Three times as large as any of the others, the command tent's purple and gold fabric stood out from the plain gray tents that surrounded it. Two guards stood at the entrance. They nodded as Jonathan escorted David inside.

King Saul was seated on a tall chair with general Abner standing beside him. The King's face was drawn, his hair and beard ragged. If the soldiers had seemed grim and discouraged, the King looked absolutely defeated.

David realized he had arrived just in time.

Half a dozen soldiers stood before their king, the cream of the Israelite army, dressed in their best war gear. Two large men scuffled in front of the high seat, while their older patrons spat accusations at each other.

General Abner stepped between the young men and shouted in a deep rumble, "Stop this bickering! We're not here to fight among ourselves."

The men froze. Although smaller than either of the soldiers, Abner pushed them roughly aside. "Don't worry. You'll all get your chance to impress the king."

King Saul hardly seemed impressed. He hadn't even noticed the scuffle, distracted by a smudge of grime on one of the buttons on his tunic. He scratched at one cheek and then the other.

"Father," said Jonathan, "I'm sorry to interrupt."

Saul looked up. Dark circles nested under his eyes. David had never seen the King look so tired.

"What is it?"

Jonathan hesitated. "It's David... from the palace." The arguments in the tent died down.

David felt everyone's eyes bearing down on him.

Saul barely looked at him. "The boy who plays the music? What does he want?"

"He says he has a message."

"Very well."

David stepped forward, his head high and his back straight. He bent to one knee. "My king."

"Get on with it," said Saul. "What's this message?"

Saul glanced down at his tunic, swatting at the fabric along the front as if knocking away a swarm of flies, but there was nothing there.

What am I doing here? Any of these soldiers is more suited to face the giant than I am. The king won't even look at me. Just when he felt his resolve about to break, he thought of Michal and knew he couldn't hesitate.

"I've come to fight the giant!"

"What?" Saul stared at him in disbelief.

Jonathan flushed red. "I'm sorry, Father. I had no idea. I shouldn't have brought him here to talk such nonsense."

"I must be the one to fight the giant," David insisted.

"Don't be ridiculous! You wouldn't stand a chance." Jonathan grabbed him by the scruff of his neck and started to drag him backward.

The crowd in the tent came alive with taunts and jeers. One soldier shouted, "My wife could beat him." Another laughed and said, "Your wife could beat you." A voice farther in the back cried out, "He must be crazy. Let me teach him a lesson."

Jonathan heaved David backward, "I'm sorry, Father."

David shook him off. "I can fight him and I can win!"

"You can't be serious." Abner grinned at him as if David were some feeble-minded fool.

"I *am* serious. If you want to win, you'll listen. I'm your best choice. I'm different from the others."

"I'll say," remarked Abner. "You're about half their size. Young man, this is a fight of champions. If our man loses, the Philistines shall have us, they will own us. We'll be their slaves. Every man, woman and child."

"Size has nothing to do with it. I'll use the sling."

Jonathan grabbed his arm. "That's enough, David! I've seen you practice. We have a hundred men who work the sling better than you."

"That doesn't matter. God will guide my hand."

A strange light kindled in Saul's eye. It's just a flicker, thought David. But if I fan it to flame, maybe he'll listen to me.

"You know it's true! You felt it those times when I played the lyre for you at night."

"I felt... something," admitted the King.

"It wasn't my song that chased away those demons. It was the power of God."

"Demons?" asked Abner, amid a startled murmur from the crowd.

"Not important," said Saul with a dismissive wave of his hand.

"This is ridiculous," said Jonathan. "David can't possibly be our champion." He took firm hold of David using both hands this time and dragged him halfway to the tent flap.

"It was the power of God acting through me! The Lord chased those demons away! You know it, my king. You know it!"

"Hold!" said Saul. He took a deep breath and looked David up and down.

David stared right back.

"You speak the truth. You have chased away dark spirits with your music. But slaying the giant is another matter. How can you be so confident?"

David straightened his tunic. "Before I came here, when I was tending my flock, I fought off lions in the mountains with only my staff."

Saul snickered. "You won't be able to chase Goliath off so easily."

"I also killed a bear."

"You fought a bear?" Abner asked.

"Well, not exactly. It came at me. There was nothing I could do. And God smote him down to protect me. I saw it with my own eyes. The power of God. Invincible."

Abner huffed impatiently. "Enough! Stories of such miracles are too many to count. Every old woman has a dozen of them."

"It's true." David stepped forward. "I saw it with my own eyes. I felt His presence. The Lord who rescued me from the bear will protect me from the hand of the Philistine giant as well. I can call upon Him to defeat this pagan."

Saul did not seem convinced. Instead, he scratched furiously at the back of his neck.

"And I also saw the prophet Samuel in Gibeah," David added.

"The prophet Samuel?" asked Saul. "When was this?"

"Months ago, during the Festival of Weeks."

"And what did Samuel have to say to you?" Saul spoke slowly, his jaw clenched tight.

David knew better than to tell him everything. Not that bit about becoming king in Saul's place, that's for certain. "He said God was with me."

"Oh, this is ridiculous," said Jonathan. "He's just a boy from the fields. He doesn't even know how to fight."

"And the demons?" asked David. "The Lord who vanquished your demons through my hand will destroy the giant Goliath. I swear it!"

Saul regarded him carefully.

"Come now," said Abner. "You can't really be considering this?"

The King didn't bother to answer. He scratched his scalp so violently, David thought he might draw blood.

David smelled the bitter stench of burnt ochre in the tent, as he had so many times before in the king's bedchamber. The King's outline grew fuzzy right before his eyes. David started to feel lightheaded. And then it all came into focus. The King was once again beset by demons. David saw them as shimmering maggots crawling over his clothes, his skin, his beard. They clung to his face, wriggling worms in purple, red and blue, dangling from his nose, burrowing into his ears.

"I know how you suffer, my king," said David. "I know what ails you."

"This is too much!" shouted Abner. "You're very lucky, young man. Lucky I don't have time to skin you alive for your insolence. Get him out of here!"

A fierce wind whipped up outside, whistling through the camp, forcing its way between the line of tents and into the command tent.

"Let me show you," David said. "I summoned God's power to chase those demons away. You know it, my king. Let me prove it to you now!"

He had no idea what he would do. He hadn't brought a lyre to play. And even if he had, he couldn't call upon the orb whenever he wanted. All the time he spent practicing had yielded no fruit. It only appeared in the tent while Saul was sleeping.

The tent flap flew open, torn apart by the wind as another gust blew into the tent.

"Show me." As Saul spoke, maggots poured from his mouth.

David knelt and raised his hands. He felt God with him, just as he had when he played for the king at night. His body felt electric as if God had brought new life to every muscle, every fiber. The wind circled and he remembered the sense of wonder he felt when he'd first seen the canyon pass in the morning.

David felt his body burn as if on fire, but it didn't hurt. It felt good and strong and righteous. He reveled in that feeling, bathing in it, rolling in it, letting it fill him with certainty. He filled his mind only with thoughts of his faith and the orb appeared in front of him.

He prayed to God for help, so he could do His bidding. The orb grew brighter and a scorching blast of heat whipped across his face. Three massive bird-like creatures flew out of the portal. They circled King Saul.

David tried to look upon them, but his eyes burned. All he saw was intense white light, a whirlwind of feathers. The three spirits flapped their wings in unison, and the wind roared, running riot within the tent, mussing the men with its invisible hands, tossing their equipment aside.

David focused on the King, and the wind from the spirits' wings swirled and raged, scouring the King clean of the demon worms. The luminous maggots flew in the air all red and purple and blue. The bird-things snapped their beaks in a frenzy, gobbling them up. The wind whipped around again and then shot straight up, blowing the ceiling flap off the tent. The luminous spirits disappeared into the sky.

As the dust settled, Jonathan asked, "What was that?"

"Mountain winds," said Abner. "Just a freak accident."

The other men murmured agreement.

David realized they had felt the wind, but had seen nothing else.

But the King knew otherwise. He looked completely different now. He sat up straight in his chair, awake and alert.

David locked eyes with him.

"Secure the flap," said Abner, "and get this boy out of here."

"Wait!" commanded Saul. "I've made my decision. David will be the one to face the giant. We need to answer the Philistine's challenge today. We can't wait any longer."

"Don't send this boy. I'll go," said Jonathan. "I'll go down there today. Right now."

"No," said Saul. "Jonathan, you are my firstborn son, you're my heir, and the finest among us, but you're not the one to fight that giant."

"And he is?"

"Yes. He is!"

THIRTY-FOUR

Michal stared hard at the carriage and bit her lip. "Just look at that wheel! It's barely attached to the cart."

The wheel leaned precariously against the axel. Luckily, Hadi had stopped the wagon just before it snapped off.

Michal kicked the cart. "We don't need this!" After three more kicks she stepped back.

Abby added a kick of her own. They were stuck on the narrow dirt trail that led into the mountains. Steep inclines crowded them on both sides.

Michal paced back and forth. Her mind whirled like a dust storm. She wanted to take one of the mules and continue on to the army camp. But what would happen to Hadi and Abby? A ten-year-old girl and a sick old woman alone on the trail. The situation was ripe for disaster.

Hadi seemed to read her mind when she said, "You can take one of the mules and go on along the trail. If you hurry, you might still get there in time."

"I can't leave you two by yourselves. Who knows who might come along?"

"We'll be okay. I've been stuck in worse places," said Hadi, but Michal didn't like the way her shoulders stooped. It looked like her legs might give out from under her at any moment. And Abby didn't look much better. All the color had drained from her face. *She must be worried sick about David.*

"I'm not going anywhere. Maybe there's something we can use to fix the wheel." Michal planted her foot against the cart's side and climbed over the edge, landing with a soft thud among a scattering of garden tools and half-baked crockery. She had just spotted a coil of rope that might come in handy when she noticed two riders approaching from behind. Leaning over the edge, she called down to Hadi. "Two men are coming on horses."

"We'd better hide," Hadi said. "There's no telling who they are, or what they want."

Michal swung down from the cart.

Abby circled around the mules. "We can hide behind those rocks. They won't be able to see us from the cart."

Michal snatched Hadi's hand and led her to the cliff wall. Bathed in harsh midday sunlight, she couldn't see the riders clearly. They looked like two fast-moving shadows. "Stay here. Don't come out no matter what happens."

Hadi grabbed her arm. "It's too dangerous, child. Even if they're Israelites, they might mean harm."

Michal shrugged her off and jumped from the rocks. "They'll see the cart. They'll come looking for us. This way you'll be safe. I can tell them that I'm alone."

Hadi started to protest again, but Michal turned and strode back to the cart. As the riders grew larger she noticed their uniforms. They wore the blue tunics of the house guard. She stepped directly into their path.

The two men pulled their horses to a stop right in front of her. The animals, bathed in sweat, snorted and danced on their hind legs.

"What are you doing out here all alone? You're too young to be unaccompanied," said one of the riders.

"And beautiful too. This must be a gift from God," cried out the other, his voice treacherous. He was tall and thin with a pointy nose that seemed too long for his face.

Michal didn't recognize him. She pushed back the hood from her shabby traveling robe and shook her curly hair free. Her eyes locked on the other rider. The Fates were indeed at work, twisting the strings of her life. It was Eliab.

"That's the princess, you idiot." Eliab smacked his companion across the side of his head.

The thin soldier bowed his head. "My apologies, princess. I didn't recognize you in those clothes."

"Never mind that," said Michal.

Abby came running from the side of the road. "Eliab! We're looking for David."

"You're not the only one looking for him. They've posted a big reward for his head."

"He's gone to the front," said Abby.

"Why would he do that?"

"He wants to challenge the giant."

"I knew he must have had a reason to take that horse. He's no thief," said Eliab with a grimace on his face. "But he's a fool. That giant will tear him apart."

"We have to stop him," pleaded Abby.

Eliab chuckled. "You don't have to worry about that, sister. Even if he finds his way to the front, there's no way they'll let him get anywhere near that beast. It's a battle of champions. No one is crazy enough to choose him as our champion. He's nothing but a skinny kid."

The thin soldier dismounted. "That wheel's about to snap. I can fix it, but it'll take some time."

"What do you know about carts and wheels?" rumbled Eliab.

"I'm a carpenter's son." The thin man smiled. "I've got tools in my bag."

"Good," said Michal. "You stay here and fix it. Make sure no harm comes to my handmaidens. Treat them as you would treat me. It won't be good for you if I hear otherwise." She grabbed a fistful of his horse's mane and leapt onto the animal's back.

The thin man stood in front of the horse, his arms out to stop the animal. "You should wait for me to fix the cart so we can all go together. The rest of the trail to the front is too steep and dangerous. The king wouldn't be happy with us if you get hurt."

"I don't care what my father thinks. Step aside."

The thin man hesitated.

She kicked the colt in the belly with her heels and spurred it forward. The guard leapt out of the way as the horse barely missed him.

Eliab caught up to her. "Why are you doing this? He's just a poor shepherd that's stolen a horse. What's he to you?"

Michal shouted back, "Everything."

Michal burst into the command tent.

The King sat alone, a cup of wine held lightly in his hand. He stood when she entered. "What are you doing here? I didn't send for you."

"I came on my own. Is David going to challenge the giant? You can't let him do this. It's too dangerous."

"I've already made my choice. He is touched by God. He will be our champion."

She froze. *I'm too late.* "You can change your mind. Please Father, David can't battle that beast."

The King's eyebrows arched up his forehead and his voice rose. "David... That's twice you've used his name. How do you know this boy?"

"We've spent time together. He's special to me." She blushed. "We love each other. Don't you see? It's all my fault. He'd never have come here if it weren't for me."

The King slapped her hard across the face. She spun back a step. Wine splashed from his cup and stained her grey robe. "You've spent time with him! With *him*! You're old enough to know better. You bring shame to our house."

She touched the bruise blossoming on her cheek, tears in her eyes. "I'm sorry Father. Punish me, if you want. Lock me in a cell. Do whatever you want to me, but stop him from fighting. *Please*."

The King's fury ebbed as he saw the tears in his daughter's eyes. "There's nothing I can do about it now. My decision is final. It's in God's hands. He battles the Philistine today."

No!

The King turned to refill his cup.

She spun and ran from the tent.

Michal found David standing on the edge of a creek with King Saul's armor carefully laid out beside him. He faced the water with his back to her, standing on a carpet of emerald grass. Tall evergreens flanked him on either side. Little purple, heart-shaped flowers dotted the banks of flowing water.

Her heart burst into flames and her legs wobbled. It all became real to her at that moment, with David's silhouette looking at the creek, standing next to her father's armor. *He's really going to fight the giant.*

A rush of memories flooded her — the first time she'd seen him playing the lyre in the practice room, his fingers dancing over the strings, the look in his eyes as he scattered the demons, the feel of his fingers and the taste of his lips. She remembered how gracefully he'd lost the game to her and how naturally he'd protected Rebecca. She recalled how his face lit up when he described the canyon near his home, and how his eyes burned with passion when he talked about his faith and their future.

Did I love him from the first moment?

Her emotions churned together. It was impossible for her to say now, but she thought she did.

"David," she called out.

He turned and she raced forward and flung herself into his arms, holding him tight and burying her face against his chest. She wanted to hold him this way forever, but after a long moment, he pushed her back.

"What are you doing here?"

"When I heard that you took that horse, I knew you'd come here. You can't face this giant. I was wrong. We can run. We can go right now. We'll steal another horse and ride away and just keep riding. No one will find us. We can be together."

"Hold on," he grinned. "I thought you didn't want to live with a poor shepherd."

"I just said those things because I was afraid and I didn't want you to get in trouble. It's too late for that now. I told my father everything. He knows about us. I don't care."

David brushed a stray lock of Michal's hair from her face and his eyes turned sharp. 'What's this bruise on your cheek? Who did that?"

"It's not important. The only important thing is for us to be together. We need to run far away from here."

"It's important to me. How did you get that bruise?"

"My father was angry when I told him about us. He hit me. It's nothing, really."

David pushed Michal gently away. He stared down at Saul's armor as if seeing it for the first time, and kicked it. One, two, three kicks. "I wish he wasn't the king."

"Will you run away with me?"

David turned to face her, and she saw again that honest look and his playful smile. "And miss out on a chance to slay a giant?

Never. I mean there aren't that many giants around, so I really can't pass up this opportunity."

"Very funny." She punched him lightly on the arm. "You don't have to do this."

"Yes, I do. This Philistine spits in our faces. He thumbs his nose at God. I can't let him do that. Even if we'd never met, I'd still do the same. God has chosen me as his champion, not your father. Why God selected me, I don't know. But I must do this for *Him*."

"They say he's twice your size and can snap full grown trees over his knee like toothpicks."

He shrugged. "Who cares? He could be the size of a mountain but he's still a dwarf compared to God's power. I've felt His strength. It will flow through me when I face him."

He seems so certain. So brave. "How do you know?"

David shrugged. "I feel it with my heart. The same way I know we'll be together after this is all over."

"And there's no way for me to change your mind?"

He shook his head. "I'll never change my mind about you, and I'll never change my mind about this. I will face the giant and he will feel God's wrath.

She saw the truth of his words on his face. She didn't know if God was truly with him, but she could tell that he *thought* God was and nothing she could do would change his mind. She turned to look at her father's armor so he wouldn't see doubt in her eyes. "Well, I guess we had better hurry up then. Do you want me to help you into that armor, or do you want to kick it some more?"

"It's useless." David waved at it. "Your father is a full head taller than me. If I put that on, they'd have to carry me down the valley to face this Goliath. I'd topple over and never be able to get up."

"I'll have them find you something more suitable, then. Maybe Jonathan's armor? He's taller than you, but he's shorter than my father."

He shook his head. "God will be my armor. I don't need bronze and plated steel."

She planted her hands on her hips. "Well, what are you planning to hit him with? Surely you'll need a sword."

He pulled out his worn leather slinger. "I think I'll use this. I just need to find a few smooth stones." He stepped toward the creek. "They should be in here somewhere. Help me look. I'll need five."

"Why five?"

"One stone will be for God, my mother, my father, Abby, and the last one is for you. That way you'll all be with me."

She looked away. She didn't want him to see her cry.

Just when she thought she could turn and face him without tears, a small shrike landed on top of her father's bronze helmet. He chatted at David, and jumped up and down. David laughed and held out his hand, palm up. The bird landed in his palm, tweeted a few more times and flew away.

"What was that?"

"Just an old friend."

"Really?" She was about to question him about it, when they heard a voice cry out, "David!"

They turned to see Abby running toward them.

She stopped right in front of David and kicked him in the shin. "You idiot. What have you gotten yourself into?"

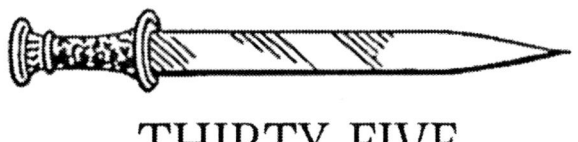

THIRTY-FIVE

David stepped back, wary of another kick from his sister. "Not you too, Abby."

"But David, have you gone mad? What are you doing?"

"What I have to do. And don't try and talk me out of it. It won't work."

Abby sighed. "Why do all of your shortcuts end up dangerous?"

"What?"

"It's just like the shortcut you took me on when I went shepherding with you. The river flooded and you had to face a mountain lion and a bear just so we could make it home."

David grinned. "True, but I got us out of it. And I will this time. You just have to believe in me."

Abby squinted and looked him over from top to bottom as if she'd never truly seen him before. "Okay."

"Really? You're not going to try and talk me out of it? Not even a little? He is a giant? I thought I was your favorite brother."

"Nope. You'll find a way to beat him. You always do. And who says you're my favorite brother?"

He winked confidently. "Okay—good, but we both know I'm your favorite." He turned to leave but a sick feeling clawed at him and he paused mid-step. He felt as if he'd been buried under a rockslide. For the first time he thought what failure would mean, not for himself but for his family. "There's one more thing. If I lose this fight, I want you to send a message to Dad. Tell him I'm sorry."

"Sorry for what?"

"For making everyone slaves. And Abby, you'll have to run away."

"Where?"

"I don't know. Somewhere. Don't go back to the palace. That's the worst place for you. And don't go back to the farm either."

Michal placed her hand on Abby's shoulder. "Don't worry. She's with me."

He grinned. He didn't know how Michal would keep Abby safe, but he knew she would.

Abby sounded confused. "Why did you tell me not to go back home?"

"Dad can't keep you safe. If I lose, they'll stone him to death."

Abby's hands flew to her hips. "You could have thought about that before you started this."

"Are you ready?" Jonathan asked.

"As ready as I'll ever be."

"You're going dressed like that? No helmet or chest-plate? No shield?"

"What good would it do? One of the foot soldiers told me he saw Goliath drive his spear through a man's shield and plate armor in a single stroke. I have a staff and a sling. That will have to be enough."

Jonathan nodded. "Come on. I'll walk you to the front line."

The Israelite troops had descended to the foot of the valley. Rather than arrange themselves in defensive positions among the rocks, the men milled restlessly in the open, line after line. As David and Jonathan passed among them, David noticed side-looks and sly glances from the soldiers. Most of them shook their heads, muttered to themselves and stepped aside.

A pair of men blocked his way.

"What's this?" David asked.

Jonathan didn't wait for an answer. "Step aside, Navi," he said.

Navi grinned but no warmth lit his face. He was a thick-set, middle-aged fighter, a veteran of many battles if the scars on his arms and face told the tale correctly. "Step aside? Step aside? So this scrawny boy can go down the valley and lose the war for us? I haven't been stuck here for forty days, boiling in the hot sun, to leave my chances with *him*."

Jonathan squared his shoulders and faced him full on. "The King has made his choice."

"Has he? And this is the best he can do? I don't think so." Navi turned toward the others gathering around. "He's not our champion, he's our doom! Are we to be roasted on a Philistine spit because of some madness of the king? I don't think so."

The others crowded in a little closer. A few in the back raised their voices to jeer at David.

Jonathan whipped his sword from its scabbard. "Step aside. I won't ask you again."

Navi shouted. "I say we kill this *champion* here. Before he gets us all killed!"

Jonathan growled and slashed at Navi's side. Navi managed to block the thrust with his own sword, though the force of Jonathan's stroke staggered him back half a step. Jonathan moved so quickly he looked like a blur as he smashed Navi in the face with the hilt of the sword and knocked him into the dirt.

Navi glared at David. "Some champion. He needs the prince to fight his battles."

Angry men pressed Jonathan and David from all sides. Soldiers of every rank offered disgruntled sneers, threats, and loose talk. David felt the anger around him rise like a bonfire.

Jonathan didn't hesitate. He stepped forward and drove his blade through the front of Navi's neck.

Navi's eyes bulged as blood bubbled out of his throat and ran down his neck.

David was shocked. Navi had been one of their own. *How could Jonathan kill him so easily? Could I ever do something like that?*

Jonathan yanked his sword from the dead man's neck and held it steady in front of him. "Anyone else? My sword will speak for our champion all afternoon if that's what it takes."

The rest of the men backed off. But just when David thought the situation was in control, a rustle ripped from the crowd as another group of warriors pushed their way toward them.

He felt his stomach twist. He didn't want any more Israeli blood spilled just so he could reach the valley.

He breathed easy when he saw his brothers, Abinadab and Shimea, pushing through the crowd. His heart swelled; he'd thought he might never see them again.

Abinadab shouted, "Make way for the king's champion."

Shimea added, "We don't have all day. There's a challenge to meet."

When they reached the front, Abinadab turned to face him. "We're a long way from the farm, David."

David touched him on the shoulder and felt a lump in his throat. "I know. I'll make quick work of this giant." He tried to add confidence in his voice he didn't feel as he glanced back at the Israeli positions and strained his eyes. "I don't see Eliab around anywhere."

Abinadab shrugged. "He's as dumb as an ox. He refused to come with us. He said you're a fool."

Some things never change. I could slay a hundred giants and it wouldn't be good enough for him. "Great. Nothing like a vote of confidence from my oldest brother."

Shimea grinned. "Oldest yes, but he's the dumbest and the worst looking." "Am not," said Eliab as he shoved a soldier out of his way. "You're crazy if you think I'd miss this fight. It's not every day I get to see my brother torn in half by a giant."

"Thanks."

"At least you can't get lost here like you do with the sheep." Eliab gestured at the great expanse of the valley.

"I never get lost with the sheep." David grinned. He could hardly believe it, but it felt good to be teased by his brothers. If he closed his eyes, he could almost imagine being back home for dinner.

"Make us proud," Abinadab said. "We really don't want to be slaves."

David nodded, and then followed Jonathan away from the front lines. "Are you sure you still want to do this? That you *can* do this? I'll take this challenge for you, if you have doubt."

Their eyes met. Jonathan was a true warrior, tall and proud in the dazzling sunlight. Certainly the best the Israelites had to offer. But David was sure Jonathan would lose. Only God could provide victory over the massive Philistine champion, and for some reason God had chosen him. He wouldn't have believed it a month ago, or two weeks ago, or even yesterday, but now he was certain.

David shook his head. "The Lord God will win this battle for us. I just have to have faith in Him."

THIRTY-SIX

David stepped into the Valley of Elah.

The valley splayed out before him, a rocky expanse of parched dirt and low scrub bushes. The distance across, only a few hundred paces, meant the difference between victory and defeat. Armed men lined both sides of the pass. Just as the Israelite forces had gathered to watch the battle, the Philistines camped on the other side. The opposing armies bristled at each other across the gap, hurling taunts back and forth. They had never been so close.

As he walked forward, he felt a remarkable sense of calm. It was a clear day, the sun hot above him, a gentle breeze blowing from the east. The Israelites didn't cheer for him; instead they seemed to be arguing among themselves again, or perhaps Jonathan was stabbing someone else in the throat. David didn't know or care. His fate lay before him.

He walked about thirty paces before he heard the rumble of thunder. The sound boomed again and again as it reverberated off the cliffs.

But the sky was clear. It made no sense, until he realized what was happening.

It wasn't thunder. It was Goliath.

The giant emerged from the Philistine ranks, each step a drumbeat against the dusty earth. But the thunder did not come from the giant's feet. Giant war drums were hidden among the Philistine ranks. The drummers matched their drumbeats with every step Goliath took.

With two great strides Goliath separated himself from his army. His shield carrier struggled to catch up. The shield was a huge rectangle of bronze, trimmed at the edges with gold. At each corner, emblazoned in bright metal, leered the bull's head symbol of the pagan god Molech. The carrier looked like a dwarf as he strained under the weight of the massive shield.

As the pair approached, David realized the shield-bearer was neither a dwarf nor a little boy. He was a large man, taller even than David, yet he appeared like a child when compared to the giant. And for the first time, David realized the true enormity of Goliath's presence.

Goliath wore the finest war gear David had ever seen. Sunlight glinted off his great metal shirt of bronze scale-armor. His shoulders were huge, his arms bare and massively muscled. He wore bronze greaves over the full length of his thighs and legs and an iron-tipped war spear slung between his broad shoulders.

Size and armor alone did not define the giant. He moved gracefully and assuredly. This was a man bred for war, supremely confident, to whom all others must seem like nothing more than pestering flies.

Dear God, thought David, what have I done? *He's going to kill me.*

David suddenly felt the full weight of his situation. He stopped walking as if he'd been punched hard in the stomach, his muscles frozen by fear. More fear than he'd ever known in all his life.

I'm going to die here today. My people will be destroyed.

Goliath stepped forward with the cheerful swagger of a soldier in his prime who has never felt the sting of an enemy's blade—his steps light, his back straight, his shoulders swaying with confidence. It looked as though he was drinking in the scene of the battle, already basking in the victory he was sure to have.

David thought of Michal, and life flowed through his veins again. If not confidence, he felt determination. Defeating the giant was the only way King Saul would ever let them be together. Of course to collect the bounty, he had to win. The alternative...

It doesn't matter. I'd rather die than lose her.

Goliath gazed across the chasm. His eyes passed over David casually as he squinted against the bright sun. There was no fear in the giant; that was for certain. He looked skyward, checking the position of the sun, then drew his immense sword from the sheath at his hip.

David had never seen such a weapon. Surely it was forged in hell. The blade was as long as an ordinary man's body and half as wide. The steel glinted fiercely in the sunlight as if its edge held the power of the sun to slice a man in half. The massive hilt, crusted with emeralds and splashed with dried blood, fit snugly in one of Goliath's hands. He raised the sword effortlessly, though it must have weighed half as much as David himself.

David gripped his staff.

Goliath's shield bearer finally caught up. Huffing and puffing, he set the shield beside his master. David didn't have a shield bearer, and no shield either, but in this dance of champions it was his turn to advance.

He had to step forward, but it was hard. Fear coursed through his veins. He wanted to run, to give up, to try and escape. The last thing he wanted was to take that next step. No reasonable man would advance on the giant. No one would want to take that step.

He waved his staff over his head, more to distract the giant than for any other reason. And he stepped forward.

Goliath shouted angrily across the chasm, "Am I a dog that you should come at me with sticks?"

Amusement twisted his face into a sick smile as he turned to address his men. "They've gone mad. They've already lost! They can't muster a real champion so they seek to insult me. With this! A petty joke. They send a child against me!" Goliath laughed and his laugh was terrible.

"Laugh all you want." David strode toward the monster. He knew he was not what Goliath had been expecting, and this could be his best advantage. The gigantic brute had been expecting a warrior like himself, thick-muscled and bull-headed, to take up the challenge and meet him in hand-to-hand fighting. That was what he was ready for. He had come to the field weighed down with heavy scale armor. He couldn't move quickly, and probably didn't expect to have to move at all.

His spear and sword were certainly deadly, but only at close range. *I can't give him that chance.*

David stopped far short of the giant. Close enough, but still out of reach.

"Come to me," said Goliath. He gestured with a wave of his free hand, more bored than impatient. "Come to me that I may lay out your flesh here on the ground, a feast for the birds and the beasts of the field."

He swung the gigantic sword in a wide arc and David heard a frightful *whoosh* as it sliced the air

"You have your sword and spear," said David, "but I come against you with a prayer to the Lord Almighty on my lips, the God of the armies of Israel, whom you have defiled. This day the Lord shall strike you down, monster, and I will give the corpses of your army to the birds and the wild animals, and the whole world will know that there is a great God in Israel."

"Judging by his champion, a puny God indeed. Come on, I said. Come you to me."

Goliath pushed his shield bearer aside and stepped forward. He moved fast for such a big man. The gigantic sword whistled through the air. David just barely ducked under the stroke and scrambled to the side.

Goliath laughed.

David turned and ran.

"Look there!" said the giant. "The son of Israel. Some champion they sent to me. He has wet himself!"

Laughter fell from the Philistine lines like a rain shower. Silence, equally as deafening, held sway among the Israelite troops.

"I won't chase after a child! If he leaves the field, this fight is over. It will be the same as if I had slain him."

He gestured at the Israelite lines with the edge of his sword. "All of you will be my slaves!"

David stopped thirty paces away and unwrapped his sling from the leather strap that held his tunic together.

"Lord my God," he said in a low, earnest voice, "I put my trust in you. Guide your humble servant in what is right, and show me the way. You are my light and my salvation. Guide my hand, that I might slay the enemies of Israel. In your name, my Lord. In your name."

David drew his arm back and circled the sling at his side. He expected to feel the same dizzy, lightheaded sensation that had come over him when he'd dispelled the demons in the command tent. He remembered the wild energy that had filled his chest, the explosive sensation that had coursed through his veins. But now he felt nothing except the hot sun and the dry, salty dirt in his mouth.

David spun the slinger faster. He had to take his best shot. The giant was thirty paces away, a sizable target, but mostly covered in scale armor. He wore no helmet, his black hair falling loosely to the shoulder. The stone would have to hit him on the head. But at thirty paces it was a more difficult shot than any he'd ever practiced against the olive tree. And he usually missed those, anyway.

It's all up to me. It's all up to me.

Time slowed. A burst of white light blinded David and he was no longer in the valley of Elah. He spun in a circle, seeing nothing but white. Below his feet, a sea of endless white; above his head a sky of perfect white that went on and on. He grew dizzy looking at it. He had no purchase here, no solid ground to step upon. *Where am I? Has the giant killed me already?*

A man appeared before him, cloaked in a brilliant white robe. His gray eyes sparkled and the sun glimmered off his white hair and beard as if they were adorned with jewels. Although the man appeared very differently from the last time David had seen him, he recognized him immediately as the seer from the festival; he was Samuel the prophet.

"Samuel?"

"You were expecting someone else? I hope you're not disappointed."

"I wasn't expecting this. Where is the valley? And the giant?"

Samuel spoke in a deep rich tone, his voice calm and soothing. "They are where they should be. The question to ask is: why are *you* here?"

"I don't know. I need to defeat the giant."

The prophet smiled. "And do you think you can do that on your own? Without God's help?"

David sighed. "I need God. I've always needed his help. I prayed for it."

"That you did. And you expected it would come?"

David looked around but there was nothing but white. "I did."

Samuel looked around too. "And that just may be your problem. You expected it would come. You bragged to Saul and his men. You assured them. You treated God as if he were your servant."

David felt his heart sink. He had done that. In his desperation to win the king's favor he had bragged of God's power. "I banished the demons."

"God did that through you, yes. He allowed you to open a portal to heaven, so He could send His angels to do His work. You did nothing on your own."

"But surely he chose me for a reason. He must see something in me."

"Perhaps He did. And perhaps he was mistaken. When you worked these miracles, did you proclaim them the workings of God? Or did you keep them secret?"

"It would have embarrassed the king."

"But you weren't embarrassed proclaiming it to the men in front of everyone today, when it served your purposes."

Though there were no walls in this sea of infinite whiteness, David felt as if he'd been backed into one. Frustration made his head spin. "I have to defeat Goliath. I can't do it myself. I need God's help. What do I have to do? How can I prove myself worthy?"

Samuel laughed. "You can't prove yourself worthy of Him. You are not worthy."

David dropped to his knees. "There must be something I can do."

Samuel studied him for a long moment. "There might be a way. What do you think He wants?"

"God doesn't want the Israelites destroyed…"

"No, he doesn't."

"So he'll help me to save them."

"Yes, but only if you are willing to do the same. Why did you undertake this challenge?"

He began to see the problem. He had to tell the truth, but he was sure it would damn him. "Because I love Michal. I want to win the challenge so I can marry her."

"Not for the Israelites. Not for God. You've taken this challenge for yourself."

"For them, too." David hung his head. "But mostly for myself. I want to be with Michal."

"You are a fool, David son of Jesse, to have disrespected God. He offers you a choice. You can turn away and run, and let the Philistines take Israel. He will protect you. You will live your life safely with Michal. A long and good life. No harm will come to you or your family. Or you can defeat Goliath here today and save Israel, but you will not profit from it."

Samuel stepped forward. "If you choose Israel, you cannot have Michal. You must choose—the kingdom or the girl."

Samuel faded, and as if touched by some invisible painter's brush, the vast white space slowly flushed with color again. Red dirt below, the craggy greens and browns of the mountains, the clear blue sky above. A horde of jeering Philistines on one side, the expectant Israelite army on the other. A giant in the middle.

He was back in the valley, the slinger's leather straps still in his hand. He knew he could run and God would provide safe passage for him and Michal. He could almost see the green, open fields, a flock of sheep, and Michal with a smile on her lips as the sun lightened her hair. Their days would be filled with happiness. He'd fulfill his dreams. He would make her happy.

And then he looked out onto the army of Israel. He could already hear their screams, feel the crunch of their bones beneath the wheels of Philistine chariots, the acid laugh of the giant as the marauders overwhelmed them. Could he live with himself, knowing he'd sacrificed God's people to the pagans?

He turned back toward the giant. God had chosen him for a reason. He could not turn his back on His people now. He would not sacrifice the Israelites for his own happiness. His heart hammered in his chest. He had to trust in God, even if it meant sacrificing the one thing he wanted most in the world.

Goliath's head cocked a little to the side. His eyes narrowed as he finally noticed the sling.

David swung the sling, measuring the revolutions in heartbeats as it whirled around him.

He tightened his grip on the straps, swinging them harder and faster.

Goliath reached for his war spear.

David focused on Goliath's massive head.

Goliath pulled the spear from its harness.

David let loose the stone.

It whistled through the air, running straight and true. The giant stood frozen, completely motionless, completely helpless. The stone hit him square between the eyes.

Crack!

Goliath blinked once, then his eyes rolled back up into his head.

He fell backward and hit the dirt with a terrific, ear-splitting thud. The whole valley shook when he struck the ground. It was the sound of an entire forest of trees falling as one. It was the sound of righteous victory.

But not complete victory. Not yet. David raced forward.

Goliath lay on his back, the small stone embedded in his forehead. But he wasn't dead. The fight wasn't over. One of the giant's fists clenched. A low murmur came from his lips. He was going to get up!

David had no sword of his own. He crouched beside the body and took hold of the Philistine's sword. He grunted as he tried to pick it up. The sword was too big, too heavy for him to lift.

Goliath rolled over onto his belly, his hands pressing into the dirt to push himself up. Once he righted himself, he'd kill David for certain.

David tugged hopelessly at the gigantic sword. His heart threatened to pound straight through his chest.

He glanced to the heavens and suddenly felt a glorious warmth fill his body, a white-hot strength in his arms. The hilt of the great sword burned in his hands, but it didn't hurt. He strained with all his might and raised the weapon over the giant's neck.

Goliath's eyes opened, glassy and unfocused. He twisted on the ground, and looked up at David strangely.

"It...hurts..."

"I'm sure it does. And so will this!" David slashed the sword down. The gigantic blade bit deep into the giant's neck. David planted one of his sandaled feet on Goliath's shoulder and raised the sword again. It seemed light as a feather. He slashed its edge down again. The second stroke nearly took Goliath's head off. He finished the job with a third stroke.

Grabbing fistfuls of ebony hair with both hands, he lifted the giant's severed head. He raised it high so everyone could see.

THIRTY-SEVEN

David looked up at the jagged, dripping mess that had once been Goliath's neck as he held the giant's head high above his own.

An eerie silence filled the battlefield as he turned the head toward the Philistine lines. Across the distance he caught glimpses of his enemies' faces—open mouths, wide eyes, pale colorless skin, confused expressions. A solitary, high-pitched voice cried out from behind their lines, cutting through the air like a blade, "No, it can't be!"

David turned to face the Israelites and thrust the massive head in the air.

Thunder roared. Energy exploded as the men ran cheering. The ground shook.

The Israelites chanted, "David! David! David!"

They surged forward all at once, crackling with confidence and fighting spirit. He had never felt anything like it. It was as if a thousand soldiers had become one, unified in purpose, fearless and bold, energized by faith. They screamed "David!" as they charged. His name had become their war cry.

David spun. A third of the Philistine army raced forward to meet the Israelites in an uneven line, as the rest turned and ran. He stood his ground as three men came barreling down on him. He swung the severed head and let it fly. It hit the nearest Philistine on the helmet and knocked him down.

David lifted Goliath's sword and ran forward to meet the soldiers. The massive weapon still felt impossibly light. Three steps brought him within arm's reach of the other two men. A tall Philistine with a dented helmet and metal breast plate lifted his long sword over his head to chop down on him, but David slashed Goliath's sword in a wide arc that cut both men in half, the huge blade biting through metal, muscle and bone.

Both Philistines went down in pieces, just as another attacker swiped at David's head. David ducked at the last instant and thrust his weapon straight through the man's stomach, pushing the mighty sword to the hilt. The soldier crumpled with the sword still in his belly.

Suddenly Goliath's weapon dragged to the ground. David tried to yank it up, but it felt it's true weight and he couldn't budge it.

A glance backward showed the Israelite army rushing to meet him but still with a long stretch of ground to cover. The Philistines were already upon him.

A sudden wave of panic took hold. He no longer felt God's strength inside him as the Philistine army barreled toward him.

David kicked the fallen Philistine soldier over and picked up his weapon—a three-quarter length bronze sword. It felt heavy in his hand but he could manage. He'd have to. He tried to remember the sword-fighting lesson Eliab had given him, but he'd been in such a horrid state that day, he hadn't really listened.

A Philistine soldier was upon him before he had time to think. The man came at him, hacking and slashing.

Watch your opponent's eyes, wasn't that what Eliab had said?

David kept his sword up and deflected the blows as best he could, but in short order, both his arms suffered minor slashes. Whenever he found the chance, he swung his blade at the man, but his blows did little good anyway. The soldier blocked them all with a round wooden shield.

He must be watching my eyes.

David looked to his left, saw the soldier lift his shield to protect where he expected David to strike, but David spun back to his right and ripped his sword into the man's arm.

The ground splashed red and David stepped forward to thrust his blade in the man's exposed chest, but another soldier arrived and both came at him. Watch their eyes, he told himself. But they had four eyes between them and no way for him to keep up.

The second soldier smacked his shield into David's shoulder and knocked him to the ground. David's sword fell from his hand.

The Philistine stabbed his sword down but the blade did not reach its target. Instead, the point of a long pike rammed into the man's chest, knocking him back.

David stepped aside as Jonathan flew across the ravine astride his great white war horse. He released the pike, taking up a long sword in his right hand and a short one in his left. He raced forward, his weapons spinning, ducking, whirling, leaving nothing but blood and death in their wake. None of the Philistines came close to touching him. He moved faster than anyone else, as if he were a lion among sheep.

Other Israelite cavalry and foot soldiers joined alongside him now, still chanting David's name. The clang of sword against sword rang out.

David heard a familiar whistling sound and ducked. The Israelite slingers had let loose a barrage of death into the Philistine ranks. One stone connected with a man's eye, leaving behind a gaping, bloody hole. The man clutched his face and fell to his knees with a scream on his lips. An Israelite soldier raced forward, chopped down into his neck, and delivered a powerful death stroke.

David's tunic was drenched with blood. Its acidic smell hung thick in his nostrils. But the smell was not the worst of it. The sounds of the battlefield—the death cries of the men, their screams of pain and pleas for mercy—were unlike anything he'd ever heard before. His brothers had told him many stories of battle, about the stench of death in the air and the terror of blood lust, but nothing had prepared him for this. It was the sound of Hell itself. And yet the blue sky hung so clear above, the gentle breeze the same as before.

As the rest of the Israelite army raced past, David thought to chase after the men to join the slaughter. But weariness replaced the energy that had been pumping through his body and he dropped to his knees.

He looked up into the bright sun.

"Thank you, God."

The Israelites swarmed over the valley and up the other side, tolling out death with every step.

David still heard their war chant.

"David! David! David!"

THIRTY-EIGHT

Bile clawed at her throat. Alzsheba took a deep breath but couldn't hold it back and vomited into the dirt with a violent heave.

Goliath. Gone. Killed in single combat by an Israelite boy. Impossible! But she had seen it. The boy had held her giant's head in his hand, her precious Goliath, his dead eyes rolled up into their sockets. The jeweled earring had still been dangling from his left lobe. And now Goliath was gone.

Alzsheba spat out the foul taste of her defeat. The Philistines were in a panic, shouting and running in a swirl of retreat all around her. The battle already lost. The last of the Philistine forces scrambled to safety in a mad dash up the slope at the far end of the valley. That dolt Bulgossa had been brought to his knees and beheaded by King Saul himself. *Pathetic. Drunken idiot.*

The witch nearly vomited again as she recalled the pompous way Saul had descended from the hill to claim victory after the fighting was finished. Bulgossa had already been captured. Strong arms held him down as Saul killed him.

Saul. Just the thought of his name filled her heart with a wild, savage hatred.

Not again. Saul victorious, holding his bloody sword high. Goliath dead. And what am I left to do? Hide. Flee. Again? She remembered her eldest sister, Szandara, circled by a crowd of vengeful Tekoans, blood streaming from wounds where their cruel stones had battered her face. Szandara locked eyes with her in a dying glance, a fearful glance, full of disgrace and pain. Szandara's eyes had urged her to run. To escape. But never to forget. Never forget what Saul had done.

She had to hurry. Most of the Philistines were already working their way up the slope. If the Israelites captured her they might assume she was merely a camp woman and treat her to a mild beating. Unless they suspected her relationship with Goliath.

Goliath. Gone. She thought of his rough, passionate touch. The way he ripped kisses from her mouth. He had been so much more than a mere man—physically perfect, strong, confident and ruthless. But in the end he was just an overconfident fool. No better than the rest of them. His contagious thirst for power had swept her up, even to the point of deluding herself.

Could she ever have been content to sit by his side? A dream broken now, as broken as the Philistine ranks. That wasn't what she wanted, to sit on some ivory throne and dine on sweet figs and treacle. She wanted blood. *Revenge.* It wasn't in her to love. She had never loved that giant imbecile with all his raging vanity and arrogance. Hate was all she was capable of. She was good at hate. And she hated Saul and all his people above all else.

Alzsheba stumbled and fell. A clumsy foot soldier had kicked her leg in his wild flight, hitting the back of her knee and knocking her down. She glared up at him and for an instant their eyes met. On any other day she would have killed him, and he knew it. But now his frightened glance was followed by a quick, mocking smile as he disappeared up the slope. She slapped angrily at the ground. *Is this what I've been reduced to? That a common foot soldier could dare look at me that way?*

She threaded her way among the fleeing men.

She'd put too much trust in Goliath. A flawed and stupid giant at the last. So vain he refused to wear a helmet. Stupid. *How else could a puny boy have beaten him?*

But it wasn't just the boy. She knew he was the same redheaded boy who had protected Saul from the demons and evaded her assassin. A greater power had helped him. This Israelite god had a hand in it. She could still smell the lingering trace of his power crackling on the air. And this god, she began to understand, was a powerful one. More powerful than Molech. But she could still win.

Goliath had been infinitely more powerful than that boy, and yet the boy had brought the giant down. And so she and Molech could still bring Saul and his god down.

How?

And then she knew — by using their own strength against them.

She slid among the trees at the rise of the valley, and disappeared into the mists of Elah.

The Israelite camp buzzed in the cool night air. No one paid too much attention to Alzsheba when she slipped into the camp. She seemed an ordinary peasant woman in a plain linen dress with a ragged shawl loosely tied around her hair and shoulders. Just one of many who had come to celebrate, or rejoin their loved ones, or play music to earn a few pims. She told the guard her name was Beth and she was looking for her soldier husband. He eyed her suspiciously when he didn't recognize the man's name.

"Travelling alone?" he said.

"I came in with the supplies from Gibeah." She gestured vaguely at one of the wagons.

"There are all types of supplies, I suppose," he said, with a wink. "Go on, and after you find your husband, maybe later you can find me."

The victory celebration gave her the perfect opportunity. Soon this would all be gone. The tents would be struck, the camp taken down and the soldiers would go back to their cities and farmlands, the campaign over. Saul would return to his palace and his sweet milk and fatted calves. After the army disbanded, only his house guard would be left at Gibeah to keep him safe.

The festivities were impressive for a hasty celebration on the edge of the battlefield, but she knew how these things went. Wine and strong drink would appear from secret kegs and storage sacks would yield up all the food that had been hoarded during the long standoff. The revelers would eat and drink it all in a single night in a careless binge. Entertainers flocked to the scene, eager to get a few copper pieces from victory-happy soldiers, just as certain women suddenly showed up to play their roles. She mingled with the crowd, just one among them.

Alzsheba avoided the huge purple command tent. It wouldn't be wise to approach Saul that closely. Too many armed men still surrounded the king. Her greatest mistake had been her desire to take her revenge personally. She had wanted to stand over Saul and slash the knife across his throat with her own hand, feel the life drain from him, watch his blood flow. She had insisted on it, making Goliath promise she would have her chance. *Fool!*

Now she realized her mistake. She must use Saul to destroy himself, and not just himself. She would use him to destroy all of Israel. They would all pay.

She need only exert sufficient power over the king. Not directly. No, she could not approach him directly. Those attempts had already failed. The demons she'd sent against him had all failed. That wretched boy had turned aside her magical thrusts. But she knew how to get inside the king's mind. That was the way. To turn a man against himself.

She needed a piece of him, a lock of his hair, to work her dark magic. It was the only way. But she'd never get close enough to the king by herself. Not now. She needed a pawn, someone who could get close.

She wandered the celebration, shrugging off lewd proposals with a friendly laugh. On the outskirts of the camp, far from the command tent, the talk and the music became rougher. She felt herself drawn to a performance under the open sky, a dance among sputtering fires.

A small ring of men had gathered to watch the rope dance. A bearded man in a turban stood in the center holding the ropes. At the end of each leash a dancer squirmed and wriggled her charms. A collection of flutes and a tambourine offered some sorry music for the women's dance. Oh, but this was tame. She'd seen this same dance performed using poisonous snakes instead of ropes in the streets of Tekoa.

As the dance ended, men tossed coppers to the performers. Alzsheba noticed a man on the edge of the crowd. He was of medium height, strongly built, his dark hair tousled and oily, his eyes already half-glazed by strong drink. He was absolutely disgusting, revolting. More importantly though, he wore the blue tunic of King Saul's house guard. He had already noticed her, of course. His kind always did.

She held his gaze as she swayed toward him. Saying nothing, she snatched the cup from his hand, threw her head back and drained it. Strong drink burned the back of her throat.

"Careful with that," he said, with a wry smile.

She laughed and pinned him with her eyes. "What's the use in being careful? Where's the fun in that?"

"If it's fun you want..." He finished his sentence with a drunken mumble.

"What else is there?" she said.

He tried to look away. She watched him struggle like any other revolting insect squirming under the boot heel of its master. He wasn't used to being held helpless by a woman's charms.

She playfully stroked his chin. He hadn't shaved in several days, and his thick stubble felt stiff as a brush. His glassy eyes shifted uncertainly as he looked her over from top to bottom.

Alzsheba released her shawl and shook her long black hair loose. "We should celebrate."

He nodded dumbly. He opened his mouth to say something, but closed it when the effort became too much for his soggy brain.

"Come."

She led him by the hand—*filthy hands*, his thick fingers clotted with dirt and Philistine blood under the nails.

They reached a wooded area, out of sight of the others.

"How many men did you kill today with these hands?" She kissed one of his filthy paws.

"More than I can count."

With an idiot like this, that could be any number above two.

She kissed his mouth, tasting his foul breath.

"Your name?"

"Eliab, son of Jesse."

"Eliab," she purred, "Eliaaab, Eliaaab." She turned the amulet over in her hand—a needle of bone, a patch of coarse fur, red with the blood of a Philistine child.

He looked suspiciously at her, perhaps disturbed by the way she had twisted his name.

Faking passion, she parted his tunic and ran her hand across his heavy chest. *How puny when compared to Goliath. Goliath's chest is stilled now. He draws breath no longer. Stolen from me.*

She raked her fingernail along Eliab's skin, drawing a drop of blood.

"Ow!" he said, with a sneer.

Alzsheba smeared the amulet in his blood. "Wear this," she purred.

"What?"

She pinned the amulet inside his tunic. "I have something here. Wear this for me. To remember me."

She bared her thin, white neck and he buried his face there, kissing and slobbering.

She couldn't help but laugh.

You've kissed a witch in the woods, she thought, so I'll make you a promise. *You'll pay dearly for your pleasure.*

THIRTY-NINE

Torches on either side of David flared into the night sky, the flames dancing their own victory celebration. The crowd that had descended on the Israelite camp showed no sign of waning. Men guzzled wine with women on their arms and laughter on their lips. Wild music filled the air as troubadours danced merrily among the tents. David had no idea where all these people had come from. He wondered if the same faces would have shown up in the Philistine camp if the giant had cut off *his* head instead?

He wandered between the cooking fires, tempted by the smell of roasting goat and venison. But he was more interested in finding his oldest brother. *Where is Eliab?* Neither Abinadab nor Shimea had seen Eliab for some time. David was happy they'd all survived the battle unharmed, but he really wanted to find Eliab. Was it too much to hope that for once, Eliab might actually be proud of him?

It would be a lot easier if his search wasn't constantly interrupted. Everywhere he roamed, men ran at him, wine skins in their hands and a hearty toast on their lips. After the toast, they shoved the overflowing skins at him. It seemed that more wine splashed on his tunic than he actually drank. His back was already sore from all the well-intentioned slaps of good cheer.

He didn't feel much like celebrating. He'd defeated Goliath and they'd destroyed the Philistines, but he had lost Michal. God granted him victory on the battlefield but the one thing he wanted most in the world would be denied him. He didn't know how yet, didn't even want to think about it, but he was certain of it just the same. He trudged down another row of plain gray tents.

Eight soldiers stood in a knot around a low burning fire with a red-haired women in their midst. One shouted, "That's David the Giant Slayer." A round of cheers followed as did a chant of "David! David! David!"

Not again. He looked for a way around the men, but the passageway was narrow and they waved him over enthusiastically. A short soldier staggered close and shoved a skin full of wine at him, splashing some more on his already drenched tunic. "We were just drinking to your good health, as it happens," he said, spittle flying from his lips. "And here you are! Head and all!"

The men laughed and took long pulls from their skins.

The red-haired woman ambled close to him. The collar of her dress was torn in a way that revealed the full swell of her breasts. "So you're our champion, Hmm? I've never bedded a giant slayer before." She glanced seductively at him. "You must be very special." She grabbed David by the back of his head and pressed his face between her breasts.

He pushed her away to keep from being smothered.

"Don't worry I won't break." She winked at him. "No need to play hard to get, sweetie. I'm the best you'll find in this sorry camp. Or maybe you don't like me." She put her hands to her hips and puckered her lips.

"It's not that. You're as pretty as..." The wine caused his head to swim, leaving him lost for words.

"As pretty as what?" She grinned and bent at the waist, which almost freed her breasts from her bodice completely.

"As... the full moon."

"You mean two full moons," joked a man from behind.

The group cheered. The woman staggered drunkenly toward David and reached for his leather belt, but he was still quick enough on his feet to sidestep her.

"Maybe next time." He waved them off as he continued his search. The men took up a parting chant of "David! David! David!" again as he moved on.

He weaved along on unsteady legs, vaguely headed toward the royal celebration space at the center of the camp. The command tent and the surrounding tents formed a vast courtyard. A handful of the house guard stood around, looking annoyed at having to stay sober to protect the king. Maybe Eliab was among them.

Enormous torches, twenty cubits high, lit the makeshift courtyard. Close now, David stared into the flickering light for a moment. His thoughts turned toward Michal. He felt a burning desire to find her, to feel her in his arms, to drink in her sweet smell. Even if he couldn't marry her, they might steal a moment; just one moment might last him a lifetime.

Jonathan interrupted his musings, greeting David with a broad smile. "I've been looking for you. You're wanted at the royal feast."

David was thankful Jonathan hadn't suffered so much as a scratch. Nothing. Stories of the prince's exploits rippled among the men, tales that varied from him killing dozens to hundreds of enemy soldiers. Jonathan deserved the accolades. *Maybe someday I'll be as good a warrior as he is. If I can't have Michal, I can still be a warrior. If I can't love, I'll learn how to kill.*

"Everyone's waiting for you." Jonathan draped his arm over David's shoulders and led him to the royal courtyard.

Men cheered when they saw the two heroes together. A small gathering that seemed to grow larger with each step followed in their wake.

Jonathan chuckled. "This is a little better than the last time we walked together."

Despite his sour mood, David laughed with him. "That was a long walk. I thought we were never going to reach the front lines."

They squeezed between two tents and reached the entrance to the ceremonial area. Two tall torches stood over them, one on each side of the entrance. Jonathan nudged David and pointed upward. Atop each torch was an iron spike. One had Goliath's head fixed on it and the other had General Bulgossa's head.

Frozen on Goliath's face was the expression he had at the last, part anger and part shock, the small stone still embedded in his thick forehead. Black flies circled his gaping mouth.

"That was my idea," said Jonathan. "One for you and one for my father. Don't tell the King, but I dare say that the general's head was easier to dislodge than Goliath's. Look at that idiot. He could have fled, but he was so confident the giant would defeat you I found him in his headquarters, half dressed and swigging wine."

David looked up at Bulgossa's head on the spike, his eyes bulging from their sockets. "He still looks surprised. I don't think he's ever going to get over it."

"He probably wasn't alone. I bet the whole Philistine army was busy toasting your demise."

"So sorry I disappointed them."

"You certainly did. My father was wary about spiking the heads, but I think everyone should see what happens to those who oppose our Lord." Jonathan straightened David's tunic. "This uniform suits you much more than those tattered shepherd robes you've been wearing."

David beamed. "I think so, too. I borrowed it from Shimea. I thought it would be too big, but it seems to fit just right."

"It does, but you'll also need a sword. A commander in the field doesn't use the sling. It's time I teach you how to wield a sharp blade."

Commander? Did he just say commander? "When do we start?"

"Soon enough. But I think you'll have to give that tunic back to your brother."   "Why?"

"I'm thinking the house guard's blue will suit you better."

"The house guard? That's for the best soldiers. I've only fought in one battle." "But what a battle! How many others can claim to have bested a giant? And when Goliath fell, you faced the entire Philistine line without flinching. Few would have been so brave."

Keeping his voice low so no one else could hear, Jonathan whispered. "Listen, this is an important celebration. All eyes will be on you. When you address the king, make sure you kneel until he gives you permission to stand."

"Of course. I always do."

Jonathan's usually carefree expression melted away as a more troubled look took its place. "But things are different now. You're a hero. I overheard my Uncle Abner warning my father about heroes. Heroes can be dangerous."

"Dangerous?"

"Certainly. These are treacherous times. The prophet Samuel was popular, and his betrayal still stings my father as if the blade had just been plunged into his back. It has weakened his rule. Some don't think my father is the legitimate ruler in the kingdom anymore because of the poison that dripped from Samuel's tongue."

At the mention of Samuel, David's stomach twisted. At the harvest festival Samuel had prophesized that someday David would be king, but he'd also told him that if he defeated Goliath he could not be with Michal. He'd gladly trade the first prophecy for the second, but he had no say in the matter. Only God could change events, and David was sure he was doomed. He realized that Jonathan was waiting for him to say something, so he added, "That's ridiculous. Your father is the rightful king."

Jonathan leaned close as they walked. "Of course it's ridiculous, but loose talk fills the camp. The men say you killed ten times as many Philistines as my father in the battle."

"How can that be? I only killed Goliath and three others."

"Exaggerations are how heroes are made. Usually there's a bit of truth at the center of the tale but the rest is exaggeration and myth. In time the myth becomes bigger than the truth and that's all that counts."

David shrugged. "I wouldn't ever lie about what I've done."

"Of course you wouldn't! But they're saying you killed hundreds of men today. In time, everyone will believe it. Even if you say otherwise, it won't matter. You'll be the hero who beheaded the giant and defeated an army all by yourself."

"I'd never do anything to betray your father. He's my king."

Jonathan slapped him lightly on the cheek. "Have your wits about you then. Sober up. You can drink your fill later." Jonathan wrapped his arm around David's shoulders and guided him into the courtyard. "Come on. Let's enter like brothers, so my father can reward you."

David trudged into the open space, his mood dark from the strong drink.

Torchlight filled the courtyard with a warm amber glow. King Saul sat on a tall wooden chair at the far end, wearing a long robe of fine white linen embroidered in purple and gold. A thin golden crown circled his head. General Abner stood beside him, a bronze breastplate still fixed to his chest and a long sword hanging at his right hip.

A fire pit smoldered beside the king. A ram had been burnt in offering to God. David thought it must have been an impressive ram too, judging by the horns. Two priests stood over the blackened carcass. The acrid smell of scorched flesh filled the air.

"Come here, David son of Jesse." Saul waved him forward.

Torch light flickered off three mounds of glittering treasure on low wooden tables—a modest fortune of silver and copper trinkets, golden rings and arm bands heaped on top of each other. Three older warriors, dressed in their full armored glory, stood behind the stacks of loot. They were the same three who were in the command tent earlier that day urging the king to pick their favorite as champion. They seemed happy enough now, each with a hand on the pile of treasure they would share with their men.

Goliath's armor was neatly stacked beside the king's high seat. The mail shirt, even empty, made a tremendous pile of bronze scales. His great shield, the size of a bathtub, had been turned upside down. The blasphemous crest of Molech had been scratched from the front. The great sword stood behind them, a glittering monument to failed conquest and overwhelming vanity, still smeared with the giant's blood.

The courtyard filled with the soldiers who had followed David and Jonathan through the camp. Most of the blood had been washed from their uniforms, but crimson splashes still stained the wool here and there. Happy conversation rippled throughout the open space. Everyone held wine goblets. A drummer and a flutist played a light tune.

A singer sang with a high-pitched voice:
"And a mighty champion stepped forward with his sling;
The giant soon felt its sting;
When he fell down dead;
Mighty David carved off Goliath's head."

David felt queasy. He'd never thought someone would compose a song about *him*, even if it was such a bad song.

When the singer noticed David stepping forward, he stopped his song and a respectful quiet settled over the courtyard. The pause lasted only a few heartbeats before chants of "David!" chased the silence away. Everyone joined in—everyone but the King and General Abner.

"*David! David! David!*"

An uneasy feeling settled in David's stomach. He saw a stern expression on King Saul's face, his cheeks flushed with ruddy color, his eyes flickering around the open space as he regarded the chanting men.

David stopped a few paces from the King and knelt in the dirt. "My king."

His words were practically lost as the chanting continued.

He spotted Michal standing in the corner with Hadi and Abby. Her smile stretched from ear to ear. She wore a brown peasant dress and simple shawl for her head. She was beautiful. It didn't matter if she wore a fine silk gown, a plain traveling robe, or a simple dress. She was beautiful. And she could have been his.

The King stood and raised his arms to silence the crowd, but they would not be so easily silenced.

"David! David!"

The King's eye twitched as the shouting continued.

David glanced at Michal again. For a heartbeat, he imagined holding her in his arms and kissing her sweet lips. Could God change His mind? Could he still be with Michal? David looked back at the king. It was obvious Saul had noticed the way they smiled at each other.

Still, the men chanted his name. The crowds outside the courtyard joined those inside. The volume soared, almost surpassing the height it had reached on the battlefield.

"David! David!"

The King bellowed, "Silence!"

The chant died a slow and uncomfortable death. When quiet settled over the space, the King forced a smile. At least David thought it looked forced based on the strained crease of his lips and the sharp look in his eyes.

"Welcome, David youngest son of Jesse. I am so pleased that you are able to join us. I feared that you might have gotten lost in the arms of one of your many admirers."

Men in the back of the courtyard chuckled.

David's face reddened. "I came as soon as I heard that you called for me, my king." He remained kneeling, his head half-bowed.

"Of course you did. As you know, I promised to marry one of my daughters to whomever defeated Goliath." Saul paused for a moment, an exaggerated frown curving his lips. "But I find myself stuck in a bit of a dilemma. When you came to me and offered to slay the giant, you said God would use you to strike down the pagan beast. Is that correct?"

"Yes, my king."

"And did God strike him down as you predicted?"

David glanced soberly up at the king. The effects of the alcohol waned. The king had set a trap for him, and he was helpless to avoid it. God was responsible for his victory. He would never claim otherwise, and he knew what would happen next.

He lowered his head and looked toward the dirt. "I was merely God's instrument. It was His power that killed the giant."

"So you see my problem? God was my champion. He is responsible for our salvation. You were just a mere tool, nothing more. I should marry one of my daughters to God."

"Yes." David's voice simmered as he kept his head lowered. He didn't want the king to see the anger on his face.

A few audible mutterings in support of David had started to grow behind him. The energy turned uneasy. The celebration was not going the way the crowd had expected.

Jonathan stepped forward. "But Father, it was David who slung the stone and chopped off the beast's head. He was God's choice, but still he was our champion. Surely he should be rewarded as such."

Murmurs for David began to swell again. This time words like "treachery" and "unjust" rose above the rest.

The King's eyes skittered among his men.

David peered over his shoulder and found that many of the faces appeared angry.

General Abner leaned close to the king and whispered in his ear.

David wondered what Abner had said and then Jonathan's warning popped into his mind. *Heroes are dangerous.*

"Father?" said Jonathan. "You were talking about the reward."

"Of course, my son. I was just explaining the situation to your young friend." Saul glanced at his three senior commanders who stood close to their piles of loot. "I am a generous king. Am I not?"

"Yes, my king!" All three responded as if on cue.

Saul returned his attention to David. "Even though God was our true champion, I will reward you, David, son of Jesse, as promised. I will give my first daughter Merab to you as wife."

The crowd cheered.

David froze. *Did he say Merab?* He glanced at Michal and the truth of it was written clearly in her angry eyes. *I can't marry Merab. He knows that. He knows I love Michal. So God hasn't changed His mind.*

Tears brimmed in Michal's eyes as she nodded her assent.

She wants me to say yes. But I won't!

Saul clapped his hands together. "The house of Jesse is honored this day. You will you marry Merab and fight the Philistines and the rest of my enemies for me and the Lord? The wedding will take place at the next full moon."

David knew what he had to do. He took a deep, steadying breath and stood. "Who am I, and what is my life or my father's family in Israel, that I should be the king's son-in-law? I am unworthy to accept your offer."

Saul smiled thinly. "You will marry Merab and in return you need do nothing more than be a valiant man for me and fight the Lord's battles."

David stood. He felt like a rabbit in a snare. "I can't."

Abner placed his hand on the hilt of his sword. "You would deny your king? Are you too important now that men chant your name? Is the king's blood not good enough for you? You insolent pig! You kneel in front of your king!"

David shook his head. His eyes narrowed as he glared at the general. "You weren't the one who faced the giant!"

"I'll kill you myself."

Jonathan stepped between them. "David, you must reconsider. You cannot refuse this generous offer."

The world slowed and David's mind spun. For a moment he was back in the hillside near his home, surrounded by sheep and grassy fields. A few months ago that was all he knew. A wedding to Merab would have seemed like a miracle. But not now. His mind spun again and the courtyard came back into sharp focus. *I must be crazy. I have the chance to marry the king's eldest daughter, and I'm going to refuse it. My heart is pledged to another and that is the simple truth that binds me.*

"I cannot marry Merab. I want to marry Michal!"

"You dare defy me!" raged Saul.

Michal raced forward to join David but Jonathan blocked her path.

"Please give him another chance," she pleaded. "Strong drink and the victory celebration have gone to his head. He's a loyal man. He'll do what you say."

Saul glared at his daughter. "You have no voice here."

Jonathan held her back as she tried to throw herself in front of David.

"Take him!" Abner signaled the men behind David.

"Look carefully!" said the King, addressing the unruly crowd. "This boy thinks he is above me. He questions me! I'm the one who has waged war after war and brought nothing but victory to our lands. I'm the one anointed by God to be your king. This is what comes of pride! Chant not his name! He is nothing but a peasant, a shepherd. I will not be disrespected. I am the King of Israel, not David of Bethlehem."

Michal lunged toward David again. This time tears streamed down her face. But Jonathan's hold was too strong.

"Remove him from my presence," ordered the King. "You are exiled from my kingdom, David, son of Jesse. I do not kill you, because I am a generous king. But you shall live outside of Israel or not at all."

David could hardly hear these last words as the men yanked him from his feet. It was useless to struggle. But he struggled anyway.

"If I see you again," Saul added, "it will be your head on the spike."

FORTY

How did everything go so wrong?

David could hardly understand it.

Exiled from Gibeah, banned from the palace, chased away like a wild dog. Stuck spending the night in a stinking cave on the lonely hillside of Elah, with a rock for a pillow and misery for a blanket.

Four strides. That's all it took to cross from one end of the cave to the other. But it was impossible to walk off such heartbreak in only four paces. He could walk until the end of time and his heart would still ache.

"What more?" David spoke to a rock formation at the far end of the cave, a rounded ridge of stone that vaguely resembled a human head with a long, pointed beard. "I chose to save the kingdom. I chopped off the giant's head. What more do they want?"

The stone head didn't answer and David turned back the other way. Only a short time ago, the Israelites had cheered his name in battle. Now everything was twisted around and he saw nothing but utter blackness ahead, his heart broken. Even his chance at being a simple warrior had been stolen from him.

He turned round and headed back toward his stone companion again. "Exiled? Now I'm exiled? They'd be overrun by the Philistines if it wasn't for me! You know it!"

The lump of stone did not seem to know it, or at least was unwilling to agree with him out loud. He spun round again.

None of it mattered—not the shattered glory of a fallen hero, nor the fat purse of silver snatched from his hands, money he could have given to his father to pay off his debts in Bethlehem. None of that mattered. All he cared about was Michal—he'd lost her forever. He must honor the bargain he made with God and would make the same one again—but still, a part of him thought maybe once he killed Goliath, he'd earn his way back into God's good graces and have a chance with Michal. Now all hope drained from him, like sand through a sinkhole and he was left with nothing.

"I won their war for them," he said to his stone friend. "With God's help, of course. But he chose me and I slung that stone. And for that I've been stabbed in the heart."

Having reached the stony face again, he swung at it with his balled fist, hitting it right where a nose would have been, and bursting the skin on two of his knuckles.

He continued pacing. The expression on Michal's face as they'd dragged him from the royal courtyard haunted him. She'd looked so pained, so full of helplessness and suffering he could hardly breathe. *I have to see her again. I can't let her last memory of me be the one where I'm dragged away, helpless.*

"David?"

He nearly jumped out of his skin.

Michal stood at the darkened cave entrance, dressed in her dirty gray traveling robe.

"Michal!"

They ran to each other and met in the center. He took her in his arms and nearly crushed them both.

Michal's hot tears slicked his neck.

"How did you find me?"

"I had a feeling you'd be here, just beyond where you took the five stones from the creek. I knew it. I had to come."

He hugged her again, then let go to wipe the tears from her cheeks. "Don't cry."

"When you fought Goliath, I was... I was so frightened..."

"You didn't think I could do it? Just because he was twice my size." David smiled. "After all, I had a sling."

She hesitated for only a heartbeat. "I trusted you, but I really didn't know what to think. He was so big. And when he came from behind the Philistine lines, the entire valley shook. For a moment I thought he was... a god."

"He wasn't any smaller up close."

"It seemed impossible." She looked away, her cheeks flushing red.

"That's all right. I wasn't so sure myself. I had a moment of doubt, but God found me."

"Promise me you won't do anything like that again!"

"Well, I'm not about to go hunting for more giants, if that's what you mean. One is quite enough for me, thank you. Although there might be some money in it, and I already have the reputation..."

She spun and her eyes brimmed with tears. "That's not funny! When he came at you with that sword, I thought he was going to slice you in half. My whole world went dark. I thought I would lose you."

David wanted to make another quip but the earnest look in her eyes stayed his tongue.

"I can't lose you."

He took her hand. "You won't."

"When you killed Goliath, I realized you were everything I ever wanted. It was the bravest thing I've ever seen—the bravest thing I could ever imagine. But then when you said you wanted to marry me, I felt something else. I felt that I was right for you. That this is right, no matter what my father says. He's got no right to stand between us. We're fated to be together."

David sighed. He could fight the king, but he could never fight God. He didn't want to tell Michal about the choice he'd made; he just couldn't. What good would that do?

"Your father has every right. He's the king. And your father."

"I'm so tired of hearing that!"

"He'll always be your father."

She smacked him on the arm. "Sure he is, but did you have to act like such an idiot in front of him?"

"It could have gone a little better. I'll give you that." David shrugged, "But what did you want me to do? Did you want me to marry Merab?"

"Of course not. Although that would be slightly better than having your head on a spike. But no, I don't want you to marry my sister."

"Then what should I have done?"

"You could have used your brain. If you were Merab's intended, you'd have free run of the palace and we'd have a better chance at figuring something out. Finding a way to escape together."

"Well…yes, of course… there's that. I'm not good at those types of details. If you hadn't noticed, I pretty much blunder forward and hope everything works itself out."

Michel smiled. "I noticed. Good thing you have me."

David hesitated. He ached to be with Michal, but he feared what would happen if he pushed along that path. The wrath of God took many forms. He couldn't live with himself if anything happened to Michal. "I don't see… how we can be together now. Not with your father exiling me."

Michal spoke in one breathless burst. "I already have a plan. We'll run away tonight. I've brought a mule and some supplies. We can leave right now."

"Your father will chase us. He'll never stop until he has my head, and I mean that literally. I don't want that kind of life for you."

Michal's sweet face grew angry. "This is my life. I get to live it. No one has the right to tell me who to marry and where to live."

"You don't need to convince me, but it's not really as simple as all that. Your father just happens to have an entire army to hunt us down with. Where can we go? Is there any place he won't find us?"

"I don't know. Is there?"

David turned from Michal. He so wanted to tell her it could work, that they could be together, but he could not risk God's displeasure. He had made a deal, and now he had to stick with it. "No. It won't work."

"We'll run. Let him hunt us. Let him chase us like dogs. I don't care. We're meant to be together. We'll find a way. Whatever it takes it will be worth it."

He turned and tried to harden his heart. "No. That's not a life for you. I won't have it. I can't protect you if we run."

Her eyes blazed with fire. "Protect me? You were willing to die for us. So am I! We'll protect each other."

He shook his head. "No. Go back to your father and forget about me."

"Why are you acting this way?"

David melted. She was so brave and strong. He pulled her close again and kissed her.

After a moment, she broke it off. "We have to hurry. We can go north along the mountain ridge and try to get to Manasseh. Hadi's going to tell them I went back to the palace. That should give us a couple of days' head start. With luck, that's all we'll need. We can do this, David. We have to try. It's the only chance we have."

David turned away. "That's our last kiss. We can't be together."

Footsteps crunched the dirt at the entrance to the cave and a gruff figure appeared, casting a wide shadow. David didn't need to see the man's face; his voice was unmistakable. It was Eliab. "Is this where you intend to live? Looks cozy."

"How did you find us?"

"Followed the princess. A little voice told me she might do something stupid like look for you."

"Well, I'm glad you came," David said. "Does anybody else know?"

"I have three men outside."

"I hope you can trust them. I want you to take Michal back to her father. She can't come with me."

"No!" Michal reached for David but he stepped away.

"No problem." Eliab walked toward them, his blue uniform nearly the same dark shade as the shadows. "I'll do more than that."

David paused at Eliab's bitter, detached tone. "I thought you'd at least be a little proud of me."

"Proud of this?" Eliab waved his arm around the room. "The great giant killer cowering in a cave? Yes I was proud of you, for a moment, for half a day. But you had to ruin it. The king offered you everything. Money, status in the royal house—"

"The wrong sister."

"That's what this is about? A silly little girl?"

"I'm your princess!" snapped Michal.

Eliab looked her up and down, a sneer on his lips. "That's funny. You look more like a beggar in the street to me."

Michal's face reddened. She moved to slap him, but David blocked her. There was no point to it anyway. He'd only told the truth. She would be an outlaw if she stayed with him.

"Fine," said David. "I don't expect you to understand. If you can just get me some clothes and a horse, you'll never have to see me again."

"Oh, you'll get a horse. Just not in the way you think. You'll be tied across the back of it as we ride back to Gibeah."

"What are you talking about?" demanded Michal.

David's heart sank. He already knew the answer. "Why did you come here, brother? You didn't come to help, did you?"

Eliab stuttered, unable to answer. His face contorted, his eyes squinting as he pulled roughly at his hair.

"What do you mean to do?" asked David again.

"I have three men outside. You brought... this on yourself."

"Eliab!" screamed Michal. "How could you? You're his brother!"

Eliab flinched as if he'd been struck. He grimaced and bit down on his lip until he drew blood. "I don't... I can't help it. This is the way it has to be. I wish..."

He stopped suddenly, like a fire that had burned to the ground after consuming all its fuel at once. His face turned hard, his brow sweaty.

"You wish what?" asked David. "What's the matter with you? You don't have to do this."

Eliab took a deep breath and looked around the cavern as if suddenly unaware of where he was or how he got there. "You're coming with me."

"I won't let you take us."

"I have three men outside. Don't try to fight us, David. I'll kill you if I have to."

FORTY-ONE

Clang! Clang! Clang!

Michal clapped her hands over her ears. "I just can't stand that racket. All day and all night for the past four days. Every time the hammer falls, it's like someone's stabbing me in the head with a spike. What's that blacksmith doing?"

Hadi slid next to Michal at the window. "He's stripping the bronze and gold from the giant's armor."

"All day and night? It's crazy. What's he going to do with it?"

"The victory feast is in three days. The blacksmith tells me your father wants the gold for the feast, but I don't know why."

Three days!

King Saul had set David's execution for the day after the feast in a public spectacle, so everyone in the kingdom could witness what happened when someone defied him. It was probably Abner's idea.

Clang!

Michal winced. Whenever she closed her eyes she saw David's neck stretched on a block of wood and her father holding an axe. David's face full of defiance, his red curls trailing down his neck, the axe falling...

Clang!

Tears rolled down her cheeks. "This is all my fault. I should never have talked to him in the first place or played those games with him or touched him or sung with him or kissed him, or any of it. I'm such a fool."

Hadi stroked her arm. "You couldn't help yourself, child. Your God has given you a big heart. You can't command it to stop beating."

"No, but you warned me. You told me what might happen. I didn't listen. I'm such an idiot." She clunked her forehead against the clay wall.

Clang!

"You never listen. You've always been that way. I knew when I warned you I was wasting my breath. Besides, I think David had something to do with this romance too. I wouldn't say he stood idly by while you flung yourself at him."

"It's still my fault. I'm the one who went to him in the cave. I led his brother right to him. I should have just left it alone."

"Really? And what do you suppose would have happened then?"

Michal shrugged.

"Do you think David would have meekly melted into the valley of Elah never to be seen again? Like he was a ghost or a vision from a dream?"

Michal shook her head.

Hadi answered for her, "Of course not. The Fates had already twisted you two together. He would have come for you and you both would probably be in the same place as you are now. It does no good to look backward. We must look to the now and the future. That's all that's important. The now and the future."

Michal saw strength and wisdom in the old woman's face. She pushed aside the ghastly images that frightened her and found resolve in her handmaid's wrinkled features. "You're right. We need to finalize the plan. I've got to save David. That's all that counts."

"What about Abby? She'll be here any moment."

Frowning again, Michal said, "If she's involved and gets caught, they'll kill her or make her a slave."

"You'll suffer the same fate as well."

"I don't care about what happens to me. I can't even think of a life without David anyway. But I don't want Abby's life on my hands also. She's just an innocent girl."

"You can't protect everyone from themselves, Michal. You have to trust that they'll make the right decisions. Abby loves her brother. They have a special bond. What would you do if Merab or Jonathan was in that cell instead of David?"

The door opened before she could answer and Abby walked into the room. Old tear tracks meandered down her cheeks; her plain gray dress was torn at the sleeve and her lip newly split open.

"Abby are you all right?" asked Michal. "What happened?"

Abby sniffled. "I went to talk to David, but they won't let me see him. I kicked one of the guards at the door and tried to get around him, but the other one grabbed my dress and slapped me. He said if I didn't get lost he'd put me in a cell too. The other one said they'd chop off my head next."

"Come here." Michal opened her arms. Abby folded into them, and Michal held her tight. There was so much of David in her. She was impulsive and fearless and honest and...

Michal shook her head. She couldn't go down that path, not now.

Hadi stared at her knowingly and shrugged. Of course with Hadi a simple shrug was never just a simple shrug. She could speak volumes with almost any expression.

She's right, thought Michal. Abby deserves to know what's going on. She'll get herself into even more trouble if we don't let her help.

Abby pulled back and wiped fresh tears from her face with her sleeve. She wasn't full grown yet, the top of her head reaching only to Michal's chin. "They can't kill David. They can't! He can be a blockhead, I know. He acts before he thinks, but he would never be disloyal to the king. They've got to give him one last chance. He deserves one more chance."

Michal placed her finger against her lips and whispered. "We're coming up with a plan to rescue him. I won't let them..." She couldn't bring herself to say the word 'execute.' "I won't let them punish him."

"I knew it! You'll beg your father to spare him?"

"No, Abby. My father won't see me. He's got me locked away in this room as if it were a prison cell."

"Then Jonathan's going to help?"

"Not him. He won't see me either. Besides, he'd never go against Father."

"We're going to have to do this on our own," said Hadi. "We won't get any help from anyone else."

"What's the plan? What can I do to help?"

Michal saw hope burning in the girl's eyes for the first time since David had been caught.

Clang!

Michal wished she had a good plan, one without so many holes. Still a plan with holes was better than no plan at all. "Hadi told me about a secret tunnel to the prison cells. I'm going to sneak in disguised as a servant and give David's guard some wine spiked with a sleeping powder Hadi knows how to make. With any luck he'll drink the wine and I'll free David. But once we get out of the prison cell, we'll need a way to escape the compound. Everyone will be distracted during the victory feast, so I figure that's the best time to go, but I don't know how we're going to get beyond the gate."

"What about Eliab?" said Abby. "I talked to him yesterday and he's really sorry he turned David in. He spends all his time drinking and muttering to himself. I know he would help us. He could get you past the gate. I know he'll help."

"I don't know," said Hadi.

Michal wasn't convinced either. "He betrayed us last time. I don't think we can trust him."

"He'll help. I'm sure of it. You don't need to trust him. Just trust me." Abby inched closer until she stood only a sliver away.

"What do you think, Hadi? Eliab did seem odd when he found us in that cave. Like he was fighting with himself. Part of him wanted to let us go. I could feel it. Perhaps he's realized he's made a mistake. Maybe Abby is right."

Hadi shrugged one shoulder. "It does no good to escape the prison and be locked in the compound. If you can't get out, there's nowhere you can hide from the house guard. With Eliab's help, you might be able to get through the back gate undetected. He's our only chance."

"I'll convince him." Abby bounced on her toes.

She's so much like David.

Clang!

Michal shuddered.

Abby found Eliab slumped against the base of an olive tree in the open area the house guard used for fighting practice. His eyes were closed, an empty jug of wine toppled by his feet and a new red stain splashed across his blue uniform.

She marched up to him and kicked him in the leg. "Wake up, Eliab!"

He grumbled, his eyes still closed, so she kicked him again. "You're drunk! Get up!"

He rubbed his face with both his hands, opened his eyes and squinted against the glaring sun. "What do *you* want?"

"They're going to kill David the day after the feast. Do you want to help him or not?"

Eliab groaned, lifted the clay jug, tilted it back, but when nothing came out, he tossed it to the side. "What can I do now? It's too late."

"Why did you turn him in the first time?"

He tried to stand but only managed to lift himself a little way, thought better of it, and slid back to the ground with his back against the tree. "I don't know, Abby. It's all a blur. One minute I was outside guarding Michal's tent and the next I was in that bloody cave with both of them. I'd take it back if I could."

"Would you help him if you had the chance?" Abby stood close to him now, her gaze piercing his bloodshot eyes. "Do you think you can sober up enough to be useful?"

He nodded. "All right. All right. I'd help him. He's my brother too, you know. I don't know what... why... I don't know what happened but if there's a way I can save him, I'll do it."

"Good," she whispered, "there's a plan to free him during the feast. They just need to get him past the back gate. Can you help?"

He staggered to his feet. "I'm supposed to be inside the courtyard during the feast, but I can switch with Zeke. He hates gate duty."

"And they'll need a horse and some supplies."

His eyes cleared a little. "I can get those too, and have them ready by the gate."

Abby wagged her finger at him. "I'm trusting you, you big dope! If you mess up, I'll never forgive you." She kicked him again in the shin.

"What's that for?"

"Just in case."

FORTY-TWO

David woke to the sound of rattling keys.

"You have a visitor."

"What?" David rubbed the sleep from his eyes. "Who is it?"

The guard didn't answer. In the six days he'd been kept in this cell, he hadn't gotten anyone to talk at all. None of the guards showed him any sympathy. Only one person had ever been to visit him—Harel, the stablemaster's son. It had not been pleasant.

The guard's head disappeared from the small square window in the heavy wooden door. The prison cells at Gibeah were cut directly into the bedrock below the palace, just a little square stone room with a straw mat to sleep on and a rough bench in the corner.

"Who is it?" David asked again.

"Your father."

My father? He leapt up from the floor. *Is good news too much to hope for?*

The guard unlocked the door. Rusty hinges squealed against its weight as he swung it open.

Jesse paused in the doorway. He looked much older and thinner than David remembered. His frock was so dirty and ragged David wondered if his father had been handled roughly. Or maybe he had just become so used to seeing the fine clothes worn around the palace that his own father looked like a beggar to him now.

"Step in," said the guard.

Jesse took a faltering step, and the guard slammed the door with a heavy thud.

Jesse flinched at the sound.

David rushed forward and hugged his father. "I can't believe you came. I thought I'd never see you again."

Jesse gently pushed him away.

David led his father to the bench before he fell down. *He looks so tired and weak. This is all my fault.*

"David, I want you to know, I've been pleading your case to anybody who'll listen. And there are a lot of them, a lot of the men, the soldiers, who sympathize with your situation. They remember what you did in the Valley, how you fought for them and killed the giant."

David forced a smile. "Oh? That's good. But it won't be enough to save me, will it?"

Jesse's voice grew stronger. "You haven't done anything wrong! Well, refusing to marry the first daughter was stupid, I'll grant you that. But there's no law saying a man has to accept a betrothal. Even if it does come from the king!"

"Meeting with Michal alone? I'm pretty sure the king didn't appreciate that part. Of course that's only a guess since he hasn't come by to visit."

Jesse shook his head. "She came to you, David. She came to you in that cave. You were in exile. You weren't doing anything. It was a very foolish thing for her to do. She is a very foolish young woman."

"Don't blame her. This isn't her fault."

"Then I'll blame that bonehead brother of yours. He's managed to avoid me so far, but let me tell you David, when I catch up with him…" The old man shook his bony fist, but had to pause to catch his breath. "There's going to be a price to pay."

David sighed. "Go easy on him. He's a total blockhead, but he only did what he thought was right. And besides, what good would it have done for him to help me? Someone else would have caught us, and he'd only have wound up rotting in the next cell over. I can't blame him, Dad. This is all my doing. Tell me, have you seen Abby?"

"Yes, yes. She's broken-hearted as you could well imagine, but your princess has done right by our little girl. She made sure Abby will stay on as her handmaiden. So there's that. Maybe something good will come out of all this one day, at least for her."

"There's a lot of good in it. We defeated the Philistines. The war's over."

Jesse eyes sparkled with a bit of their old fire. "You're a hero, David. A great hero for the people! Everyone's still talking about it, when they know the king's men aren't around to hear, that is. They won't forget about what you did. That filthy giant! Hah! Right between the eyes! I didn't know you could use the sling so well."

"Well, he had a giant-sized head, but it was a petty righteous shot at that," agreed David. "I only wish you could have seen it."

"Oh, I wish I could've!" Jesse smiled widely, showing his few remaining teeth. "You'd think they'd be grateful. You'd think that, wouldn't you? I went to Jonathan. I thought he'd be reasonable but he's not a reasonable man, David."

"What did you offer him?"

"Everything. Our flocks, our lands, even my life in exchange for yours."

"Dad!"

The old man shrugged and seemed to fold in on himself. "What else could I do?"

"I'm glad he didn't take you up on any of it."

"Well, I'm not off the hook that easily. I won't tell you what your mother said. I might have to sleep with the goats from now on."

"I'm sure you can handle it."

Jesse waved him off. "Why did you do this, David? Why?"

"Why?" David paused. He knew it would sound foolish to his father, but he had nothing else to tell him. "Because I'm in love. With Michal. How could I marry Merab? I'm sure she's nice enough, but she isn't Michal. Michal has a fire in her eyes, Dad. And in her soul to match. Who else would have tried to run away with a poor shepherd? And she's smart. Much smarter than me."

"I'm sure. Sure about that last part, anyway. She's not the one in the cell."

David ignored his remark. "Her smile lights up the room and lifts my heart. No one else has a smile like that. No one else."

Jesse patted him on the thigh. "I've been a fool for love myself too, you know. Not a complete idiot, like you've been, mind you. I remember your mother, standing by the well in town. She had some fine attributes too, but I won't go into detail. She's your mother, after all. And there were quite a few suitors for her back then. I had to fight more than a couple of them off. You wouldn't think it to look at me now but I used to be pretty good with my fists, make no mistake. Yes, son, I do understand."

"Good. Then you know there wasn't anything else I could do."

Jesse didn't answer. Instead he pushed on David's shoulder for leverage and rose to his feet. His hand and legs shook. "Nothing else for you to do. Killed a giant, insulted the king. Head on the chopping block. Nothing else, eh?"

"I'd do it all over again."

Jesse waved him off. "Neh! I'll keep trying. If Jonathan isn't reasonable, he's not reasonable. He's too young to know anything anyway. I'll look for someone older. Maybe I can get through to Abner." He stepped toward the door.

"Abner won't listen. Stay away from him."

"Someone will listen. There's still time." With his back to David, he added, "I won't stay for the… for the end of it. I won't watch you die. I can't. So I've just come to say goodbye."

"Goodbye, Dad."

FORTY-THREE

Alzsheba lay quietly in the still, dead earth. A black beetle crawled along her belly with a slow, steady progress. Each leg pressed gently against her naked flesh. The thorny head raised and lowered, raised and lowered, antennae fiddling as it crossed the curve of her breast. It paused at her collarbone, flapped its wings and stared at her with cold, black eyes.

In the beetle's wake, a small army of other beetles swarmed up her thigh and across her belly.

"*Don't worry, little sister,*" said Razana.

"*They won't bite,*" added Szandara.

I know, thought Alzsheba. They wouldn't dare.

The insects were, after all, merely curious. They had been crawling over her for days as she lay in the moist earth in the burial crypts at Tekoa. Surrounded by the restless dead, in catacombs and crypt-beds, Alzsheba wondered if any of these beetles had feasted on the flesh of her sisters' corpses. But that was impossible. Razana and Szandara had died long ago.

Alzsheba had more important things to worry about than curious beetles. She had returned here, to the burial pits of Tekoa because it was a place of power for her and her sisters. The stale, rancid breath of the demon god Molech blew through the tomb shafts here, caressing her body with his dark power. In these cave tombs the unclean were stuffed into clay pots or simply heaped among the crumbling masonry. It was a quiet place. Few dared venture here, to the lowest levels of the pits, to walk among death and darkness and the remains of nameless witches. Only empty sockets watched her from the funeral slabs. No one would disturb her.

On her belly lay the charm she had fashioned from a lock of King Saul's hair, hated Saul, the betrayer. It had been easy to have her slave Eliab bring her everything she needed. Controlling him was easy. He was less a man than a collection of petty complaints walking on two legs. He disliked his station in life, envied his betters, and collected grievances against his own wife, reciting them in quiet, frustrated moments. Yes, he was very easy to control with the amulet she had pinned to his uniform.

But King Saul, the murderer, the beast, was another matter.

"*You've made a fool of him!*" raged Razana.

Szandara cackled hysterically. "*Fool! Fool! We've won, dear sister, we've won!*"

Patience, thought the Witch of Endor as she gently stroked the talisman—the King's hair braided with those of the rat and wolf until neither could be distinguished from the other, and painted red by the blood of an Israelite newborn. Yes, this was a powerful token, the connection strong. She slowed her breathing, slowed her heartbeat, until she lay as motionless and pale as the rest of the dead. Saul. *Hated Saul.* She reached for him across rocky fields and mountain crags, past settlements and towns, farmlands and graveyards. She reached for him all the way in Gibeah.

Her eyes were his eyes now. She saw what he saw. She knew what he knew. Hated Saul stood lonely in the special room that housed the Ark of the Covenant. He had adorned the surface of the holy relic with the gold taken from Goliath's shield, the gold that had borne the mark of Molech.

Szandara cackled.

Quiet, sister! I must concentrate.

Delving into Saul's mind was difficult, even with the amulet, but this night he was already half-drunk from wine and spirits. *Still toasting his victory. Still drinking the red blood of my fallen giant.*

A wild rage flared up in Alzsheba's heart. She clenched her hands into fists, squashing the unlucky beetles that had crawled into them.

"Saul! Saul!" hissed Szandara.

"Kill him!" demanded Razana.

I will.

Saul's victory over the Philistines had brought him no confidence, only more fears and petty suspicions. He'd had little to do with the outcome, except for choosing the right champion. But had that been his choice? His God had played a hand, but Saul wondered whether God had been aiding him or the boy. He feared that his God wanted to replace him with someone younger, more deserving.

Oh how delicious. How he suffers.

Across the top of the Ark lay a slender silver dagger. Alzsheba focused her attention upon it, commanding Saul to pick it up. The amulet on her belly grew hot and her flesh started to sizzle and burn.

"Pick it up!" said Razana.

"Pick it up!" cackled the other. "*Pickitup! Pickitup! Pickitup!*"

The witch concentrated. His arm was her arm; his slender fingers, reaching out for the knife, were her fingers. Yes.

Saul brought the knife to his chin. *One slice. That's all it would take.*

Alzsheba felt the cool edge of the blade touch his throat. She felt the excitement of the kill. She wanted so much to make an end of it. Her sisters' elation raged in her mind, their chatter maddening.

"Kill him!"

"Kill him! Kill him!"

Patience, sisters. I will. You know how very much I want to, but it won't be enough. He's already ours. We can wait just one day more.

"Kill him! Kill him! Kill him!"

Stop it! We'll wait one day more. And then we'll kill them all! What will their God do? What will the powerful Hebrew God do if the King of Israel sheds innocent blood on this, their most sacred relic? It's said he wiped out Gomorrah at a single stroke. It's said he cleansed the entire world with water. What will he do in the face of such sacrilege, such insult?

He'll destroy them all, said Razana.

Yes, yes, yes! added Szandara.

It has to be tomorrow. It has to be at the victory feast. Not now. Not yet.

She withdrew the blade from Saul's neck. She made him turn the point to the line of his jaw and slice the flesh, just a small gash below the ear, just enough pain and humiliation to satisfy her sisters for a little longer. Then she made him put the knife down.

I can wait one day more.

FORTY-FOUR

Michal looked up from her sewing as Merab entered her room.

Merab frowned. "You're not looking well, sister. Aren't you eating? You seem so thin. Hadi said you needed to talk to me."

Merab wore an elegant yellow dress that twisted around her waist and draped down her body in long swooping lines. Silver hoops dangled from her ears and a new golden chain circled her slender neck.

Her sour expression didn't match her festive apparel. Her face was a sheet of ice, all angles and severe lines. Michal had seen that expression too many times over the years. Merab was disappointed in her, which was bad but still much better than being truly angry.

"I don't have much of an appetite these days. Cooped up in this room, with a guard at my door. But you look lovely. I understand you've been matched. Tell me all about him! Come sit with me." She patted the space next to her on a bench beside the window.

Merab hesitated a few heartbeats then settled as far away from her sister as the bench would permit.

"Your engagement happened so fast."

"The news proved too tempting for the gossips. When your shepherd boy refused me, word flew throughout the land as if it were carried by a flock of starlings." Merab fluttered her hands above her head. "The fact that the mighty champion would rather die than be my husband didn't exactly improve my standing among potential suitors. Gavriel's son, Nathan, broke our betrothal."

"I'm sorry."

"At least everyone seems to have forgotten that David was just a poor lyre player. Being turned down by a champion is bad enough, but a rejection from a poor musician would have ruined me completely."

"That's not fair. David's refusal had nothing to do with you. It's just that—"

"You two are in *love*. I know, but that part of the story has mostly been forgotten. He didn't want me. That's all anybody knows or cares."

Michal reached for Merab's hand, but her sister pulled it out of reach.

"So, you see little sister, we had to act fast. We had to make arrangements before tales of my disgrace became all-consuming. Father offered me to Jacob, the rich landowner who lives outside of Judea."

"But he's got to be at least fifty years old, and has such mean looking eyes. He wouldn't have been a good match at all."

"Well, it doesn't matter now, does it? After your David refused me, even Jacob decided against the marriage. It was impossible to find anyone willing to pay the bride price Father wanted for me."

"But you did find someone. Who?"

"An Amalekite named Zachary."

"Tell me about him. Is he young? Is he tall and handsome and kind?"

Merab smiled and the simple expression lifted Michal's heart. At least some good may have come out of this.

"Well, he's still young, probably just a few years older than me. I've only met him once, but he's pleasing to look at and seems gentle. He wears only a short beard and he's quite tall. Not as tall as father but taller than Jonathan. He gave me this necklace." Merab lifted her chin so Michal could see the shiny golden links.

"Oh, Merab, it's beautiful. So Father made a good choice after all?"

Her sister frowned. "Father had nothing to do with it. Mother made all the arrangements."

"Mother?"

"Oh yes... you wouldn't know. Father's been... distracted since the battle. He spends all his time with the Ark. He's obsessed. He wants to cover it in gold. The priests are quite angry with him."

"Why? He's been talking about gilding the Ark for years. I'd think the priests would be happy."

"Yes, but he's using the gold from the giant's armor. The priests say *that* gold is tainted with evil spirits, that it should never go on the Ark. They seem afraid of a bull's head that was carved into the shield, but Father won't listen... He won't listen to anyone."

"That *is* strange. A bull's head? Does it have a man's body?"

Merab shrugged. "I don't know."

It seemed like a lifetime ago when they'd caught the spy bearing Molech's symbol. That was before David, before love, before he was dragged away and put in a cell, before his pending execution. Michal twisted a long lock of her hair around her finger and tried to recall what Hadi had said about Molech. *She seemed so afraid of him, even after all these years. A false god. What difference could it make now?*

Michal and her sister stared at each other for a long moment, the silence heavy between them.

Merab spoke first. "You didn't ask me here to catch up on current events. I can tell by that look in your eyes, Michal. What do you want?"

"I need help, sister. I can't let them execute David. He doesn't deserve that fate."

"I know. I tried to talk to Father about it, but he wouldn't listen to me. He seemed to barely recognize me. Mother's had no better luck with him, either."

"Even after all that's happened, you tried to help him?" Tears welled in Michal's eyes. Even after the rumors and ridicule and loss of status, Merab had gone unasked to plead David's case.

"I'm not *dense*. I know you love him. You are my sister." Merab took Michal's hand, her touch warm and forgiving, and the frost melted from her face.

A lump formed in Michal's throat. "I intend to rescue him during the feast, but I need your help to get out of this room. Without you, my whole plan is useless."

"You want to break him out of prison?" Merab's eyes narrowed. "That's too dangerous. I'm not going to help you get yourself killed!"

"Then I'll find another way. I have to try, no matter what."

"You've always been like this. The rules were never for you to follow. As a child, you'd ask so many questions you made my head spin. Why do men get to stay out late, or choose who they marry, or..." Merab rose from the bench and looked out the window. "What will you do if it doesn't work? What if he dies?"

"Then I won't eat another bite. I'll fast until I'm too weak to stand or walk or do anything but whisper his name, and then I'll join him in the next life."

Michal stared defiantly into her sister's eyes until Merab looked away. "You're serious. You'd throw your life away for the lyre player?"

"I love him."

"I could tell Father. He'll double the guard, or lock you in a cell until after the execution. For your own good!"

"You could, but you won't."

"No... I won't." Merab turned back toward Michal. "I was so happy when you were born. I prayed day and night for a little sister. I remember when they first let me see you. You were so small and helpless, your face all red and puffy from crying. I promised I'd take care of you. That I would be the best big sister ever. I don't know if I've always lived up to that promise. But what am I supposed to do now? If I help you, you'll probably get yourself killed. And if I don't, you'll starve yourself."

"You're supposed to let me decide what's best for me. Please sister. I'm begging you."

Merab sighed. "What would you have me do?"

"I need to get past the guard outside my door. Come visit me before midday, just before the feast starts. Wear the purple dress Mother bought for you last year. I have one that's almost identical. You know the one I mean?"

Merab nodded.

"Great. I'll wrap a shawl around my head and walk right past the guard. The light is always dim in the hallway anyway. With luck, he'll never notice that we've switched places. All he'll notice is a princess in a purple dress. He'll think I'm you."

"But I can't miss the feast. Father will send someone for me if I'm late."

"True. But the guards always switch at midday. You can leave when the new one comes. He's not meant to keep you inside my room, only me. You'll be able to march right by him." Michal glanced at the floor. "Even if this works, there's a chance that Father will find out you helped me. You could get in trouble."

Merab's eyes sharpened. "Ha! What's he going to do to me if he finds out? I'm getting married in a month to the only man who would have me. He won't change that." She lifted Michal's chin. "The worst part is, if it works, I may never see you again."

"I have no choice. If they kill David, I'll die soon enough anyway."

"I was wrong before, insisting you should do whatever Father says, that you should marry whoever he dictates. That's not right for you. You aren't me."

Michal threw her arms around her sister. "I love you. You're the best sister."

Merab squeezed her tight. "I love you too, even if you've always been a pain in my neck."

"Not always," said Michal as they separated.

"Not always. Now tell me what it's like to kiss someone you're in love with."

Michal grinned. "It's hard to explain, really. My heart was beating so fast I thought it was going to explode. He was so close I couldn't help myself. Suddenly, we were joined, and I was more than just myself. I..."

FORTY-FIVE

Two tall lamps lit the entrance to the cellar, but the back of the chamber remained mostly dark. The shadows swirled, forming and reforming like dark clouds tossed by a summer storm. Only the flickering yellow light from Hadi's small lamp lit the way as Michal and Hadi weaved around baskets of food, sacks of grain, and jars of pickled fruit.

Hadi paused at a large wine cask in the corner of the room. "We need to go into the tunnel here, climb the stone steps up to the Ark room and find another tunnel in that room. It will be along the wall opposite the Ark. That second tunnel leads down to where they keep the prisoners."

"Thanks Hadi, but we are not going forward. You're staying here. You're in no condition to climb through these tunnels and I can't have you any more involved than you already are. It's up to me from here."

"But the guard might not drink the wine and—"

"And I'll have to think of something else. But you have to stay here and keep the cellar clear. It'll do us no good to break out of the prison and find three members of the house guard waiting for us." Michal took the lamp from Hadi's reluctant fingers.

Hadi handed her a skin of wine and a wooden cup. "Make sure he drinks the whole cup. It's strong enough to knock him out quickly, but only if he drinks it all."

Michal took the skin and cup, leaned down, and kissed Hadi on her wrinkled forehead. "You've been like a mother to me." Her throat tightened, making her voice a little rough. "What would I have done without you? I don't know how to thank you."

"Hush. I'll have none of that goodbye stuff now. You'll return in short order. Now let me look at you." Hadi leaned back and frowned. She wiped some dust from the top of the cask, smudged it under Michal's chin, and mussed the collar of the brown peasant dress she wore. "That's better. Now you look like a proper servant girl."

"That's all I want to be," said Michal. "A servant girl married to David."

"And he'll be lucky to get you, child. Anyone would. I have one more thing for you." She slipped a dagger from the folds of her robe and handed it over. A pair of rubies in the handle sparkled in the lamplight. "This is your brother's. I borrowed it. I thought it might come in handy."

Michal glanced down at the weapon. "I hope it doesn't come to that."

"Take it."

She took the dagger, hugged Hadi one last time, and entered the tunnel up toward the Ark room. This trip seemed shorter than the last time. It had been only a few months ago, but it seemed as if a lifetime had passed. She felt none of the hesitancy she'd experienced before. She had no choice now. She had only one chance to save David, and she *would* take it.

Reaching the end of the tunnel, she removed the slice of the plaster wall and stepped into the Ark room. It took her a few heartbeats to realize what she was seeing.

The Ark is gone!

The room, which had previously seemed magical and alive in some way she could never really have described, now seemed empty and dead. Small indents were left notched into the wooden floor where the Ark's legs had been, and little swirls of dust seemed to hang in the dead air as if searching for the lost treasure.

What did my father do with the Ark? Why would he move it?

She thought it might be important, but she couldn't think about it now. She needed to hurry.

She crept along the wall and rounded the corner, her fingers questing along the smooth surface. After a few passes, she found a small nook and used it to pull the plaster free. *There is another tunnel.*

She traveled along the tight passageway and down a flight of rickety wooden stairs, careful not to make a sound. Scurrying rats raced in front of her to disappear into the rocks underfoot. Her skin crawled at sight of them, but she steadied her breathing.

The tunnel was dark and damp, and muddy. When she reached its end, she hesitated. She didn't know where they kept David or whether the guard was posted within sight of the tunnel. If the guard stood just outside the tunnel door, he'd spot her for sure. All would be lost.

She put her ear to the crack in the plaster wall. Her heart thumped in her chest. Thoughts of David flooded her mind. She remembered his red hair shining in the sun as he entered the Valley of Elah to face the giant. *So brave.* Surely if he could do that, she could slip into a dark hallway and face a sleepy guard.

She blew out her lamp and all turned to darkness. She tried not to think of the rats. Her stomach twisted and the musty air in the tunnel caught in her lungs. *I must be brave for David.*

With a trembling hand she found the hold in the wall, pushed out the plaster square and slid it to the side. One breath later, she ducked and entered the dark underground hallway. A small torch lit the space with unsteady orange light and it took a moment for Michal's eyes to focus, but when they did, she saw no one, only a corridor with four prison cells, two on each side.

Where's the guard?

Michal strained her eyes but saw nothing. Her heart plummeted. She needed a guard. She needed a key to the cell door. Without that, how was she going to save David?

"Great," she muttered to herself. She went down the line and looked through the small windows in the doors. On the third one, she found David hunched over on a bench, his face downward.

"David!" Her voice was just a throaty wisp.

"Michal?" David jumped from the bench and raced to the door. "What are you doing here?"

"What do you think I'm doing? I'm here to break you out. Where's the guard with the key?"

"You have to go. Hurry! It's not safe!"

Clap! Clap! Clap!

Eliab sauntered from the shadows as he clapped his meaty hands together. "Very good, princess. You've got courage, I'll grant you that."

"Oh, Eliab. You startled me. You're supposed to be waiting at the gate."

Eliab strutted toward her. "I'm right where I'm supposed to be."

"Do you have the key?"

Eliab paused at the cell door and peered inside. "For him? I don't think so." David's face appeared at the square window. "Michal! Run! He killed the guard."

Eliab laughed, his broad shoulders shaking wildly. After a few moments his low throaty rumble dissolved into a high-pitched cackle.

"Michal! Run!" David rattled the door to his cell.

Sweat froze on Michal's back. She pushed the cup toward Eliab. "Some wine?"

He slapped the cup from her hand and the wine spilled at her feet. "You're going to pay for what happened to my Goliath." The words flew from his lips with the high pitched voice of a woman.

"*Your* Goliath?"

"There's something wrong with him," said David.

Eliab lunged forward, grabbed the front of her dress and pulled her close.

Michal punched him, striking his shoulders and then the side of his head.

He shook off the blows as if they were nothing.

"Leave her alone," shouted David. "Kill me! I'm the one you want."

Eliab spoke in the weirdly strained female voice. "Kill you? Yes. You're *all* going to die! When the monster spills innocent blood on the Ark, your God will turn on all of you."

Eliab swung Michal around like a rag doll and turned to face David. "But first I want you to see me chop off your girl's head. Just like I saw you kill my Goliath."

David threw his shoulder against the sturdy wooden door, but it did no good. "Eliab! Someone's controlling you. Fight it, brother. Fight it!"

Eliab cackled again. He bent Michal's arm behind her back and pounded his fist against the door to David's cell, a wicked grin on his face. "Now watch closely."

Michal wriggled the dagger from her waistband. She'd only get one chance at this, and even now, she wasn't sure she could do it. She'd never stabbed anyone before, even a monster like this.

She plunged the dagger at Eliab but misjudged the distance. Instead of stabbing him, she sliced straight down Eliab's chest. The bronze blade ripped through his tunic and drew a thin red line.

Eliab shoved her aside.

Michal stepped back, waving the dagger in a trembling hand. "Stay back."

"Ha!" said Eliab. "What are you going to do with that dagger? Poor defenseless girl, locked up in the palace like one of daddy's little treasures. What have your dainty little fingers ever used a blade for except to cut up sweet pastries after supper?"

Michal took a faltering step backward, her eyes fixed on the sword at Eliab's hip. *How can I defeat him?*

The witch's voice continued, "Are you going to cut dear Eliab's throat or stab him in the heart? Do you even think you have the nerve? I see your hand shaking. You can't do it. Because you're weak."

David rattled his cell door again, hurling taunts at his brother, but Eliab didn't seem to hear. He advanced on Michal with grim determination. Eliab's mouth twitched as if he were trying to smile, but Michal saw strain on his face. Somewhere inside, the real Eliab resisted the witch's control. She sensed an opportunity and darted forward, stabbing with the blade.

Eliab smacked Michal's hand and the dagger flew from her grip.

He grabbed her throat with both hands.

"Are you watching, David?" squealed the witch's voice with malicious glee. "I'll strangle her first, I think. I want to look in her eyes. I want to feel her die as I squeeze the life out of her with your own brother's hands."

David screamed and cursed, but there was nothing he could do.

Michal couldn't hear his words. She couldn't breathe. She could hardly struggle, her head spinning, her world turning gray.

The witch laughed and laughed. The sound consumed Michal. She thought it would be the last thing she'd ever hear.

The room darkened, but she noticed the cut fabric from Eliab's tunic had flapped down to reveal an amulet pinned to the inside. *An amulet!*

She summoned the last of her strength and snatched the amulet. Head spinning, she tore it free from the tunic.

He released her and she fell to her knees, gasping for air. Clutched in her hand was the witch's foul trinket—a needle of bone, a patch of coarse fur, red with dried blood. She tossed it to the ground and stomped on it as if putting out a burning ember.

Eliab stared blankly down at her. His eyes widened as he raked his fingers through his short hair. "No... No!" His legs crumpled and he fell to the floor.

Michal crept forward.

Eliab seemed puzzled. "What happened... Who?"

"You're Eliab, son of Jesse." She snatched the key ring from his belt.

"Eliab?" he mumbled.

She unlocked David's cell door.

He raced into her arms. "I thought I'd never see you again."

"I couldn't let them kill you."

"Well, I appreciate that, but I had everything under control."

"Really?" smiled Michal.

David grinned. "Would you believe I was working on it?"

Eliab muttered incoherently.

David slapped his brother lightly on the face. "Wake up. Eliab!"

A spark lit behind Eliab's eyes. "David?"

David slapped him again, this time a little harder.

"H-h-huh," Eliab sputtered. Then he sank to the floor and closed his eyes.

David glanced at Michal. "What do you think happened to him?"

"Hadi once told me something about witches and a dark demon named Molech. She said they use his power to control other people. Don't you see? A witch must have been using that amulet to make him do her bidding."

David nodded. "That must be why he acted so strangely at the cave. I'm sort of glad to hear it. Eliab is stubborn like a mule, but I knew he wouldn't ever betray me like that. What do you think we should do with him?"

"He's too heavy for us to carry."

"I'd say just let him sleep it off—he's used to that—but we can't just leave him here. They'll think he helped me escape." He bent down to haul Eliab up by the shoulders.

Michal felt as if cold water had been tossed on her face. "Wait, David! We can't take him with us. Not now! My father has been scraping off the gold from Goliath's shield and armor. He's used it to encase the Ark."

"So? What does that have to do with Eliab?"

"Goliath's armor had the symbol of Molech on it! That's why my father's been acting so weird lately. A witch must be controlling him, too. We have to go to the feast before it's too late. We need to stop my father before he destroys all of Israel!"

FORTY-SIX

King Saul licked his parched lips. No matter how much he drank it did no good, he could not satisfy his maddening thirst. He struggled to his feet and waved off his musicians.

"Stop! Let there be an end to music."

He gulped the last swallow of wine and threw the goblet down on the table. It rolled forward all the way to the edge and teetered but did not fall off. "How can we have such music now?"

The room remained silent.

He heard the witch's voice in his head. *No one dares speak against you. They think they've only been brought here to drink and eat their fill. They don't suspect the glory you will show them. They are weak and you are strong!*

The palace courtyard hadn't seen such splendor since the Festival of Weeks, at the start of the Philistine war. Foreign dignitaries, dressed in elaborate caftans and colorful silks, packed the open square. Saul had ordered the storehouses flung open and everything set out at once to impress the visitors. Serving trays overflowed with shanks of paschal lamb, roasted calf, fatted fowl, barley cakes, figs, dates, fresh pomegranates.

The King stood at the head of the great table, beneath a purple awning for shade against the harsh midday sun. Jonathan sat to his right, Queen Ahinoam to his left.

"Let there be an end to celebration. How can we celebrate another war, from which we've gained nothing? Hundreds of brave men lost, and our foes still lurking in the hills. And others on our southern border, just waiting to attack us. How do we stop them? How do we keep the pagans out once and for all?"

Queen Ahinoam took her husband's elbow. "Perhaps by remaining calm in the face of our guests," she suggested quietly.

The witch's voice spoke to him again. *How dare she! She knows nothing. Tell them! Tell them what must be done.*

He yanked his arm away. "There is only one way to achieve a lasting peace in this kingdom." He raised his eyes to the blue sky. "Divine providence. Do any of you deny it? Do you?"

King Saul glanced at the row of priests standing behind him. A few silently nodded their approval, but most of the others seemed lost.

Fools! They are blind men lost in false piety. You can lead them around by their noses. I will show you what must be done.

He walked around the long table, grabbed his goblet and urged the steward to fill it until wine splashed over the sides. The guests stared at him, shock etched across their faces as he drew a thin silken sheet away from the object at the front of the table.

The crowd murmured and gasped as they saw the Ark revealed. Sitting atop its chest of orange-colored acacia wood, the relic was resplendent in its new golden panels. The sun sizzled off the gold casing.

Saul stroked one of the golden cherubs at the top of the Ark with a slender fingertip.

Now is the time. Bring out the sacrifice! It's the only way.

"To be delivered from our foes we must have a sacrifice." He tipped back his goblet and let the wine overflow from his mouth to splash over his lips and down his chin.

The head priest spoke, "But we've already filled the morning with prayers. We've burned three calves today, my king, as the Lord requires. What other sacrifice?"

Still his tongue. He speaks with the voice of the prophet Samuel. He thinks you're not worthy. They all do.

"Shut up!" barked Saul. "Shut. Up." Spittle flew from his lips as he spoke.

The priest shrank back.

You must make the sacrifice. Show them how you stand in God's glory. You'll show them all. Hurry now!

"Bring out the girl!" he shouted.

Two of the house guard came forward, each holding the elbow of a young girl between them.

Abby stepped hesitantly toward the Ark, her eyes locked on the relic, her mouth slightly agape. Clouds rolled in above them, darkening the sky and dimming the Ark's dazzling brilliance. She glanced suspiciously at Saul.

Saul grabbed a fistful of Abby's hair and bent her backward across the top of the Ark. She screamed and kicked out desperately with her feet.

"Hey!" she yelled. "Stop it!"

Stop that little lamb from bleating.

Saul drew a thin dagger from his ceremonial robes and pressed it close to Abby's exposed throat. "Say nothing. It won't help." He looked out upon the stunned crowd.

Tell them again. Tell them!

"A sacrifice is needed."

Jonathan jumped from his seat. "Wait! Father?"

"Sit down!"

"She's done nothing wrong. She's just a child. Surely you don't intend to shed innocent blood here today. On the Ark? You will anger God, not honor Him."

There it is, said Alzsheba in Saul's mind. *The betrayal of your own blood. He wants your glory for himself. He wants to be king. Don't let him take what's yours. Don't let him turn everyone against you!*

"Sit down! Not another word from you!" snapped Saul. He shook his head to chase away the witch's voice, but her chatter had become all-consuming. "It's the only way. The only way to ensure our safety."

"No!" said Jonathan.

King Saul snapped his fingers and four house guards emerged from the corners of the room.

Jonathan darted forward, but the guards raced in time to intercept him before he reached the king. The first took a roundhouse to the head and went down, but the second grabbed his other arm and the third clutched the neck of his tunic.

A fierce wind tore the top of the tent away. Thunder crashed all around them.

"It's the Hand of God, Father!" shouted Jonathan. "You can't do this!"

He lies! He wants the priests to love him and all the men to follow him. He wants to be king in your place.

Saul nodded at his men. "Muzzle that ungrateful dog," he said in a low voice.

Jonathan struggled to get free, swinging wildly at one guard and then the other. He knocked another one down before someone clubbed him on the head and he fell.

"The Ark—" objected the head priest, but when one of the house guards moved toward him he shrank meekly back into his place.

"Saul," said the Queen. "You're not going to—".

"But I am. I am!"

Abby kicked with her free leg but couldn't reach the king. He held her pinned back, her neck stretched at a painful angle.

Lightning flashed. Thunder rumbled. The sky darkened so much it was as if night had fallen mid-day.

Good. Let the end come now. You must do it now or forever be the weak poor farmer, mocked and laughed at by those he would rule! Do it! Cut her throat! Let the child's blood run down and bring the black curtain down upon them all.

Saul leaned forward with the knife, his fingers tight on the handle.

FORTY-SEVEN

David and Michal burst into the far end of the courtyard. David unraveled the sling from his belt as he took in the entire scene. The Queen stood at the dais, outraged. Jonathan had been knocked to the ground and held by two men. The King stood before the Ark, his eyes wild. *And Abby!*

The dagger held to his sister's throat glinted dangerously in the light cast off by the golden Ark. David slipped a stone into the sling's pouch and ran forward, his heart in his throat.

The king's men forced their way through the crowd toward him.

He swung the sling until it whistled through the air at his side. *Please God, let my aim be right. I can't miss. I can't let him kill her.*

He let fly, his target the king's shoulder.

The stone sped true, striking King Saul at the collarbone. The knife flew from his hand.

"You dare!" raged Saul.

Guards charged forward, surrounding David.

"Take him! Take him and kill him!" ordered the King.

Two men grabbed David, ripping the sling from his hand. One drew a sword from its sheath with a metallic screech.

"Hold!" shouted Queen Ahinoam. She stood at the head of the table. Her voluminous yellow gown seemed to glow in the Ark's light. "Do not harm him! That's an order!"

The guards bent David's arms back, holding him tight, but no sword appeared at his throat. Instead, Merab stepped between David and the sword, a blur of purple in her festive gown.

King Saul's eyes roamed from the Queen to the dagger on the ground to the little girl whose hair he still held tightly in his balled fist. Abby struggled, striking his back and shoulders with her little fists, but he ignored her. He took her throat in his hand and squeezed.

The darkened sky raged above them. Lightning struck the palace turrets and Saul glanced fearfully up at the sky. Thunder crashed.

"No!" said David. He pulled with all the strength of his arms and twisted his body, but the soldiers held him tight. "Abby!"

David centered himself. He struggled to concentrate, to raise the orb from that place deep inside, as he had done all those times before. He felt the same desperation as the other times. He would use it to open the portal. But nothing happened.

Why doesn't it work, he wondered, and then the truth hit him.

God is angry. He's waiting to see what we'll do. We have to stop this on our own.

FORTY-EIGHT

Saul's features grew waxy again and a sneer crossed his lips. He tightened his grip on Abby's throat.

Michal shoved the guards out of her way. "Father! What are you doing?"

"Be quiet," commanded Saul.

"No, I won't be quiet!" She marched to the front of the courtyard, her hair disheveled, her peasant dress flowing around her. But despite her ragged appearance there was no mistaking the grace and bearing of her walk, the commanding tone of her voice.

"There's a witch controlling you," she said. "Don't you feel her? You must."

Saul shook his head and tightened his grip on Abby's throat. Abby sputtered, her face turning red.

Michal continued, "The witch wants to make you kill this little girl, but you won't do it. You're better than that. You're stronger than some petty witch. You're the King of Israel."

Saul looked quizzically at her. "I'm no king... I... I'm just a simple farmer."

She moved closer.

"Yes, a farmer. Before all this. Before you were king and had so many worries and troubles. We used to sit and look at the hills early in the morning, at sunrise, you and I. Just father and daughter. Remember?"

"Yes of course." Saul tried to clear his head. His grip on Abby's throat loosened. "Of course I remember all of those things."

"And you used to take me up on your shoulders and tell me I was your little princess."

"You are the princess."

Michal tugged at her dirt-brown homespun robe. "No, I'm not. Not really. Not anymore. Now I'm just a runaway and a peasant girl. But I *was* a princess in that early morning light on the farm. You told me so. I remember one stormy morning, it was thundering just like this. I was frightened. You said you loved me and promised everything would be all right."

"It will…"

"Then let that girl go. If you love me, you have to let that girl go."

The haze lifted from King Saul's eyes and a new light burned in its place, as if he had just returned from the far shore of a waking nightmare. He looked from Abby to the Ark. "My God, what have I done?"

He released Abby suddenly, as if unaware that he'd been so close to choking the life from her.

The sun clawed its way between the clouds and daylight returned.

A terrifying screech tore through the courtyard. It circled around them, driving a hot spike into their ears. It was the witch's scream, her rage and disappointment so intense it rattled David's soul. Then it faded away, trailing off into emptiness and impotence, and disappeared.

The gold that had been used to gild the Ark began to sizzle. It glowed white hot for a moment then bubbled and popped, running down from the holy relic in lustrous rivulets that seeped into the ground.

Michal stepped into her father's arms and spoke softly to him.

The King signaled the men who held David. "Let him go."

David pulled his arms free and breathed as if for the first time. Michal had succeeded where no one else could. Somehow she knew only love could break the witch's spell.

He raced forward and scooped Abby up into his arms.

King Saul rubbed his wounded shoulder. "Did you just shoot me in the arm?"

"I did. Everyone else was just standing around."

Saul glared at him. "Weren't you supposed to be locked away somewhere?"

"They let me go for good behavior." David chanced a half-smile.

King Saul glanced down at Abby as if looking at one of his own daughters, and for a moment it seemed he might even apologize. Instead he straightened his spine and turned again toward David.

"It seems I owe you another debt of gratitude," said the King. He looked at the shimmering Ark, and added, "All of Israel owes you this day."

"There's only one thing I want."

Saul glanced at Michal. And he smiled. "You'll have it. With my blessing."

EPILOGUE

Michal strolled through the fruit grove with David. Merab and Abby kept a few paces behind them, chatting together as they walked. The afternoon heat had faded away now and a light chill frosted the air.

Three days had passed since they'd rescued Abby and defeated the witch. Most of the guests at the victory celebration had already departed from Gibeah. Life had started to fall back to normal, although Michal knew her normal would never be the same. Her mother and all her handmaids were busy preparing for Merab's wedding. And after that there would be her own wedding to look forward to and then married life with David. No, there weren't going to be too many ordinary days from now on. Not for her.

"I'm glad Hadi's feeling better," said David.

Michal grinned, "She's back to being her old self again. Now she's wrapped up in a *secret* project. But it's the worst kept secret in the palace."

David frowned. "Really? I haven't heard anything."

"She's making me a dress for our wedding. Do you think I'll look good in white Egyptian silk?"

"I can't wait."

He wore a handsome wheat-colored tunic with elegant white embroidery, courtesy of Hadi's skillful hands, along the neck and cuffs. A dark blue cape hung from his shoulders. The early afternoon light slipped through the trees and splashed across his face. He was still the untamed youth she'd first met in the practice room, but if she squinted her eyes just a little, she saw the prince he would become.

Jonathan had appointed him to the house guard in a post just slightly above his brother Eliab. David was proud to be in the house guard, but never wore the uniform on their walks together. Michal sensed his inner conflict — half warrior and half poet. When he spent time with her, Michal got the feeling he wanted to be something different than just a warrior. Something more.

"Do you think they'll be happy?"

"Who?" asked David in an oddly distracted tone.

"Merab and Zachary," she said. "You think they'll be happy?"

"Oh…" He shot a casual glance at Merab and Abby. "Jonathan approves. Stronger ties with the Amalekites, that'll save us a lot of bloodshed."

"Yes, but what do *you* think?"

"Zachary seems a good man, for an Amalekite. And when we talk about Merab his face lights up. I think he's in love with her. He's a bit of a poet himself, you know. Pretty good one, too. I'd like to spend more time with him before I go."

"I wish you weren't leaving so soon." Michal had had enough of fighting and war and bloodshed, but Jonathan and David were leaving tomorrow for the northern lines to chase down the last remnants of the Philistine army. And after that, as sure as the sunrise, some new enemy would need to be defeated. One thing she'd learned as a princess, there was always fighting. There was always war. Her chest tightened just thinking about it. She wanted him safe, but he was a warrior and he would always be in harm's way.

They came upon a large flat rock, the same place where they'd met in secret that first time when they sang together in the fruit grove.

"Let's stop here." Michal sat on the rock and David spotted one last pear on the tree. He reached up and plucked the fruit, then sat beside her.

She locked eyes with him. A sly look graced his face and melted her heart, though she wasn't quite sure what it meant. She had memorized every line in his face, but his moods were a different story. Luckily, she had the rest of their lives to discover their meaning.

He offered her the pear, and she took a bite.

Still something wasn't right. He looked guilty.

"What's wrong?"

"Nothing."

"It's not nothing. I can tell."

David whisked a loose strand of hair from Michal's face, brushing his fingers against her cheek. He lowered his head and whispered. "There *is* something I need to tell you."

"You're not already married, are you?" Michal smiled as she said it, but David didn't laugh.

He leaned closer and spoke quietly so only she could hear. "Maybe it doesn't mean anything. I don't know. It's just that I don't want to keep secrets from you, so I want you to know."

"Go ahead." She placed her hand on top of his.

"When I first came to Gibeah, my brothers and I met the prophet Samuel. We didn't know he was Samuel at the time, but I'm sure of it now. He rolled the knucklebones for me in a seer's tent at the Festival of Weeks and told my future."

"About the giant?"

"No. He conveniently left that part out, but he said I would become the King of Israel."

"The king? You believe him?"

David nodded. "I didn't at first, but now I do. Don't get the wrong idea. I'd never do anything disloyal to your father or your brother."

"I know." It was hard to imagine something bad happening to her father or brother, but the Fates had a mind of their own. "I have to admit I've been keeping a secret also. I wasn't sure I should tell you this, but you're right. You *will* be king someday. I already know all about it."

David looked confused. "How could *you* know?"

"God told me."

He arched his eyebrows upward.

"Surprised that God would speak to a woman?" Michal grinned. "When my father held that knife to Abby's throat, when he almost shed her blood on the Ark, the Lord was there. Above us."

"The storm…"

"Yes, and He spoke to me — to me, a woman, a girl. I heard His voice in my head. It was so beautiful, David. I don't think I can ever describe it."

"What did He say?"

"It wasn't with words, not exactly. It all came in a flash. He said I needed to help my father resist the witch, to remind him who he was and speak to his heart. He also showed me some other things, and that's when I knew you would someday be king and that we could be together. He told me about the choice you made in Elah. He said it was a sort of a test and I guess you passed."

Remembering the moment, she felt a warm breeze blow through her as if it were summer again. She had seen a vision of David as an old man — a golden crown perched on his gray hair, the lines on his face deeper and more plentiful. But they were still confident and honest lines. He was not perfect, yet she knew he would grow into the man she always thought he could be — a fierce warrior, a remarkable poet, a great king. A man touched by God.

But she wasn't about to tell him all that. His head was swollen enough as it was.

David smiled. "I don't know what to say."

"Well, that's a first," Michal chuckled.

"You're amazing."

Michal glanced behind her at Merab. Her sister smiled, then nudged Abby and pointed at something in the distance to draw the girl's attention away.

Michal leaned toward David and brushed her lips against his.

"You taste like the pear," David whispered. "Sweet."

They kissed again and again, but when David moved in for a more passionate embrace, she pushed him back. "Hold on. We're not married yet."

Perhaps they laughed too loudly because Merab and Abby approached the rock.

"I saw you kissing, you know," Abby grinned. "But don't worry, I won't tell the king."

David rolled his eyes.

"I think we can let this one time slip without telling Father," Merab said. "Besides, I'm starting to like your brother. I'd hate for him to be thrown in a cell again so soon."

Abby smirked. "He's not too bad once you get to know him." She poked David in the shoulder. "If you two are done slobbering on each other we should go."

"No," said David. "We're not done. Not by a long shot."

A redheaded shrike flew between them and landed on a nearby branch of the pear tree. Abby moved to shoo it away, but Michal stopped her. The bird was a friend, and part of their story too.

Abby giggled. "Things sure ended up funny."

David grumbled. "What do you mean, funny?"

"Well, Dad sent me here hoping to marry me to some nobleman or other and he winds up marrying you off. To a princess."

AUTHORS' NOTE

We were inspired to write this story after Jeff attended a vestry retreat for his church. At the retreat, the David and Goliath story was discussed. Truthfully, we didn't know much about the tale before that weekend. Sure, we knew about the sling and the giant and maybe the five stones that David chose to face Goliath. But we didn't know about the battle of champions, the war between the Philistines and the Israelites, and the amazing love story between David and Michal.

After that weekend Jeff felt compelled to write this novel and drag his brother along as a co-author. But we didn't want to make this a simple re-hashing of the Old Testament story. We wanted to write a novel that readers will enjoy without any reference to the biblical story, and luckily, this story has some great features built into it-young protagonists, an unlikely love story, a war, witches, and a giant. We really couldn't ask for more.

Our goal when writing this story was to keep the basis of the David and Goliath story intact and to re-imagine it so that it will inspire current readers with the same themes. We obviously took some liberties with the biblical accounts, but less than you might realize. The Witch of Endor is mentioned in the Old Testament and so are demons and portals to heaven where angels might appear on Earth.

Our sincere hope is to entertain readers with a re-telling of a biblical story most don't know in detail. If we've offended anyone, we deeply apologize.

ALSO AVAILABLE:

ALAANA'S WAY

All five books in this young adult epic fantasy series are now available. To find out more visit AMAZON

In the frozen north, a land of deadly weather and unforgiving spirits, the shaman is all that stands in the way of disaster. When Alaana is called upon to become shaman for the Anatatook people she discovers a kaleidoscopic world where everything is alive, where the tent skins whisper at night and even the soapstone pot has tales to tell. She faces vengeful ghosts and hungry demons as she travels the dangerous path to becoming a shaman. And there's just one other problem. Girls aren't allowed to be shamans. This is Book One in an epic fantasy series with a unique arctic setting. All fans of fantasy will enjoy these five novels.

From *The Bee Writes*: "This is a beautiful and exotic story that leads you from one adventure to another. "Alaana's Way ~ The Calling" is an entertaining read both for adults and teenagers. Well, it doesn't happen very often that I give 5 out of 5 Bee's for a book. "Alaana's Way ~ The Calling" though is one of those books that have hooked me from the beginning."

From *The Bibliophilic Book Blog*: "The author has created a vivid world, characters (great and small), and a strong main character in Alaana. THE CALLING is the first book in the Alaana's Way series and it truly brings the reader into a wholly different world from their own. Very well done!"

From *Underground Book Reviews*: "Ambitious. That's how I would describe Ken Atlabef's saga of a twelve year old Inuit girl and her perilous journey of transformation. These journeys are wrought with wonder and peril and are beautifully written. To the reader, these spiritual characters become every bit as real as those in the flesh and blood world. I can say so many great things about this novel, from the dialogue to the sweeping scenery to its solid editing. Original in both scope and execution, I highly recommend it."

WIND CATCHER

This multiple award-winning young adult fantasy thriller is now available. To find out more visit AMAZON

Juliet can not control her fate, but will she control her destiny?

Juliet Wildfire Stone hears voices and sees visions, but she can't make out what they mean. Her eccentric grandfather tells her stories about the Great Wind Spirit and Coyote, but he might as well be speaking another language. None of it makes any sense.

When she stumbles upon a series of murders, she can't help but worry her grandfather might be involved. To discover the truth, Juliet must choose between her new life at an elite private school and her Native American heritage.

Once she uncovers an ancient secret society formed over two hundred years ago to keep HER safe, she starts to wonder whether there's some truth to those old stories her grandfather has been telling her.

All she wants is to be an average sixteen-year-old girl, but she has never been average—COULD never be average.

Betrayed by those she loves, she must decide whether to run or risk everything by fulfilling her destiny as the Chosen.

WINNER: Readers' Favorite Awards -- Gold Medal 2015: Young Adult Coming-of-Age

WINNER: Mom's Choice Awards -- Silver Medal: Young Adult Books

WINNER: Beverly Hills Books Awards - 2015: Best Young Adult Fiction

WINNER: Awesome Indies -- Seal of Approval: "A treat to read."

What Others Are Saying About Wind Catcher

"This is an enjoyable read for all ages that goes by as fast as the authors can unspool it." ~ *Kirkus Reviews*

~~~

"This very unique and refreshingly original contemporary fantasy has elements of high epic fantasy woven throughout it, and it will surprise and delight even the most jaded fantasy readers." ~ **Readers' Favorite Book Reviews**

~~~

"Wind Catcher stands out from the crowd. It's... a powerful young adult adventure steeped in Native American legend and tradition." ~ *Midwest Book Review*

~~~

"Wind Catcher is one of the best thrillers for YA that I have read in some time.... If I hadn't had to eat and sleep, I would have read it right through without stopping. It is just that good!" ~ *Bookends*

~~~

"A page turning thrill a minute, Wind Catcher kept me guessing until it's final pages. Age appropriate YA literature at its best. Don't miss it!" ~ **Judy Murphy, Masters School Librarian**